Standing Up

KATE FOREST

This book is dedicated to my hero. When I said I had this crazy idea to write a book, he smiled and said, "Okay."

Chapter 1

JILL

Oh, great. Another big, hunky one.

I sighed and shook my head. Through the glass door of the study room off the main library floor sat the latest victim of the calculus requirement. These jocks — guys with thick arms and even thicker heads — saw me as an easy target. The brainy math tutor they tried to flirt with instead of buckling down to learn calculus.

They didn't care about learning a subject they'd never use after graduation, but I couldn't complain. If it weren't for the math requirement, I wouldn't earn enough to pay for fees and books. And there was no way I could graduate Phi Beta Kappa and tops in astronomy if I couldn't afford my books.

I squared my shoulders and opened the door.

"Hi, I'm Jill." I extended my hand.

"Mike." He reached out but didn't get up from his seat. Not that I expected it. Boys these days didn't care much for formalities.

I took a seat next to him at the table. The room was bare of anything that would distract from studying. It contained only a table with scratched laminate, three unmatched chairs with various degrees of upholstery, a whiteboard that was once white, and a fluorescent light that hung over the table. If I was inclined, I could've been distracted by Mark, or whatever his name was, and his amazing shoulders and jaw line. But my focus to become a specialist at NASA would never waver.

"So, uh, Mike Lewis." I read his name off the information sheet I'd been given by the math department. "I see you're in your junior year and taking calculus. Most people try to get it out of the way sooner." I slid the textbooks from my bag.

"Yeah, well, freshman year I had to take remedial math. Couldn't even place into calculus. And last year, well, I was failing, so I took an incomplete and thought I'd try again this year." Mike had a thousand-watt smile. His green eyes shone like the radiation from the most luminous quasar.

His charm would get him far, even if his brains failed him.

"Don't worry, we'll get you to pass calc, but you'll have to do the work."

A Theta Chi frat cap sat on the table beside him. *Great, the jock house.* They fed off each other, almost taking pride in their lack of brains by thumping their enormous chests and announcing their alpha status.

"Aye aye, cap'n." He saluted and flashed his smile again.

Plenty of my students had tried flirting. Maybe they thought they could get me to do the work for them. I was immune. I could never date anyone who couldn't discuss anything other than sports statistics. If I was looking for a man, and I wasn't, he'd have to be brilliant, and not just his eyes.

"Let's start with the basics. A fundamental idea in calculus is approaching zero." I pulled out some scrap paper. "We can do an experiment right here. Let's say you start at this table and take a giant step halfway to the wall over there. Pretend the wall is the zero point."

I waited for him to get up. "I mean, let's try it." I waved my arm toward the wall.

His eyes narrowed. "What does this have to do with calculus?"

"I'm trying to explain how you can approach zero but never make it to the wall."

"Why not?"

"Listen, I want to show you that if you took a giant step half the distance to the wall and then another step half the remaining distance, and then again and so on and so on, you'd never reach the wall."

"Sure I could. I could probably make it there in about three steps. Why do you think I couldn't walk there?"

"Because." I took a deep breath. "Each step would only cover half the remaining distance. You'd get really close but still be a little bit away. And your next step could only be half the remaining distance."

Mike studied the wall. I could almost hear the gears grinding away in his head. Soon smoke would pour out of his ears.

"I think I get it. My brother and I used to play this game with my mom's cakes. She makes the best chocolate cake. We always wanted to save some for the next night. So we only took half. This first night we usually felt a little sick, eating half a cake. But eventually it did disappear."

"That's right, but only because you don't have an infinitely narrow knife."

Mike cocked his head. Stifling a giggle, I recalled our old Labrador's expression when his squeaky toy would get caught under the couch. But Mike managed to look hot and not dumb.

"Oh, cool. I see." The wrinkles in his brow eased and his eyes widened in comprehension.

The rest of the lesson wasn't as easy. Mike seemed to get the basic ideas, but when presented with an equation, the symbols and letters made him cringe like I offered him lima beans. Yet it wasn't disastrous. I'd had worst first lessons, and Mike did seem willing and eager to learn. That would make it a lot less painful. And admiring his chiseled jaw was pleasant, too. His thick, dirty blond hair fell nicely across his face when he bent over a page. His scent wasn't half bad either.

Damn, nothing good ever comes from getting distracted by a man. I should have learned that lesson by now.

"So, I think we should stop there for today." My voice cracked a bit as I pulled away from the fantasy.

"Darn, and I was enjoying myself." Mike winked.

"Yeah, right." I rolled my eyes.

"No, really. You don't talk to me like I'm an idiot. Plus I never expected the math department to send over a beautiful woman."

"Thanks, but not all of us physics majors are scrawny geeks."

"Physics? Impressive. I respect a person with real brains. Hey, why don't we hang out tomorrow? We should get to know each other. Especially since we'll be spending all this time together." He leaned back and draped his arms over both chairs on either side of him, revealing exactly how broad his chest was.

"Really? You're kidding. You're asking me out?"

"What's wrong with that?" His eyes widened with mock innocence.

"First of all, I'm your tutor. I get *paid* to spend time with you."

"When you say it like that, you make it sound

illegal."

"And second, you don't need to know me better. We have a job to do, to get you to pass the calc requirement." I looked away so as not to be pulled into his orbit.

"Jill, I don't want to just pass. I need an A." When he said my name, his eyes smoldered and his voice got deadly serious.

"An A? Why do you need an A so badly?"

"Because I'm real close to Phi Beta Kappa. And I don't want the stupid math requirement messing it up." He said it so plainly, I thought I must have misheard.

"Phi Beta Kappa?" *He must be out of his mind if he thinks I'll buy that line.*

"Yeah, I'm going to graduate with that key pinned to my gown." Gone was the easygoing charm and handsome smile. A determined stare and hard-set jaw had replaced it.

"Oh, uh. What's your major?"

"And I thought you weren't interested in getting to know me." His smile returned. "I'm pre-law."

"Oh." *A well-thought-out response.* The pre-law program was rigorous. And if his grades were close to Phi Beta Kappa… "You must have made dean's list."

"Yep, both years," he said.

"Still, calculus is different. It's probably not the type of class you're used to."

"Ahh, she figures it out." He winked again. "So how about this? If I get an A minus in the class, you have to go out with me. One date."

"Why would I agree to that?" I crossed my arms, hoping to create a barrier between his chest and mine. The room seemed awfully small. Why was I even discussing this?

"Because you want to motivate me. I happen to know you've never had a student get less than a B."

"How do you know?"

"I asked the head of the department to give me the best tutor. I told him about my GPA, and he agreed I should have the best. Your reputation is on the line."

Now it was my turn to narrow my eyes and give him a steely glare. Not that I had a steely glare to conjure. So, he'd picked me especially for my tutoring success. "I guess you're serious and determined. Fine." I threw my arms up. "What's the chance you'll get an A anyway?"

Mike laughed a good, deep laugh that shouldn't have sent a shiver through my belly, but it did.

He reached out and took my hand. Not quite a handshake, but his large, warm palm enveloped mine. Electricity shot up as if my arm were a closed Gaussian surface.

"It was an A minus," he corrected me. "And now I've got to go to my next class. It was nice to meet you, Jill."

Again, he said my name with a deep rumble and I was stuck to the chair.

Mike reached under the table and pulled out a pair of crutches. My mouth fell open as he hoisted himself up and clipped the brackets around his forearms. He planted the crutches in front and swung his legs forward to meet them. He wore cargo shorts, showcasing strong, thick thighs, but below his knees his calves were almost emaciated.

I clamped my mouth shut quickly, but too late to escape his notice.

"Don't worry. That Phi Beta Kappa pin won't weigh me down. I'll still be able to cross the stage next year." He cocked his head and with one hand awkwardly pulled the heavy door of the study room open, maneuvered half his body through the doorway, and sidled out. The door hit his crutch as it closed.

He clomped out of view of the glass door, swinging his half-atrophied legs through the crutches.

"Idiot!" I said aloud, and let my head fall to the table with a *thunk*. How could I have sat there with my mouth gaping open? That might have been the rudest thing I had ever done.

What had surprised me most about the lesson? Was it his legs? His intelligence and academic achievement despite looking and sounding like a jock? Or was it that I had broken my number one rule? Don't let a man distract me.

MIKE

Man, that was the least graceful exit ever, even for me.

I hurried as fast as I could to the "Survey of Elizabethan and Jacobean Drama" lecture. I shouldn't have stayed flirting after the lesson. I had barely ten minutes to get from the library to Stinson Hall, go up the ramp at the far side of the building, wait for the slowest elevator on earth to go up the single flight, and then clomp back down the long hallway to the lecture room. If I didn't look like a three-legged frog hopping up steps, I would take the stairs. Besides, I held people up when I took the stairs. People were too polite to say anything, but their impatience was thick when they waited behind me.

Jill caused me to linger in that study room. She was smokin' hot. Not in the way my buddies' cheerleader girlfriends were hot. No, she wore clothing that covered up all the parts I wanted to see. But her blue eyes, deep blue, almost violet, were big enough to get lost in. She had the blackest hair framing her heart-shaped face. And boy, was she cute when she got frustrated with my inability to solve functions.

I shook the image of her compact, curvy body out of my mind, as my crutches clunked down the hallway. Pain shot from my shins, because I rushed. The pain was always worse when I demanded too much from my ankles. The sound of the crutches echoed against the walls of the empty corridor. I was late. Everyone else had made it to class minutes ago. I'd have to walk in, drawing attention as I fumbled into one of the auditorium-style seats, stow the crutches underneath (probably knocking someone's coffee over), and try to catch up with everyone else.

Elizabethan and Jacobean Drama was not only easier to follow than calculus, it was infinitely more fun. Sure, ancient Professor Coulter could prattle on and get lost in his own obscure ideas. The rumor was he was present when *Twelfth Night* was originally performed. But this was the type of class where I gained the knowledge I would use.

Although I took all the pre-law-required classes to please dear old dad, my main goals — to go to a grad program for theater and starve as an actor in New York — never wavered. I had to bide my time until I built upper body and quad strength and convince my parents I'd do what I was told to do. Even if it meant making Phi Beta Kappa to mollify the old man.

When class was over, I folded my laptop away in my bag.

"Hey, buddy, want to grab some lunch?"

Steve, a fellow Theta Chi brother, had come up and clapped a hand on my shoulder.

"Sure. You can fill me in on what I missed."

"You're kidding. I need you to explain the entire lecture to me. I couldn't follow a single word he said. I only took this class because you said it was cool and there'd be hot girls. So far, none are interested in a stud like me. Come on. I'm buying, you're talking." Steve stood patiently as I waited for the rest of the students to leave the room.

It was better to hang back and be last than to trip someone with a crutch. But waiting I could do. I'd cultivated patience for two years, an expert at waiting.

Chapter 2

JILL

Without a sound, I stepped into the nearly empty office, hoping not to disrupt anyone's work. It wasn't much of an office — some cubicles, computers, and a smart board. It lacked the glamour of what most people imagined of a place where brilliant scientists studied the cosmos. I placed my things at the student desk, the one all the other undergraduates who were lucky enough to get a few hours of work in Dr. Shaffer's office shared. If working for free was still considered work. But it would be a huge advantage on my grad school application.

"Hey, Jill." Robert sauntered over. He'd been a major distraction at one point. I'd escaped that distraction with a broken heart and a potentially ruinous secret, but also a valuable lesson. Stay away from doctoral students. Or any other male students, for that matter.

"Hello, Robert." My clenched teeth kept me

from blurting out the filthy epitaph I had coined in his honor. Whatever he was about to say wasn't going to be good.

"Listen, I'm having a hell of a time with this program. I can't get it to crunch my numbers the way it's supposed to." Robert plopped his laptop right in front of my own screen, blocking my view. "Can you take a look? You're always so brilliant with these things."

"I'm supposed to spend this time gathering some data for my project. And Dr. Shaffer asked me to—"

"Great. Thanks. I'm starved. I'm going to grab a quick bite." He patted my head, and I fought the urge to sink my teeth into his meaty mitt.

I was only allowed a few hours to use the computers in the office. I tried to get as much done as possible in my small window of access. Whenever Robert, or any of the others, dumped extra work on me, that meant my own work lagged. I accepted I was low woman on the totem pole and could bear it, but that didn't mean I liked it.

I hunkered down and tried to get Robert's data set to make sense. Usually, I *was* brilliant at these things, but today I couldn't concentrate. My mind wandered back to Mike.

He was one surprise after another. I had pinned him as a jock—a no-brain jock. But with his GPA through the roof, he obviously had brains. And with his legs permanently disabled, he was no jock. He must have been in some kind of accident. With the top two-thirds of his body buff, he'd been an athlete at some point in his past.

"Hello, Jill."

"Oh, hello, Dr. Shaffer." I was so lost in thought, I hadn't realized he was there until I felt his hand rest on my shoulder.

"What are you working on?" His normal six feet seemed even taller when he stood over me.

"Robert's having a problem running his data through the program. I was taking a look at it. But I'll get to the supernovae measurements you left for me."

"Fine, fine. You're always so helpful to everyone here. I especially appreciate that you and Robert are able to work together after you two broke up."

"We're all adults." What choice did I have when Robert could wreck my career? I forced a smile, ignoring the clock ticking away my allotted time.

"I assume you're applying for the paid internship next year." He straightened up and leaned against the wall, his long legs casually stretched to my chair.

"Yes. I hope to use data from a satellite x-ray observatory to study the effect of supermassive black holes on the formation and evolution of galaxies and clusters of galaxies. I know it's early yet to start collecting data for my senior project, but if there's a chance I get the internship then it will be worth it. Since the applications are due next month, I was going to ask—"

"No need," he said, waving his hand. "I'll be more than happy to write a recommendation for you."

"Thanks. The money would go a long way, and I could quit the tutoring and spend more time here..."

"You're my star. Such a hard worker."

"I try," I said. *I try too damn hard for everyone else.* But if it was all going to pay off, and if I got the internship next year, then it was worth the sacrifice.

MIKE

I balanced the thick textbook on my lap. The lighting in the studio theater wasn't set up for classwork, and even worse, the only table in the front was being used to pile scripts. Numbers and symbols swirled together on the page. The problem set the calculus prof assigned was due in a few hours, and Acting III was about to begin.

"Hey, Mike. How are you?" Sandy took a seat behind me and looked over my shoulder.

"Good. Just gotta finish this problem set." I didn't want to blow her off, but I needed every available minute.

"Okay. You want to get together later? We're all going to the screening of the student movie from the film department. I can drive you."

"Thanks. I'll let you know."

Sandy's voice held no pity. This was one of the classes in which I could relax. My disability wasn't merely tolerated—it was nearly celebrated. Not for the first time, I wondered if a woman like Jill could accept me as much as the theater students had. Although Phi Beta Kappa remained front and center, if I could impress that brainiac hottie by earning an A, that would be the icing on the cake.

"Hard at work, Michael?" Beth Stone's scent always hit me before I glimpsed her.

She stood over me, but quickly pecked Sandy on the cheek by way of greeting and took the seat next to me. Her spun-gold hair shimmered even in the half-light. Her large chestnut eyes framed with thick lashes reminded me of those pinup girls from the 1950s. The perfect femme fatale.

"Just trying to pass calc." I closed my book. No point in trying to work now. Beth's presence always drew my attention, but not in any way I'd ever want to follow through on.

"You'll more than pass, you always do. Your class load would break a lesser man. Did you read the script?" She straightened my collar, which probably didn't need straightening.

"Yeah. A little dark, isn't it? Brecht is too heavy

for me."

"Michael." She shook her head, and the light caught the dusting of freckles she'd chosen not to cover with makeup today. "You don't fool me. Inside you're a deep thinker. And the depth of your emotions…" She sighed. "It's evident in your performances."

I shrugged. With Beth I didn't have to hold up my end of the conversation.

"You're the only one I know who takes their college career seriously. You'll have enough credits for a double major in pre-law and theater." She placed her delicate hand on my forearm. "You're an inspiration. I only wish you would see that in yourself."

I was forming a typical sarcastic comment to deflect from the direction of the conversation when Professor Shandell arrived.

He'd performed in countless off-Broadway shows and directed a few independent, but successful, films. His burly six-foot-plus stature, frizzled gray hair, and expertly rumpled clothing completed the aura. The students were in awe of him, and his demeanor captivated the class.

But I usually watched Beth instead of Shandell. Not only was she beautiful, but I learned more about acting from watching her small movements, the trivial changes in her expressions, and the shifting of her body posture.

I could get with Beth if I wanted, but it would wreck our friendship, and wreck the wall I had built around my emotions.

An acceptance existed among the theater majors that was more complete than with any other group. Yes, my frat brothers looked out for me. And no, no one had ever said or done anything purposefully insensitive. But Beth and the others had embraced my disability. In fact, it wasn't a disability here; it was a different ability. Being a misfit among misfits was an honor, and I relaxed into the seat to listen to the lecture.

JILL

It was a good thing I didn't have time for lunch. The way my stomach clenched, nothing would stay down.

The week since the tutoring session with Mike had flown by faster than a solar tsunami. I'd avoided all thought of seeing him again, compartmentalizing that hour with him into a box labeled "Do Not Open: Leads to Distractions." I hoped he wouldn't show. Maybe he'd be too angry at my stupid reaction to his crutches and he'd find someone else to tutor him.

"Jill, why the rush?" Nikki Sanchez, my best, and mostly only, friend nearly slammed into my side as she ran to catch up.

"I'm going to be late for my next tutoring session." I didn't slow my pace. It wasn't a problem for Nikki and her runway-model legs. Those of us in the barely five-foot crowd had to work our feet double time.

"You're never late for anything." She strode along the cobbled path beside me.

The sun glinted off the windows of the academic buildings and through the candy corn colors of the trees, not hinting at the bitter Chicago winter to come.

"Robert had me doing some work for him, again."

"Asshat. Why don't you tell him where to stick his optical lens?"

"I need to make a good impression in Dr. Shaffer's group and get that internship. Or I'll spend the whole of my senior year rushing to even more tutoring sessions." If Nikki knew how, in a stupid, desperate moment, I'd cheated and allowed Robert to do a project for me, she'd be obligated to turn me in to the dean's office. I didn't want to risk our friendship and put her in that position.

"He's still an asshat. Taking advantage of the fact that you guys dated."

"Exactly why I'm never getting involved with a man again until I've got my PhD."

"Just don't date anyone in the department."

"Uh-huh." Men were not to be trusted.

"I'm coming over for dinner. I can't stand the dining hall anymore," Nikki said.

"Okay." I was nearly out of breath when we reached the library doors.

"Have fun ogling the latest eye-candy jock." Nikki started to veer off.

"What do you mean?" My voice strained.

Nikki squinted in confusion. "Relax. I know you'd never go for any of those guys. But it's got to be fun to look."

"Yeah, right." I hoped my sarcastic tone worked.

The library, silent except for the buzz of the fluorescent lights, did not feel as welcoming as it typically did.

With my head bent and eyes trained on my shoes, I approached the study room. I'd have to apologize for the way I stared at his legs last week. I'd also have to set him straight—the date thing couldn't happen. But I couldn't apologize about staring and then reject the date. He'd assume I wouldn't date him because of his disability. Which wasn't the case at all.

I couldn't date any of my students. Ever.

I dared to lift my head as I opened the door.

Mike's casual posture and magnetic smile crashed into my gut.

Yes, it was good I hadn't eaten.

"Hi," I squeaked.

"Hey there. Thought you'd given up on me."
Mike tapped his watch.

"Sorry. I got held up by a professor." I stacked
textbooks, keeping the table between us.

"Don't tell me you're failing a subject."

"No. I work for him. Well, not really. It's
volunteer for now."

"The university is reaping the benefits of your
blood and sweat, huh?" The word *sweat* shouldn't
have sounded sexy.

"We all have to pay our dues." I shrugged.

Mike's smile dimmed for a moment, but that
didn't detract from his eyes, which only got greener.

"Let's get started." I cleared my throat.

"Sure. Why don't you sit down then? Or are you
going to lecture me from over there?"

I turned right and left and discovered the only
other chair was next to Mike.

"Right." I came around the table, never letting
my gaze flash down below. I wouldn't look at his
legs. I wouldn't look at his crutches. Deliberately, I
pulled the chair from the table and sat as far as I
could from Mike without seeming to want to place
distance between our bodies.

His muscular arm rested on the table, and the
back of my hand grazed it as I pulled the textbooks
close. Other parts besides my stomach clenched.

I risked a glance in his direction. His eyes never
changed from that enchanting expression. This was

going to be a long session.

Chapter 3

MIKE

I never expected a math tutoring session to fly by.
The incomprehensible subject usually twisted my
insides and muddled my brain. My brain was
muddled for sure, but it was Jill the Genius who
twisted my insides and clouded my thoughts, not
calculus. And the sensation was much more pleasant
than any math-related affliction.

The telltale signs of her discomfort were there. I
had perfected my radar for those signs. People
looked anywhere except down. They held their
bodies stiff, as if they were afraid of showing off that
they could move and I couldn't.

Jill did those things, but there was more. Her
body reacted to mine in a positive way. She might
have been uncomfortable with my legs, what there
was of them, but she was turned on by the rest. I'd
perfected my radar for that, too. Life before the
accident had been full of wide eyes and licking lips

as girls fell all over themselves for the star football player.

Jill had battled with herself during the last session. Torn between eyeing me up and staying professional. Her snarky attitude before she'd caught sight of my graceless exit showed a fire breather under her hesitance.

"Are you thinking about this equation or daydreaming?"

I couldn't keep the smirk from my face. Her attempt to look tough with a glower and squared shoulders only made her cute features more adorable.

"Wasn't Einstein accused of daydreaming in class?"

"Einstein never had me for a tutor." She crossed her arms, covering her curvy breasts. Compact women were feisty, and brainy compact women were doubly feisty.

"If he had, he'd have daydreamed even more."

"We have to talk about this." Jill shifted farther back into her seat.

Talking with Jill would be nice, but I had more physical ideas in mind.

"You're doing a great job," I encouraged her. "I really think I'm understanding the lesson."

"No, I mean...our deal."

"Are you backing out? Do you think I'll get a good grade after all?" I leaned forward to examine her captivating lips as they worked to form a response. It was a good opportunity to take in her vanilla scent as well.

"No. I'm sure you'll do fine. It's…it's…"

I leaned back and gave her space. This was the moment when people tried to come up with an excuse, something other than my legs. I never made it easy for anyone. It wasn't easy for me, and I certainly wasn't going to let Jill the Brain off the hook. If she wanted to back out of the date because I'd have to use the handicapped ramp to whatever restaurant we went to, then she was going to have to say it to my face.

"Your flirting is distracting you from the work. There's only so much I can do. You can lead a horse to water…" The snark returned. Her eyes narrowed and she leaned into my space.

"Am I the horse?" An inappropriate image of Jill riding me knocked the equations out of my head.

"At least one end of it." Her self-important grin should have felt like a jab, but her smile was too welcoming.

"All right, Jill the Brain. I'll focus more on calculus, if you promise to stop wearing that perfume."

"I'm not wearing perfume," she insisted.

"Then why do you smell like vanilla?"

Jill shrugged. "Don't know. But we've wasted precious minutes and you have homework due."

I glanced at the clock on the wall. "Crap. I also have another class to get to." I hastily shoved my stuff in my bag. Another graceless exit awaited.

"I've got to dash, too." Jill was quicker at packing her books, and made it to the door before I even stood up. "See you next week. And don't forget what I told you."

"About your perfume?"

"About derivatives, you dolt." But her glare over her shoulder was too cute to be menacing.

The swish of her ass as she sauntered out through the library was to be appreciated as fine art. She wasn't wearing perfume. She refused to watch me look like a klutz as I left. And she hadn't backed out of the date. Yep, calculus tutoring was much better than I imagined.

JILL

After I left the library, I marched up the steps of the mathematics department. These theory people could bug me sometimes, but without their work, the applied physics folks would never get the next extrasolar telescope out of earth's orbit.

Another session with Mike would send me colliding with the Hubble. Why did he have to be so handsome? Why did my body betray me this way?

I'd seen handsome guys before. But he was handsome and smart…and witty, and confident, and a flirt. And I had no time for a man like that.

I knocked on the frame of the open office where the secretary sat behind a large desk.

"Hello, Jill." Ms. Singer waved me in.

"Hi. I wanted to ask about the tutoring assignments." I fidgeted with the strap of my bag.

"I'm sorry, we don't have any more. We give you as many as we can. You're the best. But we do need to let the other tutors have a chance."

"Oh, no. I don't need any more. I think I might not be able to continue with one of my students." Sweat beaded at the back of my neck. Could I toss Mike aside like this? But judging by my reaction to him, I couldn't sit next to him one more time without losing myself in a relationship and risking my goals.

"Is there a problem?" Ms. Singer took her eyes off her computer screen.

"Not a problem really. It's Mike Lewis… He…he…"

"Did he do something?"

If sending my heart rate through the roof and invading my dreams was doing anything, then *yes*. "No. It's only, I don't see us as a good fit."

"That's a shame. He has a chance at honors and has made dean's list the previous two years. He asked specifically for the brightest tutor we had."

"I know." I looked away, unable to bear Ms.

Singer's kind, questioning eyes.

"Did he make you feel uncomfortable? I know sometimes those boys can get fresh."

Fresh would be a welcome relief from the heat. "Is there someone else who can tutor him?" I twisted the string from my hoodie.

"I'm sure I can find someone." Ms. Singer turned toward her computer again. "I'll give some sort of reason to the dean. Mike's father is a major donor to the university. Those new rooms in the student union…"

"His father paid for the rec room and bowling alley?" A chill streaked across my shoulders.

"Yes… Let's see. It looks like Russell is available."

"Mike's father knows the dean?"

"I would think so — they attended law school together. If I recall, they were high school friends as well." Ms. Singer made a note on her pad. "Can you wait while I give Russell a call? In case he says no."

The last thing I needed was any negative story about me circulating around the dean's office. As the tutor who refused to help the disabled son of the dean's best friend, I'd never get the internship.

"Wait," I yelled, and held out my hand.

Ms. Singer's finger froze above the phone keys.

"I can keep tutoring him. It's really no problem. I was thinking I might be too busy, but what's one more student? Plus, I really need the money. Don't call Russell."

"Good. Russell's an idiot anyway. But you didn't hear that from me." Ms. Singer replaced the phone.

I said good-bye and drifted out to the daylight.

Mike was well connected. He'd get into any law school he wanted. He didn't need a paid internship to keep afloat. Probably didn't need a part-time job either.

I meandered across the quad and was nearly hit by a passing Frisbee.

There was no getting out of this situation. Mike was the one student I couldn't give up.

If I were stuck with him, then I'd make the most of it. No reason a responsible, intelligent person couldn't control her urges around another intelligent person. As long as he stopped being so good-looking and funny and talking about my scent.

After two weeks, I was inured to Mike's good looks. They didn't affect me anymore. I could sit there and concentrate on the work and not be distracted by his mesmerizing, almost aquamarine, eyes. The square jaw shadowed by a day's growth of thick beard and his broad chest did nothing for me anymore. *Yeah, right.*

"How did the problem set go?" I sat across from him.

"Great—got nine out of ten correct," he said. "No thanks to you."

"What do you want? Me to do the homework for you?"

"That would be nice. It would leave me more time for other things."

"Like what?" I crossed my arms over my chest to keep from shaking. The last thing I needed was another cheating incident.

"Working on my tan." Mike leaned his head back and pretended to bask in the sun, which was really the yellow-green-tinged fluorescent light.

"Sure." But my mind wandered to Mike in a bathing suit, riding at his waist. A line of hair trailing down and disappearing. And then I brought myself to a stop. Would he be able to use his crutches on the beach?

"Let's take a look at your lecture notes for the week. The midterm is coming up, and it's one thing to be able to do the problems with the textbook open, but what's going to happen during the test?"

"Don't worry. I made a small cheat sheet. I can fit it inside the cuff of my crutch. No one will think I hid it there."

My mouth went dry. I had suspected one or two of the people I tutored of cheating. But none had ever said so. The corner of my mind where I kept my own secret pinged. The tremor in my hand forced me to lay it flat on the table.

"You're that desperate to get an A?" I forced the words out, not really wanting the answer.

Mike tipped his head back, this time laughing so loudly it echoed around the small study room. "Gotcha!" he said as his laughter subsided. "Don't know why I think that's funny. I should be insulted you believed me so easily." He pretended to look hurt.

"Just show me your lecture notes." My face grew hot and my neck tensed. I shouldn't have been put off by his teasing, but it hurt. He had no way of knowing how close to home he'd hit.

Mike didn't say anything as he pulled out his laptop. I bent my head down to get a look at the screen. He radiated warmth. His cologne was citrusy and light, and mingled with a natural musky scent. His arm brushed against mine, and damn if I didn't have to squeeze my knees together to stop the throbbing between my legs.

"Do you think you understand the differential here?" I pointed. How could my body betray me? Especially after what he had just said about cheating.

"Yeah. Listen, I'm sorry. I didn't want to piss you off."

"No problem. Why should I be angry?" I tried to keep my voice steady, but I heard it crack with embarrassment.

"Because I can be an idiot sometimes. Despite how much of a genius I am."

"If you're such a genius, why did you miss this integral problem?"

"My intelligence ends at integrals."

"Uh-huh." I wanted to stay angry at him for teasing. But I couldn't. He was too damn charming. "Let's work on these problems, genius." I sighed and accepted that Mike was Mike—charming, snarky, and gorgeous. I wrote out a few problems for him to puzzle over.

"So what do you plan to do with your intelligence?" Mike asked, his eyes widening as I rapidly listed problems. "I mean, how can you think up problems so quickly? Do you even know the answers to them?"

"Do you?" I challenged. "I'm studying astronomy. At least, that's the plan when I graduate. Physics major, then a PhD, hopefully here where we have access to all the big observatories' data."

"Cool. I'm a Virgo, what's your sign?"

"That's *astrology*. It's not a—" Mike's laugh interrupted me.

"Gotcha again. You're too easy," he said.

"You only wish I was easy," I said flatly, still keeping my eyes on the paper to suppress a grin.

Mike laughed again, this time a much more sincere laugh. "Now you got me. We're even."

"Come on, get to work. Or you'll never stand a chance at making Phi Beta Kappa."

He finally settled in, chewing his lip as he

scribbled and erased his way down the sheet. I shouldn't be falling for him. He was not only my student, but someone as driven as I was. He'd probably be going to some Ivy League law school after next year. And I would hopefully be staying here and working. Neither of us had time for a relationship.

"You made a mistake right here. See when you integrated x-squared?"

"You know, you make it hard to concentrate when you smell so nice."

"Humph!" But I couldn't keep the smile from forming on my face. "Let's try some more."

He shook his head. "I should go now. I have a class right after this in Stinson Hall."

"Oh." That was only halfway across the quad. But he didn't move as fast as everyone else. It probably took him longer, especially if he had to wait for elevators. He probably had to wait for two elevators, one here at the library to go downstairs and one to go back up at the lecture hall. "Do you mean you need some extra time to get to class?"

"Uh, yeah." Mike busied himself with packing up his things and didn't look up.

"Why are you just telling me now? We've been meeting for three weeks. Why didn't you say so from the beginning?" I stood and put my hands on my hips. I didn't mean to sound like a scolding parent, but I couldn't help it.

"Um." Mike's confidence and cocky demeanor vanished.

"Why don't we begin fifteen minutes earlier? Can you make it then?" I toned down my voice.

"Sure. Thanks," he mumbled.

"No problem at all." I continued to stare straight at him until finally he met my gaze. His ocean-green eyes still shone brightly, but this time his brow was furrowed and he looked vulnerable. That was wrong. He was supposed to be a smart-ass. He was a better person when he made jokes, even at my expense. This fragile part of him was too delicate to handle.

"Well, get going." I pointed toward the door.

His face relaxed into his normal expression. His mouth turned up into the smirk he wore so often, and I let out a breath I had been holding.

Chapter 4

JILL

"Did I tell you about my new student?"

Nikki clattered dishes onto the table in what passed as the dining area in my tiny apartment.

"No, why? Is he remarkable in some way?" Nikki was a physics major, too, but that was where our similarities ended. I probably wouldn't have sought her out to be a friend, but as we were frequently the only two women in the more advanced classes, we gravitated to each other. Nikki and her brusque manner grew on me, even rubbed off a little.

"He uses crutches to get around," I answered.

"Why?"

"I don't know. It seemed rude to ask."

"Why?"

"Come on, Nikki. Even you must understand some of the social graces we humans use to get along with each other."

"I understand them. I may not follow them or agree with them, but I get it."

I stirred the marinara sauce on the stove. At least once a week, Nikki came over for a much-yearned-for home-cooked meal. Her dorm living meant she ate anything she could microwave or choke down at the dining hall. Cooking was my one creative endeavor. Nikki wasn't an adventurous eater, but it was still a great opportunity to fire up the stove. Cooking for myself felt pathetic. But living alone was way more desirable than living with other people.

Nikki chopped some cucumbers for the salad and bumped my arm, causing sauce to splash on the stove.

"I'd apologize, but this kitchen is so small I can't take responsibility," Nikki said.

"It's your crazy-long arms and legs that are the problem. The kitchen is perfectly proportioned to the room."

"Which is why it fits in this closet."

It was true. With the bifold doors shut, the sink, stove, and fridge disappeared from the rest of the room. I put my handmade ravioli one by one into the pot of boiling water.

"Do you think I should ask him why he can't walk?"

"If you want to." Nikki bent over with her head in the half-size fridge. "You have anything else for the salad?"

"I'm curious about him, but really it's none of my business."

"Yep, it's none of your business." Nikki examined a tomato that may have been past its prime.

"But maybe it would help me understand him better. Maybe I need to know, so I can tutor him more effectively."

Nikki stood up and glared at me. "You don't believe that for a minute. And please don't expect me to believe it either. Don't tell yourself a lie. If you want to ask him, then ask him. But don't try to make it out to be anything other than your curiosity."

"You're right." I sighed. "But I don't want to seem nosy."

"Nothing wrong with nosy. If humans weren't curious, we'd never have discovered how to make fire, let alone wine." Nikki held up a bottle she pulled from the freezer. "Cossack brand vodka? Really?"

"It was all I could get Samantha to buy for me. One more year and we'll shop for our own stuff."

"If we mix in enough juice, it should be fine." Nikki twisted the cap and poured some into two mismatched tumblers.

"I'm curious about Mike. And I shouldn't be. I want to know more, because he's so charming and outgoing. Has he always had trouble walking? Was it an accident? Maybe his personality is compensating for his disability."

"Eureka! You've got a crush. You're smitten." Nikki grimaced.

"Shut up." I felt myself blush, and turned away. "Okay, you're right again, he's good-looking, and charming, and smart—but not in math. But I don't have time for a boyfriend now. Not with my senior project. And I don't want to lead him on any more than I already have."

"Any more?" Nikki sputtered her drink.

"We have this bet. He says if he gets an A in calculus, I have to go out with him. Only for dinner," I added.

Nikki rolled her eyes. "I give up. You've already made up your mind. You're in love, and senior project or no senior project, you'll end up dating."

It was my turn to glare. "What makes you say that?"

"I've seen it all the time." Nikki waved her hand. "People say they don't want a relationship. They don't have time. Blah blah blah. It's all an excuse so they can say later it was 'true love' and they had no choice but to be together."

"I may not have to go out with him anyway."

"Why's that?"

"He might not get an A."

MIKE

"Hey, dude, come over here." Rick got up to meet me at the end of the cafeteria line.

The crowded hall reverberated with the din of hundreds of animated conversations. The heat from the chow line made the skin of my biceps chafe against the crutch brackets. And if I ignored the scent of the chicken Kiev, I could get an appetite up for the pasta on my plate.

With the tray balanced at the end of the counter, I could just about make it to the nearby table. But Rick wasn't going to let me try. The Theta Chi brother grabbed the tray and led me over to where six others from the house ate.

"Hey, Mike," they all said in turn, some giving a fist bump.

"So, who's going to the Delta Delta Delta party on Saturday?" Rick asked.

As each one responded by saying who they were bringing to the party or who they hoped to hook up with while they were there, I stayed focused on my meal. There was no shortage of women to go with. Mostly because tri-Deltas and Theta Chis always stuck together. And because women seemed to like the novelty of dating a crippled guy. The novelty soon wore off when they couldn't get on the dance floor or had to take a bus on a date instead of being driven in a car.

"Mikey, Lorna was asking me about you," Steve said.

"Not my type," I answered through a mouthful of macaroni.

"Come on. You haven't been on a date since Meredith."

"Don't remind me. She was psycho," I said. "Besides, I've got my eye on someone."

"Really?"

"My math tutor, she's hot."

"Math tutor? For real? Some geek?" Steve rolled his eyes.

I had joined Theta Chi because it had been Dad's house when he was in college. And for the most part I fit in with the jocks. I'd been one once. Although that seemed like a long time ago.

"Why not Beth?" Ray asked. "She's always stopping by."

"Beth's a friend. We work on the sets and lights for the plays together."

"Mmm-hmm. She doesn't look at you like a friend. More like a tiger stalking prey."

I took a moment to swallow. I couldn't let the guys think I was giving up a sure thing. If a woman made her interests known, as Beth had, they would wonder if I turned her down because I was scared to be with a woman. I didn't want to look like a pussy.

"We simply spend a lot of time together because we take the same classes. Beth and I are like brother and sister."

"More like kissing cousins." Ray nudged my shoulder.

The conversation turned again to the party and who was bringing the keg and the cups. I did have someone else in mind. Jill. I had Jill on the mind so bad my mind refused to think about other things. This wasn't good.

In high school, I could get whatever girl I wanted. All I had to do was ask, and she'd say yes to the starting quarterback. And then... Well, for a few years I didn't even think about girls. If I ever thought about girls during that time it was only in an abstract way. Like, would I ever date again? Get married? Have a family? Be able to walk down the aisle?

And then, when I knew everything would work properly, I was glad. But the way girls treated me changed. No longer the athletic stud to bat their eyelashes at, I was cared for. In other words, pitied.

My math tutor wasn't merely good-looking, she was clever. And not just smart in a bookish way. She was bright and witty. And most of all, she wasn't afraid of my crutches.

At first, it was a physical thing. Always is at first. I'm a guy like every guy. I notice a sexy girl when I see one. But when she suggested changing the meeting time, that was what pushed me over the edge.

She didn't hem and haw, she blurted it right out,

nearly scolded me. Even my own family tiptoed around "the subject." Finally, someone who was cool with my legs. Bonus—I was going to get that A minus. And that date.

With lunch over, I moved to stand, and before I could reach out, a buddy grabbed my tray and whisked it away. I didn't say, "Thank you" and anyway, no one would say, "You're welcome."

The walk to the Health Sciences Building always took longer than it should. Late fall had settled in and it was on the edge of comfortable to be outside. The air was cool and the wind blowing across my ears urged me to galumph faster. Head down, crutches clomping against the sidewalk, I didn't look ahead until I heard my name.

"Mike, how are you?"

Jill. The scarf she wore had drooped, leaving her elegant neck exposed. Her nose was red from the bite of the wind. I forced my hands to stay where they were instead of giving in to the urge to bundle the scarf around her. Good thing the temperature kept everything quiet down below.

"Hey, Jill. Long time no see."

"I was heading to the office." She pointed toward the science quad.

"I've got an appointment." I nodded toward Health Services.

"Oh." She shifted her weight from side to side.

I winced. Normally, I didn't mind putting

people on the spot. I liked to watch them squirm with the discomfort of not knowing what to say about my disability. But Jill had proved herself and deserved better than my usual challenges.

"Is it for your legs or have you got an STD?" She smirked.

I laughed so hard the cold air went down into my lungs and sent me coughing. "STD. But don't worry, I'll be good as new by the time we're out on our date."

"Sure, sure." She waved her arm, dismissing the idea. "See you next time. Don't forget to study those theorems."

"Yes, ma'am." I gave her my best wink and watched her walk away. Her ass swished invitingly even under her coat. Again, I thanked the frigid Chicago wind.

Once inside, I didn't turn toward the medical services wing. Instead, I clunked down the hall, following the signs for "Mental Health."

Chapter 5

MIKE

"Dr. Marlow, how many more of these sessions do I have?" I took the overstuffed chair opposite the therapist.

Dr. Marlow had probably done his best to change the sterile office into a calm haven for patients to spill their guts. But the ethnic wall hanging and the earth-toned natural fiber area rug didn't do much to change the fact that he was a shrink and I had to bare my soul.

"We should continue our sessions until you're completely sure of your decision." Dr. Marlow held up his hand before I could interrupt. "Or until I'm convinced you're completely sure."

"I'm fine with this decision. We've been over it a million times. It's not like I'm going to be a different person after the surgery. I'll be the same old Mike, only better."

"Better how?" Dr. Marlow folded his hands in

his lap.

"Are you kidding?" I moved forward in the seat. "No more crutches. No more waiting for elevators that won't come. No more unbearable pain in my ankles and shins." I rubbed my lower leg where a constant ache reminded me of how my life had fallen apart. "No more having someone help me carry my tray. I'll have my hands free when I walk. You know, I could walk and chew gum at the same time."

Dr. Marlow laughed. "Your humor, we've discussed it."

I sighed. "What's wrong with a defense mechanism? And humor is a pretty good one. Right? It could be worse. I could use anger." I gave Dr. Marlow my signature smirk.

"True, humor does make it more pleasant to be around you. But either way, you're avoiding your true feelings."

"Which are?" I rolled my eyes.

"You tell me."

I had a great sarcastic comeback on the tip of my tongue, but Dr. Marlow's sincere expression thumped my solar plexus, and I fought for a breath. "Okay, I'm scared." I regained my balance and my smart-remark ability. "But who wouldn't be? It's not everyone who makes a decision to have their legs chopped off."

"Fear is, of course, natural. And I guess you want me to think that by using the term 'chopped off' instead of 'amputate' you're really comfortable with this idea."

"Amputate, chopped off, what's the difference?" My throat closed around the words.

"Yes, they mean the same things." Dr. Marlow leaned forward in his chair. "But one term uses humor. It divorces you from the reality of what the doctors are going to do to you."

The leather seat had become warm, and stuck to my back.

"I know what they're going to do. Get rid of these useless, painful legs." I gripped my knee and shook it. "Pieces of shit that ache in the winter and swell in the summer. Not good for anything anymore. I want to walk again."

"You do walk now," Dr. Marlow said.

"No, I don't. I get around. I don't walk. I swing my hips and balance as best I can. I look ridiculous." Why couldn't anyone understand? Even this trained professional didn't get it. Constant pain was exhausting. And if people were going to stare at me for my entire life, it might as well be while I held my back straight.

"Walking on prosthetics isn't the most natural gait."

"I'll make it work. I can make it look like walking. I'll be standing, upright, like a real man."

JILL

The door to the study room swung open. I forced myself to stay seated as Mike maneuvered his left side inside, held the door open with a crutch, and swung his right side in before releasing the weighted swoosh of the door. I watched the entire process.

I refused to be one of those people who looked away. Besides, the line from the nape of his neck to his shoulder was a pleasant sight.

"So I've been planning our date," Mike said as he plopped into the chair next to me.

"Pretty sure of yourself, aren't you?" But when he pulled off his sweater, his shirt hiked up, revealing a really nice set of abs. I swallowed. He had every right to feel sure of himself.

Mike grinned. "I have confidence in you." He pulled out a sheet of paper. "Read it and put on your party dress."

I took the paper and looked at the midterm. "An A minus! You did it." Then suspicion took hold. "Did you cheat?"

"Cheat? Me?" Mike laughed. "Is that what you think of me?"

"No." I laughed, too. "I'm just…"

"Impressed? Awed? Ready to admit I'm a calculus stud?" Mike spread his arms out.

"It does seem like you don't need tutoring

anymore." I smiled and sat back. He was a cocky guy. Maybe it was what got him through the day. But that confidence also made my mouth water.

"What? No, I didn't mean that. I need tutoring, lots of tutoring. Preferably over a candlelit dinner." He rested his hand near mine on the table.

"Uhn-uh, we had a deal. You need an A as your final grade. Midterm is only one step." My body wanted him to get the A. My brain warned me to aim for a B plus.

"Don't tell me there's more to learn." Mike shook his head.

"And it gets harder." I tried to mimic his overconfident smirk.

"I hate it when you look at me like that. Like a cat that's eaten the canary."

"We should get to work." I wanted to avoid any further references of eating him. He looked yummy enough that I often thought about how he would taste.

"Let's put off work. Tell me more about you."

"Why?"

"I'm interested. Explain astronomy to me." He clasped his hands behind his head. I tried not to admire his strong biceps.

"I can't just explain astronomy."

"Then tell me one thing, one thing that makes it tolerable to spend all your time in that office."

"Dr. Shaffer is studying the rate at which the

universe is expanding, inflation. We know it's speeding up, but we need to find out more about how quickly it's moving. It's fascinating work, even if most of what I get to do is boring grunt work, and sometimes other people's work."

"What do you mean?"

"As an undergrad, I get dumped on a lot. There's one grad student who's always pushing his work off on me. I hate saving his butt all the time, but I need to make a good impression." I opened the textbook. No way was I going to discuss Robert and the fiasco.

Mike's face had screwed up. "I don't get it. Then why do you do it?"

"To get ahead. Why do you kill yourself to get Phi Beta Kappa?"

"To get my dad off my back." He didn't say any more, and kept his eyes fixed on the table and the exam paper.

I sighed. *Okay, I can play that game. We'll simply do math. Mr. Bravado gets all scared when the focus is on him.*

As we went over the midterm and the few problems he got wrong, Nikki's words ran through my head. Why shouldn't I ask about his legs? After all, he was the one who wanted us to become closer. Not talking about it was almost calling too much attention to them. His crutches were the elephant in the room. Being straightforward wasn't easy though.

I did best quietly going along, nodding and agreeing, and never getting too deep with anyone.

"So, you, uh, will have enough time to get to class, right?" I asked.

"Yeah, thanks for coming earlier." He kept his head down as he packed up his things and pulled the crutches from under the table.

"Are you ever going to tell me?" I surprised myself as the words came out while I stared at his legs. I hadn't expected to say it like that. And judging by the scowl on Mike's face, I hadn't said it right.

After a few seconds, he brought his head up to meet me, eye to eye. "Car accident. Senior year in high school. My buddy was driving, drunk. I was the passenger. He walked away." Mike shrugged. "Did some damage to a tree and destroyed Mrs. McCoy's mailbox, though."

My mind raced through responses. I hadn't been prepared for him to answer. I couldn't say a lame "sorry." Everyone must have told him they were sorry.

"Was she mad?" I asked.

"Huh?"

"Was Mrs. McCoy angry about her mailbox?"

Mike let out a breath and his scowl completely disappeared. A grin spread across his face, lighting up his eyes again. And the tightness in my chest eased.

"Yeah. I don't remember much. But I could hear

her coming out on her porch yelling and screaming."

"She might have been concerned about the crash."

"Nah, she had the box all painted to look like a cow."

"She deserved it, then. I hate cutesy mailboxes."

"Yeah, we did the neighborhood a favor," he said.

"Well, see you next week." I closed the textbook and slipped it in my bag. My breath came easy. We'd crossed over that secrecy and lived.

"See you then, Jill." My name on his lips sent a tingle to places I didn't normally focus on in the library. He stood, whipped his bag over his shoulder, and crossed the room, his crutches clicking as he went. He let the door close softly as he left.

Crap. I didn't want to feel excited by him, but all he had to do was say my name and I forgot what was important.

I packed up my stuff and pointed myself toward the lab for another chance to get some work done. Provided Robert didn't foist his work on me.

Outside the library, fall had given up, and winter was just settling in. The trees were bare, but enough leaves still lay on the path along with the occasional icy patch to make the slate walkway slippery. The quad was crisscrossed with paths to the lecture halls and professors' offices. A few modern concrete buildings broke up the gray stone Gothic structures that dripped with gargoyles. A slight freezing drizzle fell, creating an eerie mist.

Midterms were over. The decision about the internship would be announced at the beginning of the spring semester. Time was rushing away, and I felt like I was hurtling through the asteroid belt. The internship, my project, Mike—all of it was coming at me and I couldn't dodge around it fast enough.

It had been the right thing to do. To ask him about his legs. It was over now. We could put it behind us. I wouldn't have to think about it again. And if I did decide to go out with him, it wouldn't be an issue. He'd explained it. We wouldn't have to discuss it ever.

With renewed confidence about the Mike situation, I marched on toward the office. Already caught up in my plans for my work, I almost tripped when I noticed some commotion ahead.

A cluster of people stood around staring at the ground. As I got closer, I realized they were staring at a person. Someone was lying on the ground. A familiar backpack stuck out from the crowd.

My first instinct was to run forward to see if Mike was okay. But I stopped, took a few steps back, and stood halfway behind a tree.

His crutches must have slipped on the slick walkway. Mike got up with some help from another student. His face burned red with shame. My gut clenched when he shook his head, letting people know he didn't need any help. Someone lifted his backpack for him and he shrugged it on.

I knew his face well enough now to see the hard-set jaw. Rage boiled in him, and he only wanted people to ignore him. I couldn't go over to him now. He'd be humiliated and probably never come to tutoring again.

After a moment, the crowd dispersed and Mike set out again toward his next class. I observed him proceeding gingerly, taking care to place his crutches in dry spots.

Yes, Mike's crutches would be with him always. Watching him struggle to regain his balance and his pride, I wondered if I could ever deal as well as he could? His disability was something he would have to constantly cope with. Whoever loved him would have to struggle with it, too.

If I loved someone, I could probably cope with it. But I didn't love Mike—not yet, anyway. And I didn't want to fall in love with him either. There wasn't time for a relationship with a man who didn't have a disability, let alone one who did. Guilt swept through me, and I blinked back tears. If this made me a bad person, then so be it. I wasn't about to give up on my goals now. I hadn't spent the last three years proving myself in a man's world only to throw it all away for a man.

Chapter 6

MIKE

Incessant bells grew louder and louder, interrupting a hot dream of being wrapped around Jill.

I squinted against the sun streaming through the window and tossed the alarm clock under my bed with more force than necessary.

Damn, I wanted to get back into that dream.

"Doesn't change the time, buddy," Jeff, my roommate at Theta Chi house, grumbled into his pillow.

"I know, I know. I can't understand why rehearsal is so early. Theater people are supposed to be night owls."

Jeff laughed and rolled over. I forced my eyes open and reached out for my crutches. One had gotten knocked under the bed, probably when I threw the clock. I reached my arm as far under the bed as it could go, my fingertips brushing the cool metal. Grunting, I got one finger hooked over the side and dragged it out. Jeff would never offer to help, and I was grateful. I grabbed shampoo and shaving stuff and went to the bathroom.

Sharing a bathroom with a houseful of guys was not a treat. The floor was always wet and slippery, not to mention the gross state of things. My buddies were sensitive enough to never leave anything resting on my shower seat and never walked in while I brushed my teeth. Although it was common to interrupt someone in the shower, no one went in while I was in there.

They let me share Jeff's room on the first floor. Normally, the president got this room to himself, but since it was the only bedroom on the ground floor, I moved into it sophomore year when I finally convinced Mom and Dad I was capable of moving out and living on campus.

I was over being embarrassed by how my legs looked. It was everyone else's problem, not mine. When the weather was warm, I wore shorts and dared people with my glare to make a comment. With the weather turning cold, I could put away one more deadly stare and wear long pants again.

As I ate breakfast in the kitchen area, my phone rang.

"Hi, Mom," I mumbled through my toaster waffle.

"Hi, Mikey. Sorry to call so early, but I can't ever get you otherwise."

"S'okay. What's up?"

"Dad wanted me to call and see if you could come to your brother's game this weekend. It's regionals."

The trepidation in my mother's voice told me she still hadn't figured out I didn't care if others could play sports. *When will they stop handling me with kid gloves?* Of course I'd go watch my little brother play football. I could be proud of James without feeling sorry for myself. In fact, in some ways, it was a relief not to play sports anymore.

"I wouldn't miss it," I said. "How's Dad?"

Dad had sent Mom to do the job of inviting me to the game. Despite his arrogant talk of courage, Dad was chickenshit when it came to my legs.

"He's the busiest judge in the area, as usual, but now with all the events and meetings for his reelection, I never see him."

"Uh-huh."

"So, we'll pick you up Saturday morning. Oh, your father wants to say hello."

Of course. Now that Mom had done the hard part, he could talk.

"Hey there, Mike. How are your classes?"

"Great, Dad. The political science class is really interesting. We're—"

"I mean, how are your grades?"

"All good," I said.

"Even calculus?" Dad didn't even try to hide his

doubt.

"Even calc. My tutor is great. She —"

"Fine, fine. You know I only ask because you're going to need perfect grades to get into a top law school. You won't have the other type of connections."

What he meant was that I wouldn't have the "well-rounded" application without having worked on an election campaign or been a part of a sports team, like he had.

"Don't worry, Dad. I think my volunteer work at the shelter and theater involvement make a complete application."

My dear old father's only response was to snort.

"Speaking of which, the play I'm working on will be in December, right before classes end. Can you guys come?"

"You're not in it, are you?" His deep voice rose with strain.

"No, but I'm the sound designer." I held my breath. Which was worse? Dad's embarrassment about my performing on stage with crutches or knowing I'd hardly be cast in any roles unless I could walk upright?

"Oh, I'll check with your mother. We might be busy."

"Sure. Okay, see you Saturday." I hung up.

I tried not to let his reaction get to me. Mostly, I didn't think about his expectations anymore. I had my own plans, and whatever fantasy Dad held on to about Harvard Law School was not my concern.

One hour later, pain shot up my calf as I stepped off the campus's courtesy shuttle, which for me was a necessity rather than a courtesy. I walked into the morning rehearsal for *Oklahoma!* and winced. The cast was warming up by singing the title song. Musicals—not my favorite. But I'd landed a job doing the soundboard, which was good experience.

Although I took all the required theater classes, and even won some roles in the small plays that were part of the classes, I was never cast in the big productions on campus. Not that I ever auditioned. Who wanted to see Curly, the lead cowboy, hobbling out on crutches? But I did get to participate behind the scenes. Once, for *Macbeth*, I even convinced the director I could do lights. It was a struggle, and I nearly fell from the catwalk. But I did it, mostly by crawling on my hands and knees. I made it work.

Being the sound designer was pretty cool, especially for a big musical. I'd even helped out on costumes, finding I had a fairly good hand at the sewing machine. I would never let my family or the Theta Chis know about that.

"Hey, Michael, how are you?" Beth said.

Beth's perfect, lithe figure was framed in the

doorway of the sound booth. She, of course, was playing the lead, Laurey. Skilled with costumes, lights, sound, sets, she was a theater stud. I was lucky she'd befriended me, and I could relax around her.

"Hey, Beth. Is that your costume?" I pointed to a pile of heavy fabric draped over her arm.

"It will be. Want to help me after rehearsal? I need to put this Velcro on for a quick change."

"Sure."

"And then I'll make you a home cooked meal, and take you to the laundromat if you need to go."

"Okay."

Confidence, grace, poise—all described her. She was never without makeup, and her outfits seemed casual but were put together to show off her figure. And a boyfriend on crutches would be the perfect accessory for the campus theater star. But as much as she came on to me, I couldn't bring myself to become her leading man.

The woman I would end up with wouldn't be emotional. She would be sarcastic and smart. She wouldn't do all that touchy-feely talk, or want to take care of me. She wouldn't mother or smother or watch out for my needs. She'd ignore my legs as much as I tried to.

JILL

"Thanks, Dr. Shaffer." I accepted the recommendation the famous professor held out to me.

He'd risen from his desk and come around to greet me when I entered the nearly empty office. In the opposite corner of the room, a sole post-doc had his head buried in a spreadsheet.

"My pleasure. I think you're a shoo-in for the intern position. It'll be great to have your help." Dr. Shaffer was not only head of the astronomy program, he had connections with NASA and seemed pleased with the work I had done so far. I would do anything to stay in his good graces.

"I'd much rather be working here this summer than waiting tables and tutoring. This recommendation is sure to help with the selection committee."

"Your talents would be wasted carting around pizzas."

I smiled and returned to the desk and computer screen. To the untrained eye, the various blurry spots could hardly be distinguished from one another. But I was looking at different types of galaxies all various distances from my tiny spot on earth.

I hadn't been at it long when Nikki came in and sat down next to me.

"You almost done?"

"No, I just started." I didn't take my eyes off the screen.

"Well, hurry up. I want to get a good spot in line," Nikki said, referring to the line that would soon start forming for a festival-seating concert later that night.

"Shaffer just gave me a glowing recommendation for the internship. It wouldn't look good if I left now." I turned to glance at Nikki. Making eye contact was a mistake, because Nikki could convince me to do anything. How many times had she come up while I was studying at the library and plunked the movie listings in front of me?

"How do you manage to get such good grades and be such a slacker?" I asked.

"I'm a natural genius." Nikki shrugged. "Those all look the same." She pointed her chin toward the screen.

"You particle accelerator people don't appreciate the large objects."

"Oh, there are some large objects I appreciate. And one of them will be there tonight. If we don't go soon, someone else will find Kenneth and sit next to him."

"So that's what this is about," I said.

"That's what it's always about."

"Give me a half-hour, and I'll meet you there." I sighed.

"Fine, but try to leave your poor attitude here."

Nikki left.

I returned to the computer, but didn't get very far until I was interrupted again. This time, someone had come up silently behind me. When I felt that person's presence, I jumped in my seat.

"I didn't mean to startle you," Dr. Shaffer said.

"It's okay. I was concentrating."

"I saw your friend come in. You know, a young woman should be out having fun. Don't hang around here too long."

"Really?"

Dr. Shaffer should be the last one to talk. He spent hours in his office. Everyone joked that his wife wouldn't recognize him if he ever went home.

"The data will still be here." He placed a hand on my shoulder and gave it a gentle squeeze. "But you're only twenty once."

I nodded and agreed to finish up. My own parents were great, but not the loving, touchy-feely types. Rarely did they offer a supportive or nurturing word.

It was comforting to have a mentor who cared. And Dr. Shaffer showed an interest in my future. I didn't want to get my hopes up. I figured I stood a good chance at that internship. It would start this summer and continue through the next school year. The summer would allow plenty of time to work on my senior project, build more of a reputation, and earn a spot in the graduate program.

I'd enjoy working with Dr. Shaffer. He was kind and understanding. He went out of his way to support me. He seemed to understand the difficulty of being one of the very few women in the department. In fact, Dr. Shaffer had the only female graduate students from the department in his group, and seemed to make sure they received an even footing with the men. I took a deep breath and realized I was really lucky. I had everything I could want.

Except Mike. Any attempt to wipe away the images from our last session failed. My name on his lips, the sincerity when he told his story. I could have him. He'd made that obvious enough. But did I want him? Okay, I wanted him. But did I want the distraction he'd be? I needed to stay focused.

The one time I'd lost focus, Robert had wowed me with his brains and charm. As a sophomore, the attention from someone so much older and more experienced had been heady. After dating a few months, he'd whisked me away for a long weekend to his parents' cabin on the lake. Of course, I'd brought my work with me. My final project in Dr. Shaffer's cosmology course had been due. But hiking and boating and screwing seemed to take up so much time. We'd headed for home later than expected and then the distributor in his beat-up Camaro had died on Lake Shore Drive. We'd finally arrived back on campus at two a.m. with barely time to get any work done.

Robert's "help" on my final project seemed like a fair deal, since I'd paid for the tow. A deal with the devil.

Sure, Mike wouldn't hold anything over me like Robert did. But a distraction was a distraction.

Even though I trusted him, I didn't want to walk on eggshells around Mike, always vigilant about what to say. Would I hurt his feelings? It was the hard truth; I hated to admit it. But no matter how sexy, smart, and charming he was, I didn't want to take on the burden that went with Mike.

Chapter 7

MIKE

If anyone had told me two months ago I would look forward to tutoring, I would've laughed in his face. It was time to pull out all the stops—hair fresh from the barber's, the expensive cologne Mom gave me, and a t-shirt tight enough to show off the results of my upper-body work. If there was one thing I could boast about my body, it was my pecs. I was ready for Jill's arrival. No other woman had ever seemed as comfortable with my disability. And not since the accident had I had the confidence to pursue a woman.

I'd never had a problem asking a girl out in high school. Heck, I never had to ask—they came to me. The accident cured me of that cocky confidence. But with Jill, some of my old bravado returned.

"Miss me?" I said as Jill swished into the study room.

She rolled her eyes and fell into the strategically

placed chair close to my side. "You don't give up."

"Eventually, I might. But I haven't even started yet." She was adorable when she was exasperated. Her blue eyes peered straight to my heart. Yep, I was whipped. She was an intelligent, bright woman. With enough fight in her to keep me interested.

"Let's start with calculus, shall we?" She said it with determination, but I detected a hint of a smile.

"Who made this rule? Where is it written that I need to know calculus?"

"The student handbook, I believe," she said flatly.

"But I'll never need it for anything," I insisted.

"That's not my problem." She flipped through the textbook pages with unnecessary force.

"What's with you?"

"Sorry, my friend had me up late last night. I'm grumpy without enough sleep."

"Where'd you go?"

"That campus emo band concert." She shrugged. "Not my thing. Nikki was looking for a guy."

"Any guy or someone specific?"

"A specific guy. She found him, but he was with someone else."

"Bummer for her."

"Not really. Nikki went right up to him and asked if he was in a serious relationship."

"She did?"

"You don't know Nikki. He admitted he and the

other girl were on a first date. And Nikki said, 'Well, then I stand a chance,' and I ended up driving Kenneth's date home, while Nikki stayed with Kenneth."

"No way."

"That's how it is with Nikki. I had to hold Kenneth's original date's hand all night as she cried." Jill yawned.

"Does Nikki always use you?" My fists clenched and my stomach tightened — automatic response to get ready for a fight.

"What?"

"You call her a friend. But it seems like she uses you. First, dragging you to a concert you're not really into, then ditching you for some guy, and then leaving you to take care of his date."

"You make it seem worse than it is."

"Do I?" I peered at her.

"Let's get on with this." She banged the textbook on the table with a thud.

I let it drop. No point in antagonizing her. But she was too good to let someone, a "friend," treat her that way. Why didn't she stand up for herself?

She always took charge of the tutoring sessions, would never let me lead her to other topics. Although I tried. She stood her ground. That was what I liked most about her. She wasn't mealy-mouthed when it came to the crutches, but came out and asked. And she'd demanded to know why I hadn't spoken up about needing extra time to get to class.

But with her friends she seemed different. Nikki walked all over her, and what about the day she'd dragged in an extra bag packed with someone else's data she'd agreed to analyze? Why didn't she say no to these people like she said no to me?

As usual, with our lessons I paid as close attention as I could to what she said. It wasn't difficult to look like I was paying attention—I was. But not to the actual words. Mostly I liked to watch her lips form syllables and listen to the sweet tone of her voice. She had a great voice, not high-pitched but light and breezy. She probably could have been a singer. I found myself focusing more on the shape of her face, the line of her cheekbone, the space behind her ear, and the smooth skin of her neck.

I shifted in the seat, hoping to quell the growing sensation beginning down under. Thinking of dead puppies usually worked. Luckily, all I had to do was look at the page of symbols and numbers and it was like a cold shower.

How was I going to maintain my GPA? I was hopeless at math. I only got that A minus on the midterm through sheer brute force. It took studying way into the night for several days leading up to the exam. Not that I'd ever tell Jill.

"Are you pondering the answer, or have I lost you?" Jill's voice broke into my thoughts.

"Sorry, just wondering again why the university has decided to torture me this way."

"So, now my lessons are torture?" She half smiled.

"Your lessons are sweet torture."

Her blush spread down her neck, into her t-shirt, and past what I imagined to be the most perfect tits.

"Relax." She straightened her spine. "This is the last requirement you've got. Senior year you'll apply to law schools with your Phi Beta Kappa key, and calculus will be a distant memory."

"I'm not applying to law school," I said.

"But you're pre-law." She squinted.

"That's to get my dad off my back. My minor is theater. My real plan is to star in Broadway. I'd settle for Hollywood."

"Oh!" After squinting at me for a moment, Jill looked back to the books.

I dare you. Go on say it. No one ever says it. No one I had ever told of my acting desires had ever come out and said, "Are you kidding? How are you going to walk across the stage?" Except for my father, no one had ever dared challenge this. They'd all been too polite, and scared.

Her head jerked up. She met my eyes. "Is there much call for actors on crutches?"

I was stunned, for a moment. And then I felt freer than I had in the three years since the accident.

"None, but I won't be on crutches." I let the

words hang there. I could wait out the longest, most uncomfortable pause.

Jill narrowed her eyes and squared her shoulders. "All right, stop beating around the bush. Tell me how a guy whose legs were wrecked in a car accident is going to get rid of his crutches and become an actor."

"I'm glad you asked. So few people do. They're too polite to point it out. Or they say something like, 'You can do anything you put your mind to.' I'll tell you what few people know. I'm going to have my legs amputated from below the knees."

Jill's eyes widened and her mouth fell open. "Oh, uh." And then she returned to her squinted, challenging stare. "And how will that help?"

"I'm going to work with the best prosthesis maker in the country. Right here in Chicago. I'll be almost bionic."

Jill considered this and looked down at my legs under the table. It was the most forward, brash, rude thing anyone had ever done. Blatantly staring at my skinny, shriveled legs. And it felt good.

"I guess that makes sense." Jill shrugged. "When are you doing this?"

"This summer, if all goes well. If the doctors all agree and the shrink gives me the all-clear."

She laughed, and I couldn't help but notice as she did her full breasts wiggling in a way that brought back the discomfort in my pants.

"I never thought I'd hear anyone say, 'If all goes well, I'll have my legs amputated.' I suppose I should wish you luck, then?"

"Sure."

"Good luck on getting your legs amputated." She nodded and held out her hand.

"Thanks." I accepted her hand. It was a feeble word, not enough to convey gratitude to someone who wasn't too polite to be sincere.

JILL

My nerves jangled more than if it were my own final exam. Maybe it had been a mistake to wait around for him while he took the test. I paced by the door again and attempted a casual glance into the room. Mike and two other students I'd tutored had their heads bent over their papers, along with about a hundred others. Although he sat in the far corner, I had no problem picking out his concentrating face, with half his bottom lip between his teeth.

When he'd arrived for the test, I'd been waiting outside. Surprise crossed his face for an instant, but then his sexy, charming self took over.

"I came to wish you good luck."

"I don't need it. I've got you." He'd touched my arm, singeing my nerve endings, and then joined the rest of the class.

Now I patrolled the hallway, checking and re-checking the time. The heat inside the building was blasting to compensate for the drafty windows, but I still felt the chill. Goosebumps pricked my arm where Mike had touched me. I was falling for him despite what I'd told myself. Mike came with too much baggage. When he smiled, however, I forgot all the warnings.

Shuffling noises came from inside the classroom, and the first test takers filed out. My other two students came up to report on how they had done. Both felt confident that they'd passed, and thanked me again and again for the help. Out of the corner of my eye I saw Mike waiting a discreet distance away. I tried to thank them and dismiss them without seeming rude.

"Well?" I asked as he finally approached.

"Well what? You know I aced it."

I rolled my eyes. "Okay, hotshot. Wait until next semester and we cover primitive integral."

"Mmmm. I love it when you talk dirty. Let's go out to celebrate tonight."

"Celebrate?"

"My grade—you know I got an A."

"I'll believe it when I see it." I almost agreed to go out with him. It seemed natural and right, friendly almost. Luckily, I came to my senses.

"Okay, then at least come to the performance

tomorrow night. I can take you backstage after and show you how the soundboard works."

"That would be cool. I'll try if I'm not too busy at the office—"

"And if no one gets you to do their work for them…"

I shoved my hands into my jeans pockets to keep from slapping him.

"Sorry, that was rude of me." His brow creased. "It's none of my business. You work hard because you have to. Forgive me?" He laid his hand on the sleeve of my sweatshirt, but my skin picked up the heat through the thick fabric.

"Sure," I said. Those words stung. He was right, of course. But that didn't mean it didn't hurt to hear how much of a pushover I must seem.

"Anyway. Look for me at the side door. If you come tomorrow night."

"Okay, and if I don't see you, have a good break."

"Yeah, merry Christmas."

Unsure what to do next, I took my hands out of my pockets, but my arms remained awkwardly at my sides. "Merry Christmas. See you for tutoring."

Chapter 8

MIKE

From the sound booth at the back of the theater, high above the seats, I had a good view of everyone coming in. I scanned the crowd, not sure who I was more anxious to see, my parents or Jill. What had started as some innocent flirting had turned quickly into a real obsession. I had two ways of dealing with people when I first met them. One was to be mean, ornery, and distant. That way, people were too scared to comment about my legs, or make eye contact long enough to convey that pitying look I despised.

The other approach was to be overly friendly and outgoing. If I really laid on the charm, people were captivated and impressed. They thought, *Here's a guy who doesn't let his disability get to him. See, he's not bothered by it at all, so I won't be either.*

Neither of these tactics allowed people to get close. After all, who the heck wants to hear a sob story about a youthful, athletic guy whose life was ruined in a few short moments? I hadn't been sincere with anyone since the accident. Certainly not my parents; they still acted like the car crash happened yesterday instead of three years ago.

"Hey, you all set?" Beth posed in the doorway. She was dressed in a peach-colored costume, complete with petticoats. Her pancake makeup was thick and looked unnatural, but would show off her even features onstage.

"Hey, yourself. What are you doing up here?"

"I wanted to say thanks for all your help with the costume. What do you think?" She turned in a circle.

"It looks great. If I do say so myself."

"We make a great team." She emphasized the word *team*, and her gaze was meant to penetrate.

I wanted to stay teammates and nothing more. A relationship with Beth would be too intense. Wild and fiery, sexy and fun, but intense. She would want to talk about feelings all the time. It would be like another Dr. Marlow session.

"Well, break a leg," I said.

"You too."

"Too late." I tapped my crutches. A sure fire way to keep some distance.

"Oh!" Beth put her hand over her mouth. "I didn't… I…"

"Beth, it's me you're talking to. Don't worry.

Now focus on the show. Go warm up your beautiful voice and wow them out there." I pointed to the audience below.

"Thanks." She leaned over to give me a peck on the cheek.

I misjudged where she was headed and turned, taking the kiss on the mouth. I was too stunned to move; our lips lingered for a moment too long.

"I. Uh." My head swam with her scent and the brush of her chest against my arm.

Beth laughed. "Theater people are always kissing each other."

At least she wouldn't make me deal with relationship potential tonight. "Knock 'em dead, *Laurey.*"

Beth gave a demure finger wave and flounced out in character down the rear stairs to the dressing rooms backstage.

In some ways, Beth was one person I could be authentic with. Most of the time, I could talk to her about my frustrations with my legs. She knew why I wanted the surgery. She shared my dreams of acting on the stage. And she rarely felt awkward around me.

I went through my checklist once more, although I still had plenty of time before the overture. Glancing down, I spotted Jill. She wore a blouse that wrapped around her and tied at the side. From this vantage, I had a nice view down the front of it. She was a small package, almost a foot shorter than I was. Than I had been. But the strain of the fabric across the front promised big things. Her hair was pulled back into that silly ponytail. She had gorgeous black hair that framed her face. When she let her hair loose, I had to cover my lap to hide my hard-on.

Jill was another person I was beginning to feel natural with. She never backed down when I challenged her to say some contrite remark about my disability, and she never offered sympathy. She'd do more than merely capitulate to go out with me. She'd never want to talk about my feelings, and she'd expect nothing in return. She was too busy to want a long-term relationship. On the other hand, one night with her wasn't going to be enough.

The assistant director came in to check, and I said I was good to go. One last look through the now-seated audience showed that my family hadn't come.

I put it all out of my mind. Time to get to work. The lights dimmed, the conductor raised his baton, and I focused on the controls. This was what made me zing. There probably would never be a person in my life who could get me as jazzed up as being part of a show.

JILL

I stood with the rest of the audience to applaud as the actors came out for curtain call. Their professional-like production could impress anyone, not only the friends and family in the audience. Particularly that actress who played Laurey. She was amazingly beautiful, and her voice matched. No doubt Beth Matthews, as her name was listed in the program, would go on to stardom. I had also read Michael Lewis, sound designer, in the program. Reading it sent a surprising jolt of pride to my chest.

As people filed out, I headed for the side door Mike had told me to look for. He had invited me backstage for a tour, but I simply wanted to tell him I'd enjoyed the show. Spending too much time with him outside of tutoring would only lead him on.

A few other people were also headed through the side door. Family members and friends of the cast carried bouquets, also looking to give their congratulations.

I stood at the side of the mass of people greeting each other, not knowing anyone and holding up the wall. The woman who played Laurey hugged and kissed a couple who must have been her parents, and they presented her with a dozen roses.

"Jill, over here."

I turned toward Mike's voice. He pushed his way through and approached my tiny corner of the area.

"Mike, the show was great." I was relieved to see him—a familiar face, a familiar, handsome face.

"Thanks. I think it went off without a hitch. No one noticed that Ado Annie missed her cue in the second act?" He nodded toward one of the actresses at the other end.

I laughed. "No, no one noticed."

"Hey, can you come to the cast party? We're all going over to a—"

"Mike! Son!" A voice boomed above the excited and raised voices.

"Dad! I didn't see you guys come in." Mike unhooked his arm from his crutch to reach over my shoulder and shook his father's hand, then kissed a woman who had come up to his side. She shared the same green eyes and thick hair as her son.

"Oh, Mikey, it was a lovely show. We could only come in after intermission. Your father had a fundraiser to attend."

"Hey, this is my math tutor I was telling you about, Jill." Mike nodded toward me.

"Hello, it's nice to meet you both." I plastered a smile on my face. I guessed I didn't rate *friend* status. Being introduced as his tutor threw me off balance.

"Well, Jill," the large man who towered over everyone in both voice and stature said. "Mike tells me you're helping him a great deal. His weakness has always been math, but overcoming a weakness makes you stronger."

I wondered if anyone else caught the significance of this statement, but Mr. Lewis didn't seem to notice.

"Did you enjoy the show, Mr. Lewis?" I asked to change the subject.

"Sure. Mike, ah, I could hear everything perfectly." Mr. Lewis nodded and looked around. He seemed to be searching for the nearest exit.

"It was just like when I saw it on Broadway years ago," Mrs. Lewis gushed.

"Kathy, we need to leave," Mr. Lewis said.

"Mikey, we'll come back in two days to pick you up for the break." His mother kissed him on the cheek.

They said their good-byes, and I noticed Mike's grip on his crutch and his posture relax once they left.

"It was good they could make it to part of the show," I said.

"Yeah, Dad's busy these days." Mike turned to look me in the eyes. "So how about it? Want to come to the party?"

His gaze, his thick, dirty-blond hair brushing his ear—both battled my wish to say no. In the time it took me to think of an answer, we were interrupted again.

"Oh, Michael, I saw your parents leave. I wanted to say hello. They're always so pleased with the performances." The woman who had the lead role, Laurey, was still in her costume, although it was undone a bit in back, and fell off her shoulder, exposing more of her perfect alabaster skin.

"Beth, this is Jill." Mike reached out and briefly touched me on the arm.

The beaming smile on Beth's face disappeared, but only for an instant. "Oh, the math tutor. Michael says you've been a big help." Beth reached out and took Mike by the elbow—claiming him.

"You were great," I said with the smile still plastered on my face.

"Thank you." She turned to face Mike. "I'll go get changed and then I can drive you over to the party."

"Jill's coming, too," Mike said.

"Oh. Sure. I have room in my car." Beth pecked Mike on the cheek while keeping her eyes trained on me. I didn't shift my gaze. I had no right to be pissed—Mike was my student; that had been made clear. But damned if I was going to blink first.

Then Beth left through the door leading to the dressing rooms.

"Mike, I can't go to the party." I wasn't getting between Beth and Mike, especially in Beth's car. This was not a game I wanted to play.

"Why not?"

"I have work, at Dr. Shaffer's office."

"Your work or someone else's? I bet one of the

grad students left for vacation early, but not before dumping their work on you." Mike narrowed his eyes.

If Ms. Perfect Body with the beautiful singing voice hadn't raised my hackles, this certainly did. "I wanted to let you know I saw the show. It was a nice break from working. But I do need to get back." My jaw nearly locked in place.

"That's okay. I understand. Thanks for coming. I really mean it. I'm glad you were here." Mike leaned over and pecked me on the cheek. "Theater people are always kissing each other."

I wished my stomach didn't flutter when he did. Damn, I wanted to stay pissed off at him. "I'm not a theater person, but have a great holiday. I hope Santa brings you something good."

Mike laughed. "Jill, my present will arrive when the grades are posted."

His wink sent shivers through my body. I wasn't sure what I wanted for Christmas this year. But I hoped I'd get some clarity on what the heck I was going to do about Mike.

It took five days for winter break to grow old.

I got up from the couch in my parents' living room, walked into the kitchen, looked in the cupboard, found nothing to eat, and returned to the couch. I tossed aside the magazine and tried once again to find something on television.

It was the same every winter break. Desperate for my mind to work on something, I became antsy. I'd brought home some data from the lab to analyze. But it hadn't taken long to get through it.

Maybe if I had a large family, siblings, cousins, I'd have others to hang out with. But as the only child of two only children, there was no one around. Some friends from high school were having a party later, and I said I'd go, only to escape the boredom at home.

My parents, Jack and Linda Kramer, were both at their jobs at a financial investing company. They'd take a week off around Christmas and New Year's, but otherwise, I was on my own. My phone beeped. It was Nikki texting to say she was bored out of her mind and would be returning to campus early. I texted back and admitted I'd probably return to my own apartment before break was over, too.

I slumped back on the couch and opened up my laptop. I checked once more to see if the grades had been posted. Of course not. Classes only ended last week. Professors were barely done grading papers. I shut the computer with more force than I intended.

The front door opened and my mother walked in. Linda carried two shopping bags at her sides.

"Hi, sweetie. Have a relaxing day?"

"Yeah, I guess."

"I thought I'd bake pies to take to Great-Aunt Eleanor's house."

"Okay." This was my mom's way of trying to ask for help. But she never came out and said it. My parents were masters at avoiding direct comments.

"So I'll be in the kitchen…"

I sighed and closed my eyes. *Why do I tolerate this?* "Do you want some help, Mom?"

"Oh, only if you want to. I'll need to make about three. I think. I don't know. Maybe more."

There would be about twenty people at my great-aunt's house, all of them in their fifties or older. I really was the last of the line. Three pies would never be enough. Mom was trying to make it seem like no big deal.

"I'm not busy," I said.

"Are you sure? I don't want to disturb you if you're resting."

"I've done nothing but rest all day," I muttered to myself, and followed her to bake what was sure to be at least seven pies.

Mom unpacked the ingredients and I grabbed the pie pans from the cabinet.

"What do you think? Should we make an apple cranberry?" Mom lifted the bag of apples.

"I thought Uncle William couldn't have cranberries." I took the bag from her and brought the apples to the sink to wash.

"That's right, he takes diuretics." Mom moved

the bag of flour to the end of the counter and positioned it in perfect parallel to the butter.

Her maddeningly slow pace in the kitchen had been what drove me to learn to cook.

"Are you getting together with any friends while you're home?" Mom shuffled her feet.

I handed the washed apples to her, along with a peeler. She let out a breath, relieved she had a task.

"Yeah, there's a party tonight. But I won't be home late."

She nodded but kept focused on her work. I found the recipe book, but a piecrust I could do from memory and the feel of the dough.

"What about that graduate student you were seeing. Robert?"

"Mom, we broke up last year, before the summer. I told you."

"Oh, right. I remember." She stood back from the bowl of apples. "I think they're turning brown."

"Here." I handed her the lemon. The woman might be a genius economist, but she was hopeless outside a spreadsheet.

"He seemed so nice."

"He wasn't. He isn't. I still work with him." I gently rolled out the first batch of dough, enough for three pies. If I could finish this part of the recipe with Linda without stabbing myself with the paring knife, I'd do the rest alone.

"Didn't he take you away for a grand weekend?

I thought he was very interested in you."

"He was. He might still be. But I don't want to get distracted by a man."

"I found your father when I was in college. We had shared interests. Economics majors. That's why we have such a secure, nonvolatile, and durable relationship."

More like a slow plod.

"Do you always use economic terms to describe your life?"

She raised an eyebrow — the extent of any scolding I ever received. If she ever raised her voice at me, I might fall down dead from shock. An arched eyebrow was Linda's version of losing her temper.

"Here, mix in the sugar and cinnamon." I pushed the measuring cup toward her — my version of an apology. "I'm focused on the internship and my senior project. I need to get a good start before grad school applications are due next year."

"Hmmm. I know you'll do great. You always accomplish your goals. We don't expect anything less."

Would I ever get congratulated for any of it?

"But you don't want to neglect your social life. I read a study that the most financially successful people have stable and secure relationships."

I squeezed my eyes shut and counted to twenty-three using only prime numbers. I opened them to find Mom forging ahead with the baking.

"No, Mom, I'll do that." The last thing these pies needed was Mom's ham-handed touch to putting the dough on top.

"So there's three apple pies done." She nodded as I put them in the oven. Her eyes glazed over at the cans of pureed pumpkin.

"How about I do the next batch. You go wash up. You've had a long day at work."

"If you're sure you're okay by yourself."

"It's my pleasure." Because cooking would distract me. Because doing other people's work was what I did best. Because getting my mother out of my way made everything easier.

Chapter 9

MIKE

"You keep checking for your grades. Are you worried about them?" Mom hovered over my shoulder as I typed on the computer in Dad's den. My mom had always been overprotective. Her elder son's reliance on crutches only caused her to fret more.

"Just calculus," I said, waiting for the page to load. "Crap, not posted yet."

"I'm sure you passed, honey. You said that tutor was very helpful."

I couldn't hide the smirk. "Yeah, she really motivated me."

"See? You put too much pressure on yourself for a perfect GPA. You'll be able to get into any law school you want with the grades you have. They'll overlook one C in math."

"Sure." It wasn't the law schools I was thinking of. It was that promised date. What could I do to convince Jill to go out with me even if I didn't get an A?

"He'd better get more than a C." Dad's voice reverberated through the walls, then he entered the room. Michael Lewis Sr. was used to commanding a courtroom. Even without his gavel, he called a room to order. "That tutor cost money on top of the tuition."

"I'm sure it was worth every penny," Mom said.

My grin turned into a full-blown smile.

"What's gotten into you?" Dad asked.

"Looking forward to Christmas dinner. Mom, that pie smells great."

"Thank you. Can I get you something now? Are you hungry?"

"No, I can get my own food."

Mom had stopped fetching things for me when I was in seventh grade. She'd gone back to work part-time at the library and had given the family a whole speech about how we all had to do a little more around the house.

Then three years ago, she quit her job, and our relationship reverted to when I was in sixth grade.

"I know you *can*, but I can help too."

Dad harrumphed. He was about to launch into his usual speech, something like, "Kathy, the boy needs to learn to take care of himself," when the front door opened and James walked in.

I always liked my younger brother, even when I

hated him. I'd never been jealous of the attention my brother received as a baby. Being older had more advantages. Still dressed in his football uniform, James looked tired and sweaty, and like he had that wonderful spent feeling a person gets from exerting himself, pushing your body faster and harder. It took me until adulthood to grow jealous of Jimmy.

"So how'd it go?" I asked before he'd even closed the door.

Mom was busy helping him with his equipment bag, and already fussing about the dirt he brought into the entryway.

"Lost," James said.

"What happened? You were supposed to take that team easily," Dad said.

"I threw two incompletes." James didn't make eye contact, didn't even glance in Dad's direction.

"Yeah, but how many yards did you complete?" I asked.

James turned his head toward me. "I threw for sixty-four yards and not one intercepted. I avoided a sack attempt and made two running plays for first downs."

"Give it up." I held up a fist, and James bumped it with a smile.

"Still, you lost. The quarterback takes the responsibility on his shoulders. Even if you are backup quarterback." My dad pointed to a shelf over his desk in his den. "I've cleared off a space for the trophy from regionals. You've got another game next week."

The shelf still held the trophies I'd won during my reign as starting quarterback. The star athlete of the school, I did well in basketball, too. I'd known no other identity. Until it was all taken away in about seven seconds.

Dad came to stand next to where I sat and handed me a magazine. "You should read this."

I scanned the article on para-athletes. People in wheelchairs playing basketball. Cheetah-legged amputees dashing around a track. "Thanks, Dad." Bile rose in my throat. Sure, I wanted my freedom back. I'd give anything to have the body I once had. But it wasn't going to happen. I'd never be an athlete. My goal now was to walk without crutches. "Not sure I'm going for the cheetah prosthesis."

"Why not? Why not get back into it?" Michael Sr. stood over my chair, taller than me once again. I'd grown so that I was barely taller than my father, but not anymore. Now hunching over crutches, I had to look up to meet Dad's eyes.

"Let's get through the surgery," Mom said, but the tension in the room only increased.

This was how my family referred to the pending amputation, "The Surgery." I smiled again, thinking about what Dr. Marlow would say if he could hear my family's defense mechanisms.

JILL

"Jill, quit checking your email," Dad said under his breath from across the coffee table.

Dad didn't need to keep his voice down—after myself and my parents, the youngest person there was seventy-five. I loved my family, really I did. I adored Great-Aunt Eleanor and the rest of my long-lived relatives. Listening to their stories was a college course in itself. These people had not only witnessed history, they took part in it. Great-Grandmother, ninety-six on her last birthday, had served as a nurse in World War II. One of the few women to serve in a combat zone at the time, she had a lot to tell.

Most kids on Christmas spent time playing with their toys with all the other children in their families. But since everyone in my family lived to ripe old ages and had so few children, I didn't have those kinds of Christmas memories. The few relatives that were my age always spent Christmas with their "other side," somehow escaping the long stories, the too-quiet Christmas day, and the endless complaints that older people liked to share.

"I'm looking for my grades." I looked up from my phone.

"I thought you found them yesterday," he said.

"Yeah, they were posted. I, uh, had forgotten

what they were."

Jack Kramer snorted. "I find that hard to believe. All A's. I think you like looking at them. Well, you should be proud. We are." He tapped my shoulder in what passed as affection.

"Yeah. Thanks, Dad." He must be in the holiday mood. I was really checking to see if Mike had looked at his grades. He'd probably text if he saw them. But maybe he'd bombed the final and was too embarrassed. I convinced myself that I was merely concerned because he wanted his near-perfect GPA to stay intact. But a small part of me had selfish reasons for wanting his success.

I dashed off a quick text to him, wishing him a merry Christmas. Before I could stop myself, I hit send. And immediately regretted it. He would know he had the upper hand if he thought I was wondering about him.

"Shit," I muttered.

"Watch your language!" eighty-seven-year-old and usually deaf as a stone Great-Uncle Howard shouted at me. "A young lady shouldn't use those words. When I was courting Pearl…"

I nodded politely and wore my "I'm following along" look. I'd perfected it. But all the while I was kicking myself. Sending a message on Christmas, he'd realize I was thinking about him when I should've been too busy to give him any thought. A cool, uninterested girl wouldn't be wishing him a merry Christmas.

This would only fuel his ego. Now he'd think I really did like him. Inwardly, I groaned, still nodding along to Great-Uncle Howard's story. So what if I really liked him? I could go on a date with a guy. I'd been on dates before. I'd had boyfriends. Some were even non-disastrous, unlike Robert.

But now I was at a critical time in the lab, and applying for the internship, and planning for grad school. I didn't want to lead him on. And when it didn't work out because I worked too much, he'd think I was bailing because of his legs.

My phone vibrated in my pocket, jolting me back to the present.

"I know I was shocked to learn what Pearl had done, too. But that didn't stop me. True love…" Howard went on. His eyesight was poor. Maybe I could get away with checking my messages.

As unobtrusively as possible, I held the phone at my side, away from Howard, and glanced down.

The message from Mike said, *Call me, I'm buried under family.*

I giggled.

"See, I told you it has a happy ending," Howard concluded. "Have I told you that one before?"

"No, never," I lied. I leaned forward and gave him a peck on the cheek. "Excuse me, I need to use the bathroom."

I sprang from the couch and ran up the stairs to

the third-floor bathroom, as far from the "party" as I could get.

I dialed the number. It rang three times before he answered.

"Hi, Jill." Loud voices and terrible piano playing sounded in the background.

"Oh, is this a bad time?" I asked.

"This is a perfect time. Hold on a sec." The noise grew louder then faded away. "Sorry, I had to find a quiet spot."

"Where's that?"

"Um, I, uh…the bathroom," he admitted.

I laughed. "Me too. Only the quietest spot in the house might be the living room right now. I think it's nap time at Happy Meadows."

"Huh?"

"Never mind. So?"

"So what?"

"Come on. Don't tell me you haven't checked."

"Oh, my grades. How did you do this semester?"

"Fine." I sighed with frustration. "You're going to make me ask, aren't you?"

"Of course. You must be dying to know. Listen, if it's any consolation, I'll still go out with you even if I didn't get an A." I could hear the smirk in his voice.

"That's not… Oh! You are so annoying." I couldn't keep the amusement out of my voice either. "Okay. What was your grade in calculus?"

"Don't you want to hear about my other classes?" He feigned disappointment.

"Fine, whatever."

"No, I won't keep you in suspense any longer. I got an A."

"In calc? An A? Not an A minus?"

"Don't sound so shocked. I did study all night for the stupid test. And I had the best tutor on campus."

"Well, congratulations. Next semester should be that much easier."

"So where should we go?"

"Go where?" I asked — my turn to feign confusion.

"Our date. We had a deal."

"If I remember correctly, I think we shook hands, and the deal was an A minus. An A, well, I think I get out of the date because of the overachievement clause. Check your contract, counselor."

"What? No, no. It was at least an A minus, that's what we said. Besides, it's implied if I did better, the terms of the deal are still enforceable."

"Hmm. Not sure about that. Let me consult with my attorney and I'll have him get back to you."

"You're kidding, right?"

I heard real apprehension in his voice and couldn't help feeling a little bit sorry for him. "Gotcha! Man, I've been waiting to get you back."

Mike laughed, and I heard someone yelling. "I'll be out in a minute! Really, my family doesn't give me a moment's peace. If it's not helping assemble all the toys the cousins got, it's reading stories or singing along to my Aunt Jenny's awful piano playing. Holidays can be exhausting, right?"

"Yeah, it's more laid-back with my family."

"So, your choice. Anywhere you want to go."

"Well, my favorite restaurant is The Four Seasons."

"Oh, uh, okay."

"Gotcha again. Did you really think I'd make you take me to the most expensive place in Chicago?"

"Not sure, but I would have."

"I know." My heart sank. His interest was only increasing along with my uncertainty. "How about Oasis, the Middle Eastern place?"

"You sure?"

"I love that place. The food is amazing, and I won't have to dress up."

"My kind of woman."

"I'd better go. I think they're serving dinner now." I imagined all the soft, bland food, and many glasses filled with dentures lining the sideboard. I hoped people retrieved the correct ones, avoiding last year's fiasco.

"Yeah, I don't want to miss my mom's cooking. She makes the best stuffing with sausage."

I sighed. "See you when we get back."

"It's a date."

After a disastrously awkward New Year's Eve party with high school friends I no longer stayed in touch with, I was back in my apartment.

Classes hadn't started, and campus was quiet. I was able to get some extra hours in at the office, and I was happier than if I'd stayed at home.

Tonight was the date with Mike, and I oscillated like a high-frequency sine curve. Should I treat it as a real date? Or go along as friends? I didn't want to hurt his feelings, but I didn't want to lead him on either.

An icy wind smacked my face as I walked out of my apartment building. The nighttime darkness would last for a few months. On a clear night I might be able to use the land-based telescope to gather some data. I wrapped my scarf tighter as I put my head down against the wind.

I would be a good date, an attentive date, but that was all. I had to put my foot down tonight. It wasn't fair to let Mike think I was interested. He'd only get hurt when I had to choose my research over him.

Mike waited for me at the Middle Eastern restaurant. He sat in the rear, his crutches stowed under the table. I wore my hair loose and, despite the cold, had dressed in a skirt to honor the event.

Mike smiled when he spotted me, and waved a hand toward the chair opposite him.

"You look amazing," he said when I sat down. He reached out, took my hand, and kissed it.

The act was so old-fashioned and sweet, I laughed. But inside I turned to jelly.

"Are you laughing at my chivalry?"

"Yes. But it's cute."

"Cute is not what I was going for. I was hoping for dashing and charming." Mike held his chin up dramatically.

"Oh, that too."

"Hey, I never had the chance to properly thank you for coming to the show."

"Oh, no problem. I enjoyed it."

"Really?"

"It was fun. And your friend Beth is very talented." I took my hand back and placed my napkin in my lap.

"She sure is. I learn a lot from her. She's been acting since she was a kid. While I was wasting my time on the football field, she was taking drama classes."

"Football was a waste of time?"

"Well, it's not like I can use it now." He looked down at the menu.

I gave him a hard stare, trying to bore into him

with my eyes.

"What?" He shifted in his seat.

"I never thought you were one for self-pity."

"I'm not. But what did all those years get me now?"

"I suppose you learned good body mechanics, how to exercise and build your muscles, how to work with other people on a team. The lessons of sportsmanship—"

"Okay, okay." He held up his hand to stop me. "You're right. I was having a rare sorry-for-myself moment. It won't happen again."

"See that it doesn't," I said with a smile. I didn't like this vulnerable side. My childhood hadn't prepared to cope with strong emotion.

Mike shrugged. "Did you have a good break?"

I shook my head. "I survived. Mostly it was boring."

"Boring?"

"I have a small, very small family. And mostly elderly relatives. They're great to be around for a while, but then…"

"I get it. Only my family is huge and loud and they're great to be around for a while and then…"

I laughed and cleared my throat. I smoothed the napkin on my lap and met his eyes. "Mike—"

"Uh-oh. That's the serious tone you use when I make a stupid mistake." Mike looked around. "Let's see. I put my napkin on my lap. I didn't drink from the wrong water glass, and I promise to use the correct fork."

Why did he have to have this natural lure? Like some brightly colored animal waiting for prey to happen by. Beautiful but deadly. I took a deep breath. "I'm glad you got an A, and I think you'll do great next semester, too."

"All thanks to you." He lifted his glass to toast me.

"Yes, well. You see, I can't go out on a date with you again. I'm your tutor. And besides, I don't have time for any relationship."

Mike waved his hand dismissively. "You keep saying that, but how can you not have time? How much time does it take? You have to eat dinner sometime, right?"

"Listen, it's true. My responsibilities to my research will always come first. My last boyfriend…" How could I explain that even a weekend away could lead to a catastrophe? "I'm only going to get busier."

I had to stop while the waiter came over to take our orders. I was on a roll. I wasn't going to let his charm derail me. I had to set the rules for this date. Otherwise I'd be swept away by his humor and those aquamarine eyes, and his well-muscled chest…

"I love falafel, don't you?" Mike asked as he picked up one of the appetizers he had ordered before I arrived.

"Yes, but you're changing the subject."

"Yes, I am. Because I want to enjoy myself tonight, and all this talk about goals and responsibilities is killing it for me." He took a piece of the spicy fritter and held it out toward my mouth.

I opened up and he popped it in, allowing his finger to caress my bottom lip as he pulled his hand away.

The spice from the warm food and the heat of his touch sent fire through my core. I exhaled, letting go of the tension I had held.

"And I would never do anything to jeopardize our professional relationship," he said.

"Yes, you would."

"Yes, I would, but only if you give me the green light."

His hand hovered over mine resting on the plastic table cloth. I turned my hand palm up and he brushed his fingers against my wrist causing sparks to zing up my arm. It would be so easy to clasp ahold of his hand and never let go. The arrival of the waiter with more water provided my escape. I gently placed my hand in my lap and avoided his eye contact. I didn't want to be pulled into his orbit.

The rest of the meal was easy. Mike could talk about any subject. Not only was he knowledgeable about many things, but he was also interested in learning everything. It was so relaxing to be with him. Mike, more than anyone else, made me feel like

I mattered, like my dreams mattered. He showed an interest in me. He tried hard to get me to let my guard down, but he would respect me no matter what limits I set.

"I still don't think I understand what you're saying," he said when I tried to explain my research.

"It would help if you could look through a telescope while I explain it."

"You have a telescope?"

"Just a small one at my apartment."

"Does size really matter?" Mike slid his hand across the table to run his fingers over mine.

"Oh, size matters, the bigger the better." I met his gaze and we were locked, eye to eye.

Suddenly, all my concerns vanished. I was a young woman on a date with a man I liked. Who cared about research? Who cared about his crutches? "Do you want to see my telescope?" My words tentative and barely audible.

Mike didn't react at first. Maybe he didn't hear me. I couldn't bring myself to repeat the offer.

"Did you just invite me up to your apartment?" Mike flashed the smile that melted my heart.

I could only nod. Mike placed some bills on the table and reached down for his crutches.

Chapter 10

MIKE

Even pushing myself as quickly as I could go, the two blocks to Jill's apartment seemed so far away. Each step sent a shock of pain tearing up my legs. The cold only aggravated the crooked bones in my ankle. What I wouldn't give to be in the hot whirlpool of my physical therapist's office.

But despite the pain, I focused on my unbelievable luck.

Jill had started the evening so hell-bent on keeping things professional, I had only continued flirting out of habit. I'd given up hope of winning her over. But it was difficult to keep those unprofessional thoughts from my mind.

That skimpy skirt showed off her incredibly shapely legs, which I wanted wrapped around me. And although it covered everything, the tight sweater's buttons strained against what was underneath.

"Oh, it's a flight upstairs," she said, a worried expression marring her beautiful blue eyes and furrowing the brow of her smooth skin.

"I can do it if I go slow."

She walked ahead and had her front door open. Stairs gave my ankles the most difficulty, and balancing on one leg at a time, even with the crutches, left me feeling unstable.

Jill left me unstable.

She hadn't waited for me at the top of the steps, where she would have to watch my snail's pace ungainly progress. The door to her apartment was ajar. When I finally reached the top, I entered and shut the door behind me.

"Crap. It's too cloudy tonight." Jill stood by the window, her head bent over the eyepiece of a telescope, her back to me. She was short, but good things came in small packages. The sweater outlined her soft shoulders and ample bust. The skirt clung to her bottom, leaving little room for my hand to slide up under it.

"Too cloudy?" I approached her, maneuvering around her furniture.

"Yeah, usually this is a good time of year. Sorry I invited you up for nothing." She turned around and sucked in a breath.

"Nothing?" I moved a step closer.

"Unless..." She licked her lips, and my own mouth went dry.

"Jill, I can do everything any other man can." I brought my face down to hers.

I caught her scent of vanilla, and the warmth of her body radiated against mine.

Hovering above her mouth, I waited. She had to let me know to proceed.

It was her mouth that claimed mine first. The eager kiss was all the green light I needed.

Standing meant my arms were essential for support, so I did what I could to press into her, to feel her breasts against my chest. I pulled back and searched her face for a sign.

"Should we move to the couch?" I asked.

"How about the bed?" Her mouth curved into a half-smile, and she sauntered past me into the next room.

I thanked my lucky non-visible stars and followed her.

She perched on the edge of the bed with a questioning look.

I sat next to her and dropped my crutches on the floor.

"I meant it," I said. "I can do anything any other guy can. It might take me a few seconds longer to get there."

"I'm hoping it does take longer." She reached out and undid each button of my shirt. Her tantalizing fingers working their way down. She pulled off my shirt and drew in a breath.

Her warm palms flattened against my chest and the tension left my body. Whatever fears my mind had been hanging on to flickered away with her soft breath against my neck as she trailed kisses along my skin.

I returned the favor by removing her top. The now-exposed black lace bra got me so hard I thought I heard the seam on my pants rip. She had centerfold breasts, the kind that wouldn't be out of place on a porn site. But no airbrushed photo here; she was alive and breathing, and stood to unzip her skirt.

Taking hold of her hips, I pushed the skirt to the floor and she stepped out of it. I trailed my finger along the strap of the matching panties and her muscles rippled beneath my hand, like the light flutter of a baby bird. I pulled her closer and kissed my way down her stomach. She gasped, but I kept going, with a final kiss on her mound, and taking in her scent through the black lace, fragrant and sweet.

A primal part of my brain took over until she stepped back. She knelt in front of me and opened the fly of my jeans.

For a moment, ice went through my veins. Stripping off my pants hadn't been a sexy move of mine in years, and revealing my legs up close would put a damper on the events. But when Jill started to tug at my waistband, I lifted my hips off the bed and she deftly slid my pants, along with my boxers, off. With a flourish she tossed them aside and ran a hand up from my calf to my thigh. A gratifying ease slipped along the muscle. Nothing had felt good there in years.

"Does it hurt?" Her blue eyes shimmered, a lock of her ebony hair draped over one side.

I allowed my jaw to unclench. "Not when you touch me."

She broke into a wide, wicked smile I'd never seen before and proceeded to caress my legs. The soreness melted away, and when her hand stopped at my cock, I let out a breath, and with it, released any worry.

Her petite frame was simple to lift off the floor and swing onto the bed. It was effortless to hoist such a small person after years of using my arms to support my weight.

Once I had her prone, I could work my magic. On my knees, I could do anything. And I did. I may have only been with two women since college. But years of making out with girls in high school had left me with some skills. Without any fumbling, I rid her of the bra and panties, and tortured her skin and sensitive places until she writhed against the sheets. Her eyes closed under my touch. Her mouth parted and little pants escaped, assuring me I still had what it took.

Holding her close and having her soft skin mold into mine, I was any normal man.

"I have a condom in my pants pocket." I moved

to retrieve them.

"I have some right here." Her wicked smile reappeared as she reached into the bedside table and pulled out an unopened box.

She rolled one down over me, and I couldn't help but shiver against her light touch.

When I entered her, I went straight to the heavens she spent her life studying. Her legs wrapped around my waist, and I was caught in the perfect embrace. As slowly as I could and as gently as possible, I stroked her from the inside. Only when I saw her face flush, heard her cry my name, and felt her sheath tighten around me did I lose control.

Increasing my pace, I pulsed into her until the explosion that gripped her moved to me. Surging with fire, my body racked when I came.

Panting, I lay beside her and pulled her in so she fit snugly against me. Her face was damp with sweat and her scent had changed from vanilla to musk, all because of me. With the right woman I could be a real man.

I kissed her temple and she turned those devastating blue eyes on me, which made me want to start from the beginning and do it all over again. She smiled, the Jill smile she wore after I teased her or told a joke.

"I guess I'll need to get a new tutor." I smiled back.

JILL

I rolled over and there he was. I placed a hand on his chest. The hard plane rose and fell with his steady breaths. I wasn't worried, not about what would happen this morning, not about what would happen tomorrow. Asleep, his face lacked that edge, the smart-ass smirk. His hair falling away revealed his entire face; with his long lashes brushed against his ruddy cheeks, he looked almost childlike. A little vulnerable.

He opened his eyes. He oriented himself, remembering where he was waking up. Then he turned those verdant eyes toward me.

"Good morning, gorgeous," he said, reaching out to stroke my hair.

"Good morning." I closed my eyes and relished his touch as his fingers slid down my face.

"I don't think I ever want to get up," he said.

"Never get up?" I tried to mimic his usual wry smile.

"I meant leave your bed." He rolled over on top of me. "I'm already up."

"I can see that, but let's have breakfast."

"Really?" He pasted his sad puppy face on.

"Yes, I never get to cook for anyone. Well, once a week Nikki…comes…over. What…what are you doing?" I tilted my head back so he could have better access to the places along my neck that he was kissing

"Convincing you to stay in bed."

"It's working."

After another round of fiery sex, I thought I'd never walk again.

But then my stomach growled.

"I can't satisfy all your needs?" Mike ran a lazy finger along my belly.

"Mmmm. If I can stand, I'll cook breakfast."

I slithered out of bed, threw a t-shirt on, and pulled on some sweatpants. I glanced down at Mike in bed. His broad chest was barely covered by the quilt, the line of fine hair trailing down below.

"Having second thoughts, aren't you?" He smirked.

"Oh, I can't afford to feed your ego any more than I already have." I laughed and then cut myself off. "So, do you need anything in the bathroom?"

"You have soap in there?"

"Yeah."

"That's all I need." Mike swung his legs over the side and reached down for his crutches.

I turned my back on him and walked over to the kitchen alcove. I had everything I needed for blueberry pancakes, if I used frozen blueberries. I could make a cheese and spinach frittata.

I got to work and ignored the clumping sounds

coming from the bathroom. The bathroom was tiny, as was the rest of my place. But the warning in Mike's face when he'd gotten out of bed let me know to keep my distance. I wouldn't offer to help him. If the laundry basket was in his way, then he was going to have to move it himself. I heard a muttered curse as something dropped. I held tight to my spot in front of the frying pan.

The water in the bathroom turned on, and I imagined he was using my little pink razor to shave with. The picture made me smile. Cooking for him made me smile. My cheek muscles hadn't had this much of a workout in years. Not to mention other muscles. I whisked the batter and tested the oil in the pan.

If he was willing to put up with my work schedule, this relationship might be okay. He was busy as well. Not only did he have a demanding class schedule, but he was aiming for perfect grades and working on the theater productions. It wasn't like he had a lot of free time either.

I set the table by the window and looked out onto the snow-covered street. We'd been so preoccupied last night, we hadn't noticed the heavy blanket of snow the wind had blown in. It must have started right after we got home and kept going all night. Just like we had. The smile burst out again, and I wasn't surprised to find my desire stoked.

Breakfast first. We needed our strength.

Mike came out of the bathroom, looking better than he should, considering how little we'd slept.

"What smells so good?" He walked over to where I stood, beating the eggs and cheese for the frittata.

"Breakfast in about ten minutes. Look outside." I pointed with a spoon toward the window.

Mike swung himself over to the table and sat looking outside. "Whoa, it really came down."

"Yeah, I didn't notice until this morning."

"That's good to hear. I'd hate to find out I didn't have your full attention," Mike said, but with less than his usual cockiness. His eyes were glued to the window. "It looks like the plow came down the street. All the snow is piled up between the sidewalk and the road."

"Yeah. My landlord doesn't like to get out too early to clear the walkway," I said. "Here's some juice to get you started." I handed him a glass.

"Thanks." Mike took it and drank it down.

"The rest will be out in a jiffy."

Mike's cell phone rang in his jacket pocket. His coat hung from a hook near the door. Mike wasn't going to reach it in time. But I stayed busy at the stove.

I kept my back to him as he clomped to the doorway and clomped back to the table.

I heard him check his messages then dial a number.

"Hey, Jeff… Yeah I, uh, stayed at a friend's last night…" He laughed uncomfortably. "Well, a good friend." I smiled and then did turn around to catch his eye. He winked at me. "This morning. I, uh, hadn't figured it out yet… In about an hour…great… Listen, man, I appreciate it… Yeah, okay." He recited my address and ended the call.

"Who's Jeff?"

"My roommate at the house. He got worried when I didn't get home last night. He thought I might be stranded in the snow somewhere."

"That's nice of him to check on you." I laid out the food as best I could on the tiny table. "I made too much for the table."

"But not too much for me. I'm starved and this looks amazing." He reached up, pulled me onto his lap, and kissed me.

My mouth absorbed every soft sensation of the kiss, and it addled my brain. And when he pulled back, I ran my fingers through his hair and studied his face.

"Hey, I'm going to have to eat and run. Jeff said he'd pick me up, and, well…"

"Oh sure. I could give you a ride. If you give me a few minutes to shovel my car out." It would be impossible for him to walk anywhere today. The sidewalks would be barely cleared, and when people did shovel they left drifts of snow piled at the corners. Pedestrians practically had to climb over the snowbanks to cross the streets.

"No, Jeff will be here soon." Mike's jaw tightened and his voice held the tone that told me I wouldn't be helping him to do anything.

We dug into breakfast. Mike complimented me again and again with his words and grunts of approval through mouthfuls of food.

"How am I going to go back to toaster waffles and Pop-Tarts?" Mike swiped a napkin over his mouth.

"I hope you don't." I leaned over to kiss him. He tasted of maple syrup and smelled of my floral soap mixed with his masculine scent.

A horn beeped outside.

Mike looked out the window and texted on his phone. "I told Jeff I'd be down in a minute. Can I see you tomorrow?"

"Sure. Well, let me see what's happening at the office…"

"I know I'll come in second to your work, but I hope a close second." He leaned into me, ravishing my lips one more time, leaving my knees quaking.

I held the door open as he shrugged on his jacket, kissed him once more, and shut it so I wouldn't watch him struggle with the stairs.

I cleared the dishes and filled the sink with water. On my last trip to the table to gather the leftovers, I glanced outside. Mike and his friend, Jeff, stood together on one side of a huge pile of snow. It was the heavy, wet snow your feet sink into easily, and could suck your boot off if it wasn't on tightly. They were discussing and motioning toward the end of the block. The city plows had indeed left the same pile of snow all along the sidewalk.

Mike held out an arm to Jeff, who lifted him up under the shoulders. Mike's crutches dropped to the ground as Jeff hauled him up to carry him, like a bride over the threshold, to the car on the other side of the snow. They both ended up slipping in the snow and getting damp. From one flight up, I could see the wetness had seeped through their pants.

It must be icy cold. Mike held on to the side of the car as Jeff climbed back over the snow to retrieve the crutches. As Jeff helped Mike slide into the backseat, Mike looked up at the window. I'd been caught staring; my ears rang and I felt the frittata threaten to come up. But I waved and smiled.

Mike scowled but gave a brief wave back as he shut the car door.

It was nice that Mike had such great friends to help him. He sure needed some assistance once in a while, and I was never going to be big enough to lift him over a snowbank.

This thing we had together, it could work. It could last until graduation. I liked him well enough, and as long as he understood how demanding my research was going to get, we should be fine. He'd said so himself. He knew he would come second to my work. He didn't have expectations. There'd be no demands or distractions. Just fun.

I'd seen a brief glimpse of self-consciousness in him last night, when he spoke about playing football and when we'd first got undressed. But he overcame that pretty quickly. And as long as we never spoke about things, and let Jeff do the heavy lifting, it would stay fun.

With the glow of recent sexual satisfaction, I sprang into the office. The snow had melted enough for me to slip my way to campus, which was still empty for another two days, so I could use the student computer with abandon. Soon, everyone would return from break and take up my time. But for now, I couldn't get rid of the smile stretching my cheeks. Not even when I thought about the work ahead of me.

Robert, of course, had left a list of things to get done. Mostly the boring tasks of data entry he didn't want to handle himself. I sighed. Sure, I was at the beck and call of the grad students, but having to kowtow to Robert was getting old. He couldn't be oblivious to how much he took advantage of my situation. If I said no to any of his "requests," all he'd have to do was hint that I had cheated. All it would take was the dean of students looking into a suspected cheating incident to wreck my chances. So

I sucked it up. He couldn't manipulate me forever.

Dr. Shaffer entered, shaking the snow from his boots. He stopped short when he spotted me at the students' desk.

"Oh, Jill. I didn't expect anyone to be here."

"Welcome back from break, Dr. Shaffer. I hope it's okay; I've been coming in these past few days to make some progress on Robert's work." I pointed to the screen.

"No problem." He came up to stand behind me and read over my shoulder. "I'm glad you're here." He placed a reassuring hand on my arm. "Did you enjoy your break?"

"It was fine, but I was anxious to come back here."

"I understand what you mean. I can only take so much family time."

A giggle escaped me, although I regretted the acknowledgment of the rumors about him.

"It's all right." He waved his hand. "I know what everyone says about me. It's true. My wife is surprised to see me at dinner some nights. I'd rather be here than at home. People like us, Jill, we need the stimulation from our work. Our families don't understand us."

"My parents are so involved in their own careers you'd think they'd understand why I want to work so hard."

"But they don't. Intellectuals, we need to stick

together." He pulled a chair over and sat next to me. "I think I'm supposed to wait to let you know until it's official. But I can't. You were awarded the internship. You'll start this summer and continue throughout your last year here."

"Really? Me?"

"Yes, you. There wasn't any doubt, was there? I mean, you must have known—none of the other applicants have even come close to your level of dedication."

"Wow, Dr. Shaffer. Thank you so much. I'm so excited. I can't believe this." I jumped up, and Dr. Shaffer stood as well.

"Congratulations," he said, and embraced me.

I was caught up in the moment and returned the hug. It wasn't until I noticed Dr. Shaffer holding on a little too tightly that I thought about what I was doing—hugging my boss. Sweat broke out under my arms and I wobbled back.

"In some ways, you're like a daughter to me. A family member in work and in spirit, someone who understands."

"Thanks, Dr. Shaffer. That means a lot to me." I mentally kicked myself for doubting his intentions. He was a lonely, overworked man who thought of me like a daughter.

He went into his private office and shut the door. Leaving me alone to think about my future. It was all coming together. I could give up the tutoring.

I wouldn't be able to take any more students anyway. Not after word got out about my sleeping with one of them. My face grew warm. It was then I realized the only person I wanted to share the good news with was Mike.

Chapter 11

MIKE

Her name flashed on my phone. I ignored it. I couldn't face Jill, not yet. The shame of this morning had to fade away. It would. I knew from the past that these episodes became less painful over time.

All the images still swarmed in my brain. Jill across the restaurant table, looking prettier than anyone I'd ever seen. Her whispered invitation, which was more than an invitation into her bed. It was an invitation into her life. Her busy, crowded life. Could I really be a part of it? And the amazing time in her bed. I'd had sex since the accident. But never had it been so easy. She wasn't gentle, didn't care if I was comfortable; she took what she wanted, as if I were any man, no mincing around.

And then the awful exit. Why did it have to snow so much? Damn the city and its plows. I'd looked like a fool, a child, weak. I didn't mind Jeff helping out. Jeff had helped before and I was used to it. Jeff was a man's man and knew how to keep himself distant from the situation. We would bump fists and be done with it.

Soon I'd be able to walk down the street, snow or no snow. I'd lift my feet over puddles, climb over steep curbs without a hitch. I just needed to get through this next semester, and then right after Memorial Day I was headed to the hospital.

My phone rang again. It was Beth. I answered.

"Hey, Michael, are you back from break yet?"

"Yeah, I've been back for a few days. You?"

"Got back last night. I'm headed over to the shop to paint some scenery. You want to come help?"

"Yeah, sounds good." That was what I needed — some mindless activity to occupy myself. I'd work up a bit of sweat, clear my mind.

"I'll be over in ten minutes to pick you up."

I put on some old clothes to paint in, and Jeff came in to say the walk was shoveled completely.

"Thanks, man." I wanted to convey how much it meant to me that my frat brothers looked out for me this way.

"Whatever," Jeff answered. Jeff's reluctance to acknowledge my gratitude was almost as important as the shoveling.

Beth pulled up right outside, and I got into the passenger seat, tossing my crutches into the back.

The short drive over to the theater shop was taken up by Beth's chatter about her break. She'd spent the time getting headshots and working on her vocal exercises.

"You know, Michael, there's a theater in New York that specializes in actors with different physical abilities. Sort of like Theater of the Deaf, but—"

"It's not going to be an issue soon," I interrupted her.

"I know, I'm just saying... We've got to apply to NYU grad program next fall. You're not going to back out, are you? I don't think I could face the theater program there without you. And you know I've got your back."

"Thanks, Beth. It means a lot to me, especially since I still have to tiptoe around my dad about it."

"Why don't you come out and tell him?"

"Because I need the health insurance. He'll disown me for sure when he finds out I'm not going to law school." My chest tightened. "But I'll be damned if I don't get my surgery. I've waited until my growth plates closed. I've gone through endless tests and counseling sessions." I turned to keep my face away from Beth. "The pain in weather like this is almost unendurable."

"I know, I know. But it's so drastic. Don't you want to wait? I mean, maybe they'll come up with something else."

"Beth, I appreciate your concern. And I know you care about me, but I thought you understood." I didn't turn toward her. The chance that tears would rise in my lids was too high to risk. Better to stay angry than feel sad.

"I do. I want you to be happy."

"I am. Or I will be. Sorry I snapped. I had a rough morning." I did face Beth now, as she pulled the car into the lot. Her brow was creased, and guilt washed over me. Beth did have my back, and she never came out and asked for anything but my friendship, even if she wanted more.

"What happened this morning?"

"You know that math tutor I told you about?"

"The one who is so driven she refuses to pay any attention to you and lets others walk all over her?" Beth raised one eyebrow.

"She's not all bad. Well, anyway. I kind of made an ass of myself with her this morning."

"This morning? But it's only ten o'clock now." She turned to look at me, and her eyes were wide.

"Yeah, well…" Suddenly, I felt uncomfortable sharing with Beth. Usually, I could tell her anything. She was my confidante. Certainly the Theta Chis weren't good listeners, and I couldn't share anything with my parents.

"You have to protect yourself from women like that. Believe me, I know. She's only into you for as long as you serve some purpose for her. Once you get in the way of her goals, you'll find she's not so understanding."

"Yeah, you're probably right." I wasn't sure if I

agreed, but I didn't want to hurt her feelings. Beth would put her relationships with friends before her work. Sure, she was driven to make her mark, and she had the determination to stick it out through audition after audition, rejection after rejection. Her name would be on a marquee at some point. The way she took care to understand and listen, she'd throw herself completely into a relationship. But Beth would want my soul, not just my heart. Too many emotions. Too many entanglements. And I wasn't going to be her costar.

Too bad Jill's work came first and she wasn't holding auditions for a leading man.

JILL

The flutter in my stomach warned me — if his name simply flashing on my phone could tingle my sex, then I might be in real trouble.

"Hey." I hoped the waver in my voice couldn't be detected on his end.

"Congrats! I got your message about the internship. You must be thrilled."

"I am. I still can't believe it. I've gotten the brass ring."

"You worked hard enough for it."

"True, but still there was a chance I wouldn't get

it. There's no other feeling like this. Everything I want is falling into place. I used to think I'd trudge along like my parents. Nothing ever bringing too much excitement or too much disappointment. But now the next year is all easy street. I have work to do, but that's the fun part—coasting downhill." Words had never tumbled out of me like that before. A longish pause followed. Crap! Mike had a year of struggle ahead of him.

"I'm really happy for you. Do you want to celebrate?" It was difficult to tell over the phone, but his voice didn't reflect a celebratory mood.

"Of course I want to celebrate." I scrambled for an idea. "I want to celebrate with you, here, at my place." I tried to copy the sultry voice Nikki used when she was on the phone with a guy.

"How can I pass up that offer? But are you sure I can't take you somewhere?" If he was challenging me, then I would step up and meet it. I could keep a man busy in my apartment for the entire evening.

"I never get to cook. I'd like to make you something *special*."

"Then I'll see you tomorrow night. I'm counting it as a date, even if we're inside the whole time." He matched my suggestive tone, and as blood throbbed between my legs, confidence rushed out of my chest.

"It's a date, then." My breathing was ragged with the memory of last night. Was it really less than twenty-four hours ago? Because it felt like another lifetime when I'd kept Mike at arm's length, never more than a student. And now he was…he was. Well, he was more than a student, that was for sure.

We ended the call, and I gathered my laundry and counted out enough quarters for the creaky machine the landlord kept duct-taping together.

My phone chirped a text.

Nikki: *Are you home?*

Me: *Yes. Why?*

Nikki: *Buzz me in.*

A nanosecond later, the intercom buzzed and I pressed the security lock to allow her to come in.

Her boots thudded up the stairs, and she knocked before I had a chance to unlock the door.

"Did you take the steps two at a time?" I asked as she stomped off the snow before she entered.

"What did you expect? You texted me you had sex with Mike and got the internship all in one day."

"We had sex last night. I didn't find out about the internship until this morning."

"I'll congratulate you for one. But for the other, are you sure you want to spend the next year with people who will continue to take advantage of you?"

"Seriously? You're more pleased I slept with my student than receiving an honor and paid work?"

"Sleeping with a student is nothing new around here. You slept with Robert. He was the TA in Dr. Shaffer's cosmology class you took."

"Don't remind me." The irony was not lost on

me. But Mike would get another tutor, and he and I would never cross paths in our careers again.

"So how was it? Could he get it up?"

"Nikki! It's just his legs that are injured. And it was great. I won't go into the gory details, but let's say we made a dent in my condom supply."

"Nice." Nikki nodded. "You need a good guy. A corrective emotional experience from Robert the shithead. I still don't see why you let him walk all over you. He was the one who violated the rules by dating you."

"It's more complicated. I don't have much of a choice." My lungs constricted. I went from reveling in images of Mike to having to keep the secret from Nikki.

"Sure you do. You could go to a different group. Your internship can be used for a different study."

"I can't go, that's all." I didn't want to yell. Nikki's confused face was more than about why I worked with Dr. Shaffer and Robert.

"They gave *you* the money, not Dr. Shaffer. Why do you take their crap?"

"Because I have to. Because I'll get kicked out of school. Because Robert can ruin my reputation, my chance at a career, everything." I sank to the couch, and tears spattered my pants.

"What's up?" Nikki sat next to me and waited.

"The weekend before I broke it off with Robert." I gasped and took a deep, shaky breath. "I let him distract me. He convinced me I didn't need to work on the final project. His car broke down." I gulped air. "I didn't have time. He did it for me. I handed in work that wasn't my own."

"Oh." Nikki's blank expression didn't help me.

"Shaffer gave me an A." I blew my nose and avoided Nikki's gaze.

"So Robert's been holding this over you? Threatening to expose you?"

"He told me he'd say I copied his old paper when he wasn't looking. That's what he said when I ended the relationship."

"Asshat," Nikki hissed.

"Now I've put you in it. Sorry. I think the wild sex has short-circuited my brain. I didn't mean to dump this on you."

"Dump what? I never heard you say anything. I came over to talk to my best friend about her love life and her internship. She said some crazy shit about her ex-boyfriend. But who doesn't?" Nikki grinned and held her palms out.

"Really? You'd forget all this?"

"All what? Now, let's go out tonight and mingle with regular people and do what those women in romance novels do. Don't they go dancing or drink fruity martini crap and bitch about men? I think we're supposed to do our hair and wear chunky jewelry and flouncy skirts. Do you have a flouncy skirt I can borrow?"

I laughed. "We could go to the documentary at the student union. It's about science curricula in elementary education."

"Now you're talking." Nikki slapped her leg and stood.

With a friend like Nikki, the burden of my secret seemed bearable. And the possibility of an entanglement with a man with a disability almost wouldn't be a burden on my work—it was just what I needed.

Chapter 12

MIKE

I clomped up the steps of the 1907 building to the math department office. There was an elevator somewhere in the back, used mostly as a service elevator. But the hassle of tracking down the custodian and walking all the way to the back of the building made the slow, unnatural ascent up one flight preferable.

"Hello, Ms. Singer." I entered the outer office where the secretary sat.

"Hello, Mike. Did you have a nice break?" She indicated a chair opposite her desk.

I settled into the seat. "Yeah, great food, Santa gave me new headphones, slept a lot."

"I saw your grade. Congratulations. I told you Jill was the best tutor we had." Ms. Singer's big smile reminded me of my kindergarten teacher, overly kind and perky.

"Jill is great, but I need a new tutor."

Ms. Singer's smile vanished. "I thought something might be wrong. Jill had come in to ask that you get reassigned. What happened?"

"Jill asked to have me reassigned? When?" I clenched the armrests.

Ms. Singer shook her head. "A few weeks before break, maybe. I can't remember. If you don't feel comfortable talking with me, you can see Dr. Williams." She pointed to the closed door of the department head.

A buzzing clouded my thoughts. Jill had wanted to get rid of me before our date. That meant she never wanted to go out in the first place. She couldn't bring herself to tell me to my face, afraid to hurt the crippled boy. My palms began to sweat.

"Mike? You okay?"

"I'm sorry." I straightened in the chair. "Jill and I don't have a good working relationship. It's nothing against her. I wouldn't want her in any trouble. It's me. I have trouble looking foolish in front of girls. And calc makes me look foolish." I raised my palms out. "You know, a guy has his ego."

Ms. Singer's smile returned. "I understand. I'll have to let Judge Lewis know. He called specifically to ask about your grades and the progress of your tutoring."

"My dad called?" I grabbed my crutches and hoisted myself out of the chair. "Tell him whatever you want. And please call me when you've found another tutor. Thanks for your help, Ms. Singer." I strained to keep my voice even. It wasn't Ms. Singer's fault. She was one of the many people cowed by the wealthy and powerful Judge Michael Lewis, donor to every stick and stone of the university.

My father's interference was something I thought I'd grown used to, even if it did rankle me from time to time.

But Jill was supposed to be different. She seemed to understand, to not want to "take care" of me. She treated me as crassly as she treated everyone else. And that's why I was drawn to her. She wouldn't let my disability change the way she told me off. Except it did. She went along with it. Too scared to turn me down in person, she had tried to run out the back door. A pity date and a pity screw.

I wouldn't accept anyone's pity.

JILL

I cut the butter into the flour that would be the crust to the potpie.

There was nothing like a warm chicken potpie on a cold January night to make everything cozy. The chocolate cake (made from scratch and the expensive cocoa from the specialty grocery) had been iced and sat on the bookshelf, the only available surface.

I hummed along to the radio and swayed as I pressed the dough into the deep pan. Cooking in my family had been reserved for special occasions— Thanksgiving, birthdays. I longed for those events when scents from the kitchen mingled with the anticipation of food not poured out of Styrofoam containers. It was those times I felt most loved and acknowledged by my parents.

Having my own apartment had been essential to maintaining my sanity through college. As long as I could make a good home-cooked meal once in a while, I would survive the heavy course load, the hours slaving in Dr. Shaffer's office, and the endless stream of students in need of a tutor.

The intercom buzzed and I set down the spoon to answer it.

"It's me." Mike's voice sounded tense through the box.

"Come on up." I pressed the buzzer for an extra few seconds, giving him time to maneuver inside.

I unlocked the door and went back to the stove.

The clunking of his crutches echoed off the stairway walls. When he entered the apartment, I could barely find his face behind the scarf.

"Cold, huh?"

"Yep." He swiped the knit hat from his head.

I didn't move to help him take his coat off, merely waited until he had hung up his outerwear and shut the door behind him.

When I turned to face him, I noticed his usual grin had been swapped for a hard-set pair of lips, almost white, and probably not from the cold.

"What's up?" I took a step toward him.

"I went to get a new math tutor today." Mike's gaze zeroed in on me. I was in a target zone, but for what I couldn't guess.

"I figured you would. We talked about how I shouldn't tutor you anymore. Not if we're going to, you know…" I went back to the stove. Stirring the pot gave me an excuse to break free from his stare.

"No, I don't know. What are we, Jill?"

"We're sleeping together. We're seeing each other? Hooking up? I don't know. Do we have to define it?" I hunched my shoulders over the bubbling pot. The chicken had simmered in the sauce with the veggies until it was tender and the aroma carried along with the steam to my nose. This home-cooked meal suddenly wasn't so comforting.

"Why did you ask the secretary to get me a new tutor before we started to 'you know'?" The sneer of his lip was enough; he didn't have to add the sarcasm to his voice when he quoted me.

"What are you getting at?" I put my free hand on my hip.

"That you wanted to get rid of me from the start. Guilt wouldn't allow you to kick the poor disabled guy to the curb, so you stayed on. You went out with me because you felt sorry for me. Sad case, that Mike, who would want to date him, he can't walk. I don't need a pity fuck."

"Mike Lewis, what makes you think I slept with you out of pity?" I brandished the cooking spoon, spraying drops of gravy along the cabinets. "Yes, I asked to have you moved to a new tutor because things were getting pretty hot and heavy in that study room. I wasn't going to do you any good, and it certainly didn't help my self-esteem knowing I wanted to sleep with one of my students." I advanced on him and he shuffled back.

But his retreat didn't stop me. "I've told you and told you. I'm a busy woman with a major goal to achieve. I want to spend time with you. I want a repeat of the other night, many repeats." My voice rose and I didn't care what the neighbors heard through the thin walls. "But you cannot march in here and accuse me of not being honest with you about my feelings."

"Then why are we staying in. It's fine to go out as friends, but you don't want anyone to know you're dating the crippled guy," he barked back.

"I made a potpie." My throat rasped as I yelled. Then the tears came. I stalked back to the stove. If that was what Mike thought, then he could leave. I'd allowed him to distract me. I could've spent my time at the office catching up or preparing lessons for the last few students I needed to finish with. But instead,

I took an entire day to shop and cook for him.

"Jill." His voice had grown gentle, but I could hear him clearly as he approached.

"No." I shook my head.

"Jill." He placed his hand on the small of my back, and damn if I didn't still want it to travel down from there. "I forgot who I was talking to," he rumbled in my ear. "I forgot you're my Jill. The woman who is always brutally honest with me. And that's why I like her. Forgive me?" He placed a kiss on the nape of my neck.

"You can be a real shit," I whispered.

"I know. I'm so used to being on the offense with people. It's a habit I'll have to break." He stepped back, and air rushed between us, erasing the heat. "Do you want me to go?"

"No." I filled the pan and used the last piece of dough as the top crust.

"Can I make it up to you after dinner?" The smirk was back in his voice.

"Dinner won't be ready for twenty minutes." I turned to face him. His hair, mussed from his winter hat, the tilt of his head, and the smile in his eyes all sent a jolt to my belly.

"Twenty minutes." He nodded. "Not much time, but I'll see what I can do."

I placed the pan in the oven. I sauntered toward the bedroom and called over my shoulder, "I set the timer. You'd better get in here."

Chapter 13

MIKE

"This feels weird." Jill scanned the coffee shop from our small table in the corner.

"Thanks, and here I thought you liked it when I held your hand."

"No, I mean meeting you here, and not at the study room."

Since the two weeks after that first incredible night, we'd spent most evenings in her bed. Most days were wrapped up in the start of a new semester and Jill toiling away at the astronomy department.

"Well, get used to it. It's what people do. They meet somewhere besides the library."

Jill blushed. "I can get used to it real quick."

I loved seeing that color rise in her pale skin. It reminded me of when she came. Her flush started at her neck and spread… I had to pull my mind back or I'd take her there, spilling the lattes on the table next to ours.

"Do you want to come to the Theta Chi dance? It's a fundraiser for the local food bank." I pulled my hand away to take a sip of my drink. But I didn't lean back—being close to Jill was like warming myself on the beach.

"Why are all the frat parties fundraisers? Do they feel the need to dress up the drunken orgies to look like legitimate parties?"

"Why do all people not in a fraternity or sorority assume that all Greek parties are drunken orgies?"

"They're not?" Jill cocked her head, exposing the side of her neck.

"Only the good ones." I willed my hand to stay wrapped around the coffee mug instead of reaching out to stroke her skin.

"Oh, all right. With an invitation like that, how can I refuse?" Jill leaned forward and pecked me on the cheek. It was enough to keep the image of her flush clogging my brain.

"Hello, Michael."

I looked up into Beth's amber eyes. Her hip pressed against my shoulder, her smile perfectly symmetrical.

"Hey, Beth. You remember Jill."

"Sure, your math tutor. Nice to see you again." Beth's voice rang with the confidence of someone who could do a nude scene in front of an audience of hundreds.

"Good to see you again." Jill's face flushed

again, but this time her lips were set in a tight line. This wasn't a good flush.

"I, uh, well, we…" I searched my brain for how to correct Beth. Did I call Jill my girlfriend? Did two weeks make a girlfriend?

"I'm glad I found you, Michael. We were *all* wondering where you've been. We were *all* hoping you'd help out with the costumes. It's like you've fallen off the earth."

"Just been hanging out." I tried to direct a wink at Jill, but her piercing stare was aimed at Beth.

"You've got such a talent for designing costumes, plus we need your nimble fingers at the machines." Beth laid her hand on my shoulder and gave it a squeeze.

"Yeah, I have to bow out of this one. Busy with other things. But I'll be there for the next show."

"Sure. See you later." Beth nodded and left.

Jill dropped her gaze to her latte.

"Sorry," I muttered.

"It's okay. She's looking out for you. She doesn't know me yet." Jill still didn't meet my eyes.

"Jill, you've got to help me out here. How should I introduce you to people? When we get to the party, I don't want my frat brothers to think you're my math tutor."

"What do you want to tell them?" Now she looked right into my face.

I hesitated too long. She threw the ball right back

at me and I flinched.

She shrugged. "I guess you could say we're seeing each other."

"I guess." I took her hand again, and she allowed me to caress the inside of her palm.

"So when is this big event? I'll have to prepare myself for a roomful of jocks and silly cheerleaders."

My smart-mouthed Jill returned. "Next Saturday. You need to bring canned items."

Jill checked the calendar in her phone. "Damn. Next Saturday night is my night with the telescope. I had to sign up for this time slot way in advance. There's no way I can change it. I'm sorry."

"Really, you can't switch it? I'm on the planning committee for this party and the main contact with the food pantry. I volunteer there a few times a month. They're counting on me."

"Can't you go without me?"

I didn't want to go without her. I'd been to plenty of parties without girlfriends—no problem. But now that I had a…a…someone, I didn't want to go alone.

"Sure. If you're not afraid some busty cheerleader will steal me away from you."

"I think I can handle the competition. Besides, I can always distract her with a shiny piece of metal and grab you back. They're not too smart."

It was true. No one would match Jill's intelligence. But would I ever be able to distract her from her work long enough to want me as much as I wanted her?

JILL

"It never stops amazing you, does it?"

I jerked away from the computer screen. When it registered that Dr. Shaffer had come into the office unnoticed, I let out a deep breath. This computer was kept separate in a smaller room, and had a strict timetable. I'd signed up for this slot, and I was sure the post-doc scheduled for the spot after mine would be hanging over my shoulder during my last minutes.

"Oh, Dr. Shaffer. You're here."

"I hope you don't mind. But I had some news to deliver and I wanted to see you in person."

"The internship?" My voice rose with anticipation.

"It's official. Got the letter right here." He patted his blazer pocket. "I think you'll be particularly pleased at the stipend."

I approached Dr. Shaffer. The white paper protruded from his pocket. He turned to show me, indicating I should take it, and I plucked it out.

My mouth went dry as I read the letter. It was more than enough money to stop the tutoring, more than enough to cover books and fees — even some left over so I could get new tires for my car.

"I can't believe it." I reread it.

"You deserve it." Dr. Shaffer's smile was as wide as mine.

"I didn't expect it to be so much."

He held his palms out. "I pulled a few strings for you. I thought you merited more than the past interns."

I flushed from the embarrassment. "I don't know what to say."

"The amount of work you put in at the lab says it all. You can look around and see no one else comes close." He paused and placed a reassuring hand on my arm. "In a lot of ways, you remind me of myself."

"Thanks." My throat got tight. I wasn't used to this kind of emotional display.

"Your dedication, your insights. Not to brag, but you and I are the only ones around here with original ideas." He laughed and pulled me in for a hug. "You're like the daughter I never had."

Bedtime in my house had always been a reading from the financial section followed by a pat on the head. Kisses were reserved for when I injured myself. I knew most parents and mentors were more affectionate. Most humans could respond in kind.

Uncertain, I didn't respond. Getting the internship, the outpouring of feelings from my boss. I awkwardly patted his back until he released me.

"Hey, Jill." For the second time that evening, someone entered the observatory without my noticing.

"Oh, Mike. It's you." Really, I was going to have to do better when surprised.

Mike approached us by dodging around the chairs. He stood mere inches away from Dr. Shaffer, and not only because the space was small. Alpha male Mike had made an appearance.

"Dr. Shaffer, this is Mike Lewis. He's...he's..."

"Your boyfriend? Hello, Mike, nice to meet you." Dr. Shaffer extended his hand.

Mike gripped it until his knuckles turned white.

"Dr. Shaffer came to tell me that I got the internship. Isn't it great?"

Mike finally looked away from the professor, whom he'd been trying to stare down, and fixed his eyes on me. "Congratulations, baby, I knew you would."

"I knew it, too." Dr. Shaffer didn't budge from his place, despite the crowded space with three bodies so close together. "I was just telling Jill how she's like a daughter to me. I feel very protective of her." Again the two men met eye to eye, each not moving a muscle.

I needed to interrupt the staring contest. "Mike, I thought you had the fundraiser to go to tonight?"

"I was there to set up and make sure it got off to a good start." He still didn't look away from Dr.

Shaffer. "But I wanted to come visit you to keep you company. You said you'd show me the telescope and that you'd be alone."

Dr. Shaffer smiled and took a step back. "I must be going. Despite the rumors, my wife does want to see me at home sometimes. Mike, it was good to meet you. Jill dear, congratulations again. I'm proud of you, and I'm looking forward to working with you much more now."

"Good night, Dr. Shaffer. Thanks," I said as he walked out the door.

The tension eased from Mike, his body relaxing as the door closed behind the professor.

"What was all that about?" Mike asked.

"All what?"

"The big bear hug and the 'I'm so eager to work with you more' stuff."

I rolled my eyes. "You heard him. I'm like a daughter. It's nice for him to mentor young scientists. And it's good for me. Not only do I get a sweet internship out of it, but he'll promote me in the department. My projects will get attention and I'll probably get into the grad program with a huge grant."

"I'd watch myself with him. I'm not convinced all his motives are fatherly."

"I can't believe you're jealous of my boss. I told you from the beginning, my work was going to come first. It has to. And this is the first adult in my life who has taken an interest in me. My parents couldn't care less about what I do. Here's a kind man who wants to help me succeed and you're trying to turn me against him. What are you doing here anyway?" I put some distance between us. The small office and the heat from his body made it hard to stay angry, but I tried.

"I came because I missed you. I hated being at the party without you. I thought you'd like the company. I can see I was wrong." He pointed to the telescope and monitors. "Your instruments are all the company you need."

Tears stung my eyes. Two men in one night came to see me and profess their feelings. One as a father figure and one as a lover. They probably expected me to express feelings to them. Mike was looking for reassurance that I cared about him, that I wanted him.

"You don't believe that." It was all I could come up with. Expressing emotions was not my strong suit.

"No, I don't believe it. I think you need more. But maybe you don't know what you need. I'm worried Dr. Shaffer will take advantage of that naiveté."

"You don't need to worry about me. I'm just fine."

Mike shifted uncomfortably. He couldn't reach out and touch me with his hands bearing most of his weight. I pecked him on the cheek.

His mouth was set tight, but a forced smile appeared.

"Will I see you tomorrow?" I asked.

"Sure, dinner at your place with your crazy friend Nikki and the stolen boyfriend. Sounds like a blast."

"Come on, it won't be that bad."

"I'm only joking. I'll see you then," he said.

We kissed, and I wrapped my arms around him. This hug was different. Sure, Mike couldn't return it, but my hands didn't awkwardly pat him on the back. His muscles rippled through his shirt, my palms receiving the heat he was giving off. This hug was natural and easy. Mike did that, brought out the true emotion in me.

Images of what could happen in this secluded room with the stars above us ran through my mind. But I pulled away. I only had so many hours with this image feed. I could fool around with Mike anytime.

"I'll head back to the party," he said.

"Okay. I have a lot to do here, but I'll see you tomorrow."

"Yeah, see you then."

I studied his movements around the commonplace furniture, which were extraordinary obstacles for Mike.

Now I could get to work. The usual sense of

urgency, however, had vanished. It was a little too quiet now, by myself. The eerie hum of the machines let me know I was alone, really alone.

Chapter 14

MIKE

I thumped back across campus. The wind was bitter and I hadn't bothered to zip up my coat. But the place on my back where she laid her hands was still warm. I left Jill as fast as I could.

Stupid.

I was stupid to think I could distract her from her work. Hadn't she said this was an important time? She'd explained how hard it was to get a time slot with the telescope. How would I feel if she came to the theater when I was working and tried to keep me company?

I'd love it.

Except for maybe feeling weird around Beth, I'd love to show her off to all my friends. I wanted to tonight. As I approached the frat house, the sounds of the party reminded me of what I had planned.

I imagined Jill meeting my brothers. They'd barely be polite, probably making some inappropriate joke. But she could handle it. And she'd stick by my side all night. We'd work at the refreshment table, sit on the porch, huddled together for warmth. And all the world would see me with a beautiful, brilliant woman.

I opened the door to Theta Chi, and the heat and music hit me with a blast.

"Hey, Mike, over here." Steve was doling out cups of some sort of punch. The only thing you could be sure of was plenty of alcohol and sugar. After that, it was anyone's guess as to what was in it.

"Hey, Steve. How's the collection going?"

"I've got two crates full of food, over two hundred dollars in donations, three phone numbers, and one pair of purple silk panties." He twirled them around his finger.

"I don't think purple is your color," I said.

Steve grinned his wolfish smile and went off to seek out his next conquest. I surveyed the room and contemplated my next move. Would it be helping the DJ or collecting the empty Solo cups?

"Hey, Miiike." Lorna was drunk. She listed to the side as she shuffled toward me.

"Hi, Lorna. Looks like you need to sit down." I led her to a couch in the corner, only slightly damp with what I hoped was beer. I plopped into it and sank close to the floor. I forgot this was the one without a frame at the bottom.

She flung her legs over the side and placed her

head in my lap. Her makeup had run a bit, but she was pretty. A perfect tennis player's body, a pert nose, puckered pink lips, and a mane of chestnut curls.

"Why didn't we evvver go out again?" She searched my face but couldn't seem to focus on my eyes.

"I don't remember ever going out the first time." I grimaced as a blast of warm, beery breath wafted up from her face.

"Aww, Miiii-iiike." She nuzzled her face in my abs.

Shit. My body was going to decide all on its own that we needed some. It was no use trying to reason with my dick. It would stand up and make its plans known. But I could still control the rest of me.

"Maybe I should have someone take you home." I trusted the Theta Chis. We had a code about girls too far gone to consent. But codes could be forgotten in a whisky haze.

"You take me home." She sat up and licked the side of my neck.

"I can't." I ground my teeth together.

"I *know* that you can," she whispered, her voice a whine in my ear.

"That's not what I meant." I pushed her off, tugged at my pants, and leaned forward. "I'm with someone."

"Who-oo?" She blinked slowly. "It's not Debbie

or anyone I know."

"No, her name's Jill."

"Where is she?" Lorna sat up and flapped her arm from side to side to indicate the crowd in the room.

"She's working." Activity had subsided downtown, so I could sit back.

"Working? Instead of here with you? Are you sure she's working on a Satur-Saturday night?"

"Yeah, listen, Lorna—" I stood as she did.

"You don't have to insult me, Mike." The flirty, happy drunk had turned into the touchy, angry drunk. "I know when I'm getting the brush-off. It's not every girl who would hang with you all night instead of dancing."

A siren blast sounded in my head, but I gripped my crutches with enough force to bend the metal rather than react to her slight. She was drunk. She no more meant what she said now than what she'd said about wanting to screw me.

"Debbie!" she called, and her Tri-Delt sister came over. "We're leaving."

Debbie shot me a questioning look. I turned away. Better for everyone to think I'd turned her down than to think I couldn't get a girl in the first place.

I was relieved in many ways to see the two stagger out and head for their own beds to sleep it off.

Once again, without a good plan or place to be, I went into the kitchen.

It was a little quieter in there, and I could look busy setting things out without having to talk to people.

"Mike, I thought you were heading over to see your hottie scientist?" Jeff was at the sink cleaning out cups.

"Nah, she was busy, and turns out staring at the stars doesn't get a woman all hot and bothered if she's taking measurements."

"Maybe she's not into *your* measurements." Jeff playfully splashed some water at my face.

"Nice one," I conceded.

"Seriously, Mike. There are plenty of women out there who will really be into you. Don't go chasing after someone who'll break your heart."

"Thanks for looking out for me, but I can take care of myself."

"Dude, I know you can. It's just…" Jeff shrugged.

"It's just you think I'm more vulnerable to getting my heart broken because my legs are. I don't want a woman to pity me. And Jill doesn't feel sorry for me at all. She also doesn't want to date me to show how politically correct she is. Besides, this time next year, I'll have the best prostheses in the world and walking around like Homo erectus. Don't even say it."

Jeff smirked. "Man, it's tough not to comment on that one. But I get it. I'll back off."

Jeff rejoined the party and I had some solitude again. It was more than the lack of pity that I appreciated in Jill. She didn't think I needed her. She didn't try to help me, or mother me, or smother me. She didn't try to carry things for me or tie my shoes. She expected me to be independent, and she wanted her independence in return. That was what hurt the most.

I couldn't sweep a woman off her feet, literally. But I wanted my girlfriend to be lonely without me. I needed her, and I desperately wanted her to need me.

JILL

"This is ridiculous," Nikki said. "How are we supposed to fit?"

I put the finishing touches on a chopped salad. The garlic bread was warming, the lasagna was bubbling at the edges, and the cheese was browned on top.

"It'll be fine. We'll pull the couch over to the table."

"This café table? You want to fit the four of us at one café table?"

"What are you carrying on about? Balance a plate on your lap. If I didn't know any better, I'd say Nicole Wilson is nervous." I smiled.

"Just because you've walked around with a Mona Lisa smile on your lips doesn't mean the rest of us are happy about having a boyfriend."

"Nikki, you practically stalked Kenneth for months. You even audited that Ancient Greek Language class to spend time with him. Now that you've hooked him, you're a wreck about having him around."

Nikki flopped on the sofa. "I know, it's terrible. The things one has to go through for sex." She shook her head. "What the heck do I know about being a girlfriend? Do I cut his meat for him? Buy cutesy gifts? Should I be wearing sexy underwear?"

"No, no, and yes. Honestly, Nikki, I normally wouldn't say this applies to you, but be yourself. For whatever warped reason, Kenneth has decided he likes you. Don't do anything different than what you have been doing. Except maybe changing to some sexier underwear. What do you usually wear?"

"Nothing."

I struggled for an answer as the buzzer on the intercom sounded. *Please let it be Mike.* I needed a few moments to come to terms with Nikki's lack of panties before I looked Kenneth in the eye. I heard voices and clomping on the stairs. The guys must have arrived at the same time.

Hopefully, Mike and I could put last night behind us. How was I supposed to cope with this messy part of the relationship? Nikki and I had more in common than I liked to admit.

Did Mike really want me to drop everything last night and fall into his arms? That was ridiculous — giving up precious telescope time when we could spend any other evening together. Besides, he was supposed to be busy running his fundraiser. Sure, I'd been happy to see him. But that didn't mean I should give in to every feeling his presence stirred.

But as the flutters in my stomach began as he opened the door, I was in danger of doing just that.

"Hi, guys." I took a bakery box from Kenneth and a bottle of wine Mike had pulled out of his backpack.

I helped them with their coats. Mike cocked his head. I leaned in.

"Sorry about last night," he whispered as Kenneth and Nikki greeted each other with a kiss.

"No, I'm sorry. You caught me off guard. Next time, tell me when you're going to surprise me." I laughed.

"Okay, here's fair warning. You're going to get a *big* surprise tonight, when your guests leave."

"Really?" My eyebrows arched. "Something I haven't seen before?"

"I still have a few tricks you haven't seen yet." Mike winked and joined the others.

I took a moment to try to get the blood flowing to my brain again. It seemed to have rushed between my legs.

Once we were settled around the table with full plates, Mike raised his glass.

"I'd like to propose a toast to the chef." He nodded toward me.

The others murmured their agreement.

"And I have great news to announce." Mike cleared his throat. "My surgery has been approved, and as soon as classes get out, I'm having my legs amputated!"

A thunderclap of silence fell on the room, as Kenneth and Nikki held their glasses halfway to their mouths.

Jerk.

Blurting the news out like this when I was trying to have a grown-up dinner party. What did he think? That he'd avoid me bursting out in tears or having some big emotional response? Okay, I did want to cry. I did want to be emotional, but I wouldn't. Not now, at least.

"Great. I know it's what you were hoping for." I kept my voice even. "Mike is going to have his legs amputated below the knee," I explained to the others. I turned to look at Mike, who hadn't waited and dug right into the food. "He'll be using prostheses to walk around."

"Oh, I, uh, guess that's good," Nikki said.

"Not just any prostheses," Mike said around a mouthful of garlic bread. "State-of-the-art, science-fiction-type stuff. I'll be walking around and you'll barely notice a difference in my gait than someone with two good legs."

"Oh," Kenneth said, and looked down at his plate.

My eyes burned with tears. I was unsure whether it was happiness for Mike or fear for me. The amputation had been an abstract idea, a possibility somewhere in the future. Now it was only a few months away. And Mike sat there feeling as pleased as he could be. Simply shoveling food into himself.

Fine, we won't talk about it.

If he didn't want to think about what it meant, it wasn't up to me to discuss it. That's what his psychiatrist was for.

Not my problem.

But it would be my problem.

If we were going to stay together past this semester, it would be my problem as well his. That's what Mike was waiting to see. Would I stick with him through the amputation? Through the rehab? Would I date someone without legs?

Luckily, Nikki never let an awkward moment stop her.

"I think we should talk about the university regents' plan to spend money on a new athletic facility instead of updating the biology labs. I mean, where are their priorities?"

Everyone was grateful for the distraction, and dinner came off without a hitch. I accepted the compliments on my cooking.

"It's nice to have people to cook for," I said. "You can't know how depressing it is to cook a three-course meal for myself."

"Have me over anytime," Kenneth said, but his eyes were fixed on Nikki. He hadn't taken them off her all night. Maybe he would soften Nikki's rough edges.

After the dishes were cleared, Nikki announced, "Well, we've got to get back to Kenneth's dorm before his roommate comes home. That only leaves us two hours' use of the room." She looked at her watch, grabbed his hand, and pulled him toward the door.

"Thanks for inviting me," Kenneth said as Nikki shoved his hat on his head and yanked him away.

"You're welcome," I called as the door banged shut. "I guess we're stuck with the dishes."

"The dishes can wait." Mike smiled and jerked his thumb toward the bedroom. "I haven't had my dessert yet."

"Kenneth brought cookies."

"I didn't eat any." Mike's eyes smoldered, and he had that deadly serious look.

By now, I knew what that look would lead to,

and I had been waiting all night.

I led him to the bedroom, pulling my sweater over my head as I went. I reached behind to unhook my bra, but found Mike's hand already there. With only two fingers, he released the clasp and my bra fell forward.

"How'd you do that?" I turned to look at him, but his gaze was lower down.

"Bobby Franks used to steal his sister's bras and we'd practice in his basement." Mike sat at the edge of the bed, his face in line with my bare stomach. He placed kisses along the waistband of my jeans, each brush of his lips sending quakes along my skin.

"I have to thank Bobby someday." My voice was rough as he let his crutches fall and used his hand to pull me closer to him, his fingers dipping inside my pants to tug at my panties.

"Sweetheart, you'll be thanking me in about an hour."

"An hour?"

"Shhh." He pulled me down on top of him. "Undress me. Like you did that first time." His voice held a note of questioning.

"My pleasure." I slid off and worked on his pants over his hips. When they came off, his erection sprang out of his boxers. "Mmmm, eager?"

"Babe, watching your lips close around a forkful of food is torture."

"No, this is torture." I engulfed him with my

mouth. He shivered and raked his hands through my hair.

With slow caresses of my mouth, I felt his groan reverberate through me. I pulled back and his face was wild with desire.

"Lie back." His voice rasped.

I peeled off my remaining clothes and waited as he positioned himself between my legs. I knew what was coming, but couldn't prepare for the slick sensation of a tongue against my most sensitive flesh. I gripped the bedsheet, tearing the corner as he worked his magic with his mouth and a single finger. I bucked and almost tumbled toward orgasm when he pulled away.

"No." I whimpered.

"Baby, that's just the beginning," he rumbled.

The ache had built in my core, and I couldn't wait for anything else he had in store for me. But he left me no choice as he languidly placed kisses up from my belly across my breasts, up over my chin, and finally settled on my mouth. Our tongues explored each other, and as he pulled back, I bit gently on his lower lip.

His arms could suspend him over me while on his knees, so I grabbed a condom from the side table, tore open the package, and rolled it on.

The pause as Mike shuffled to the right spot allowed cool air to blow across my damp sex. A tremor of anticipation jetted through me.

And when he entered me and the strain on his face melted away, I knew this was what love was about.

He could use one hand to balance and the other worked my clit. But even the building orgasm wasn't enough to distract me.

My mind had chosen that moment to fall in love. A cry caught in my throat. It wasn't only the release when I came, it was the elation of joining with a man who could match me in wit and who offered understanding and compassion.

It was a cry of anguish as a small part of my goals disappeared, threatened to be replaced with new ones and with the needs of a man who was about to take on life-altering change.

Chapter 15

MIKE

"So how's the new tutor?" Jill asked as we lay together on her bed, the only light coming from the TV screen.

I halfheartedly watched the Bulls as she stroked my hair.

"He's not nearly as smart as you are. But almost as pretty."

Jill hit me on the head with a pillow.

"That's it." I retaliated by tickling her sides.

After a fit of her giggling, I stopped and pulled her to me. She smelled of the honey soap she used, and of the musky scent of our lovemaking.

"There's something I want to tell you," she said.

"Uh-oh. Nothing good ever comes after that sentence."

"It's not bad." She propped herself on an elbow. "My parents are coming into town. They have a conference and we're going out to dinner."

"You want me to meet them?"

"I don't want you to feel pressured. They're difficult people. You've heard me talk about them. They're a lot like Nikki. Not a lot of emotion going on inside." She avoided my gaze and fiddled with the bedsheet.

"They're your parents—however you want to handle it." I held my breath, hoping she'd be honest.

"I'm not ashamed to have them meet you…I'm ashamed to have *you* meet *them*."

"Jill, it's you I like, not your parents. Nothing they can say or do will change my opinion of you. I'll still think you're an ogress who eats small children and trips old ladies as they cross the street."

Jill smiled. "You say the sweetest things."

"I'm charming that way."

"There's something else I need to say." This time she pulled on her shirt and took some deep breaths before she continued.

This was the moment when she'd say something about the amputation. This was when she was going to tell me not to do it. We'd just had leg-cramp-inducing sex and she didn't want my body to change. I held my breath. I couldn't change my plans, not even for Jill.

"I love you," she muttered.

"Huh?"

"I think you heard me. I love you, you idiot. Whatever you need during the summer, I—"

My head clanged. I pulled her, probably too forcefully, and squashed her into my chest. I smashed her lips with mine and kissed the crap out of her.

I didn't care if our teeth clacked together. I didn't care if she could breathe.

"I love you too," I said into her mouth.

"Could you crush me a little less?"

"No." I held on. She was going to stick with me; that was what was important. We didn't need to talk about the details. They would work themselves out.

Ringing from my cell phone interrupted our kiss. "Your phone has rung three times this hour. Someone's trying to reach you." She pulled back.

"Crap. That's my mom's ringtone. I should get it."

"I'm hopping in the shower. You talk to your mom." Jill scurried into the bathroom. The water turned on almost immediately. She wasn't going to be one of those girls who wanted to eavesdrop on my conversations. She wasn't going to be clingy or want to talk.

My mom had called three times. What could she want? I called back and she answered immediately.

"Everything okay?" I asked.

"Mikey, why haven't you called? We heard from the insurance company. You must know they've approved the surgery."

"Of course I know. Dr. Marlow and I talked." I

found my boxers and pulled them up.

"Shouldn't we discuss the plan?" Anxiety altered Mom's usual kind tone.

"What's there to discuss?"

"I don't know. But it's really going to happen now."

"That was the point, Mom." I took a deep breath. "It's going to be fine. I know it's hard to understand, but this is a relief for me."

"We should schedule it with the hospital for after our Memorial Day trip to the lake house." I detected a sob.

"Mom, I've never been happier."

"Really?"

"Yeah. And there's someone I want to invite along for Memorial Day. Can I?"

"Beth?"

"No. Her name is Jill. She's my girlfriend. You met her at the play."

"The math tutor."

I laughed. "She's not my tutor anymore. She's on board with the surgery and she's brilliant."

"Okay, if you want her to come. Are you sure she should spend the entire weekend with the family?"

"If things go as planned, she should be spending a whole lot of time with our family."

JILL

Dr. Shaffer frequently hosted parties in his house for the office or the department. This one was for all the students and faculty who were spring break orphans. People who either didn't have the funds to go home or who chose to stay on campus.

The large TV mutely played the preseason game between the Cubs and the Cardinals. Spring should show up in Chicago in a month, but that wouldn't help the Cubs any.

Not surprisingly, I was one of the few undergrads in attendance. I had enough gas money to drive back to Madison, but why bother? It wasn't as if I would be partying at my house.

I stood by the drinks table, filling my cup with more iced tea. There was harder stuff, but still only twenty, I didn't want to make the faculty feel uncomfortable. I kept my eyes on the game. Nikki had gone off with Kenneth on a camping trip to the Dells. They were probably freezing their butts off, but happy.

Painful, polite conversation with the professors had run its course, and now the talk of grant applications and department politics took place without me, since I had nothing to contribute.

I wandered into the kitchen and recognized the woman working at the counter as Mrs. Shaffer from her photo on the professor's desk. Instead of that smiling, well-coifed woman, her mouth was pinched and her hair was falling out of its clip as she furiously sliced more fruit to add to the platters. A timer went off. She slipped one hand into an oven mitt, deftly removed a sheet of cookies, and closed the oven with her knee.

"Need some help, Mrs. Shaffer?" I asked from the doorway.

Mrs. Shaffer turned a glare upon me, but quickly softened her look.

"If you have a moment, that would be very kind of you."

I stepped forward and accepted a spatula and plate to move the cookies. "I'm Jill Kramer. I work in Dr. Shaffer's lab and I'll be his intern this summer and next year."

Mrs. Shaffer briefly scanned my body. "It's nice to meet you. Call me Ellen."

"Thank you for hosting us tonight. Campus is dead this week, and it's nice to have some home-cooked food."

Ellen let out a heavy breath. "The way to a student's heart is through her stomach. And Ron knows how to reach a student's heart."

I almost giggled thinking of Dr. Shaffer as Ron. Ronald was even funnier. He was such a father figure to me that to think of his first name seemed silly. "He's been a great mentor to me. I'm grateful for his guidance."

Ellen barked a laugh. "I'm sure you deserve it. Ron always picks the brightest kids to work for him." She handed me a box of crackers and a plate of cheese, wordlessly indicating I should arrange them.

The understanding of what Mrs. Shaffer must go through hit me like a meteor shower. Dr. Shaffer's dedication to his research and his students came at the expense of his private life. I knew that, he'd even joked about it. But witnessing his wife's frantic hosting of a party for people she didn't know brought it to reality.

How could I ever ask someone to share that kind of life with me? Not everyone would be as understanding as Mike.

"Shall I take these out?" I asked, looking for an excuse to leave the kitchen.

"Yes please. I can see why Ron has taken you on. You're very helpful and…bright." She smiled, but I caught a glimpse of her jaw setting.

"Thanks," I mumbled, and scurried back out to the party, feeling like an elephant was pinning my chest to the ground.

"It's so kind of you to help Ellen in the kitchen." Dr. Shaffer approached as I set the platters down.

"It's no problem. I should probably be going soon."

"Too many old folks for you here?" He chuckled.

"No different than at home." The knot in my chest loosened and my muscles relaxed. Dr. Shaffer might not be the ideal husband, but I couldn't ask for a better teacher.

"I'm glad you came. It's good to put in an appearance. This is the cabal who review grad school applications." He nodded toward the clutch of graying profs, heads bent together in deep discussion.

I laughed, and my anxiety dissipated like protons flying off faster than a stellar wind. "Then I need to thank you again for inviting me."

"You didn't bring your boyfriend with you." He scrutinized my face.

"I, uh, didn't think he'd fit in. He's not the science type."

"I see. It must be difficult for him to get around."

"Not really." I didn't want to be talking about Mike. It seemed wrong somehow for me to have a boyfriend and focus on trivial things when Dr. Shaffer was only interested in my advancement. "I hope I didn't say anything dumb to any of the other faculty."

He waved his hand. "I'm sure you made a good impression. And that's a feather in my cap. And Jill, you make a good impression."

I felt my face get red. Why couldn't my parents compliment me, praise me, recognize my accomplishments?

My eyes stung a bit as I said good-bye and left the Shaffer household, wondering if anyone had a house in which people loved each other and supported each other and were free to follow their goals.

MIKE

"You'll be proud of me." I took the seat across from Dr. Marlow.

"Why do you feel the need to impress me?" Dr. Marlow answered.

"Can't you turn off that psychology stuff for a minute? I mean, I think this is our last session. You could at least recognize the progress I've made." I flashed my trademark smirk. I liked playing around with Dr. Marlow, but I had to admit he had been a help. "I told my girlfriend about the approval for the surgery."

"That is good news. What did she say?"

"Nothing."

"Nothing?" Dr. Marlow said. "She was silent?"

"No, she said it was great and her friend started a different conversation."

"Her friend? Her friend was there?" Dr. Marlow leaned forward in his chair.

"Yeah. We were all having dinner at Jill's

apartment."

Dr. Marlow shook his head. "You told Jill about the approval at a dinner party?"

"You make it sound like I broke a law." My temper rose. I liked Dr. Marlow well enough, but he was scolding me as if I were a child.

"Mike, I hate to break this news to you. But I don't think you handled that very well. You didn't give Jill a chance to talk about it with you."

"She could have said anything she wanted. And once her friends left, she could have brought it up." I folded my arms.

"Did you tell her? Did you invite her to talk about it when you were alone?"

"Well, we were busy with other things, if you know what I mean." I winked.

"So you dropped this bomb of news in the middle of a dinner party. Then when you were alone and she had an opportunity to bring it up, you distracted her with sex." Dr. Marlow paused. "What were you afraid she would say?"

"It doesn't matter. She invited me to meet her parents. Plus, she said she'd be around all summer."

Dr. Marlow didn't respond. He nodded and kept a blank expression.

"She's got this big internship, so she'll be here all summer," I continued. I waited. Still nothing.

"I mean, she wouldn't invite me to meet her parents and remind me she'd be around all summer if she didn't mean she'd stick with me."

"Yes, she could have meant that." Marlow nodded.

"She said she loved me. That means something." My voice cracked and sweat broke out on my forehead.

"It does. That's significant." He nodded again.

"And I told her I love her. She's going to come for Memorial Day to my family's vacation home. This is a real relationship."

"I never said it wasn't." Dr. Marlow kept his cool as I was losing control.

"She knew from the beginning this was the plan. I told her before our first date that my legs would be amputated." I tried to tamp down the uncomfortable thud in my chest.

"You know, we could extend our sessions. This doesn't have to be the last time we meet. You might want to continue so you can adjust after the surgery."

"Why do you think I need to adjust? You approved me for the surgery." I rubbed my face hard, to rid the flush and sting in my eyes.

"I know, and I still think you're ready for your new body. But I'm not sure if you're ready for your new relationships."

"New relationships?"

"You're going to have to renegotiate your relationships with your family, and your girlfriend." Dr. Marlow placed his palms out.

I stared out the window and willed my jaws apart when I felt my teeth gnashing. "What if she doesn't want to stick around? What if the rehab takes too long? What if my stumps gross her out?"

"Those are all real possibilities. Jill sounds like a great young woman. But it's a lot to ask of anyone, especially someone with as much ambition as you describe."

The love of my life, the rock that Jill was, the promise she had made—a fracture slid in. I knew all too well that my world could crumble in an instant. I wanted nothing more than to believe this time it never could again.

"What if no one wants me?" My eyes no longer stung because the tears washed out of them.

Chapter 16

MIKE

I always figured I'd see Jill's weak side at some point. I just never thought it would be at a comfortable Chicago restaurant waiting for her parents.

A week after we'd cemented our relationship, things had only gotten better. I felt bolder and more confident the more time we spent together. And Jill relaxed as well. She still worked like a maniac at the astronomy office, but she carved out time for extracurriculars. And now the big intro to the parents. I could charm anyone's folks — she had no need to be nervous, but she was.

She realigned the silverware so that it was parallel with the plate. She re-folded the napkin in her lap and took another sip of water, careful to place it back in the same spot so it matched with the condensation ring left from the base.

"You're acting like they might be bringing weapons." I squeezed her knee.

Jill shot me a dirty look. "You're the one who wanted to come along. I said you didn't need to meet my parents."

"Relax, they'll love me. And if they don't, I'll challenge your father to a duel."

"Okay, see, I love your humor. But they might not get it. Can you tone it down?"

I nodded. "Sure, no jokes. That leaves me little else to say."

"You can talk about anything you want." Jill glanced around the room.

"Jill, did you tell your parents about me?"

"Of course I did. They know you're joining us tonight."

"What did you tell them about me?" I was beginning to feel as nervous as Jill was.

"I told them you were pre-law, Phi Beta Kappa material, and minoring in theater. I said you were local, from Chicago, and had a wonderful sense of humor, that your father was a judge, that—"

"Hold it right there. I'm guessing you left out the part about my legs." I narrowed my eyes, challenging her like the day she'd asked about my disability.

"Is it important? Does it change who you are?"

"No, Jill, it doesn't. But I don't want to make this any more awkward than it has to be."

"You're the one who said it would be no big deal." She shrugged, but I spotted the pulse in her neck.

I took a deep breath. "That was before they were about to be shocked to find out that their precious only daughter is dating a cripple."

"Don't use that word. I don't find it as amusing as you do. And I'll bet you ten dollars they don't even notice."

I laughed to keep from yelling. "Don't notice? You're living in a dream world. *Everyone* notices. Did you see all the heads turn our way as we came in? Did you see the wary look the hostess gave me as I maneuvered between the tables?" My lower back began to sweat, always did when I got angry and had no way of working it off. "I think you're making excuses so you don't have to have a confrontation with your parents."

"Like you're so honest with your father about law school," Jill hissed. "The curtain rises, Mr. Thespian. You're on."

I followed her gaze to the middle-aged couple who stood scanning the restaurant. Mr. Kramer was tall and thin, but her mom was petite, like Jill. Both dressed in severe, dark suits, not like the bright colors Jill favored. Mr. Kramer's large glasses obscured a good part of his face. Mrs. Kramer had once been as beautiful as Jill. The same heart-shaped face and deep blue eyes were there. But she lacked the unmistakable Jill-spark. In fact, it seemed as though their gazes passed by us once or twice before they recognized Jill and headed over to the table.

Jill didn't stand to greet her parents, but if she thought that was going to give me an excuse to remain sitting, she was kidding herself. I reached down, grabbed the crutches for support, and lifted myself up. I made sure to get in a good glare at Jill, guilting her into standing as well.

After she embraced both parents, Mr. Kramer held out his hand and said, "You must be Jake."

"It's Mike, Daddy," Jill corrected.

"Of course, Mike," Mr. Kramer said.

"Nice to meet you." Mrs. Kramer held her hand out, and I released the crutch so I could shake it. It was soft, and she barely returned the grasp or made eye contact.

"I'm so glad to meet both of you. I've been waiting for the honor to meet Jill's parents for a while now."

"Oh." Mrs. Kramer seemed confused, and sat down in the chair her husband had pulled out for her.

I settled myself in the chair again, making a big show of stowing the crutches under the table. They didn't comment. Not even, "Oh, did you hurt your leg?" —the usual response when people were unsure. Her parents lacked the minor curiosity to even glance down as I bent to shove them out of the aisle where the servers walked.

Jill had a smug grin on her face. And I seethed.

She had been right about her clueless parents, and I was robbed of the opportunity to make my point.

"How is your conference?" Jill asked as her parents looked through the menu.

"The same talks every year. Quantitative easing, deregulation." Mrs. Kramer waved her hand.

Silence.

"My classes are going well. I've made real progress on my research."

"That's great," Mr. Kramer said as he intently buttered a roll.

"I'm pre-law," I offered.

Mrs. Kramer nodded. "Jill told us."

"But I'm not going to law school."

"Oh. Okay." Mrs. Kramer perused the menu. Nothing. Usually one of my best baits. No bites from these fish.

Jill jabbed me in the thigh with her finger. She sensed I was on a roll.

"I'm applying to theater programs."

A curt nod from Mr. Kramer.

"Mike wants to be an actor," Jill said with a futile air. Maybe conversation was impossible.

"A high-risk, unconventional approach," Mr. Kramer said without a hint of disapproval, merely an academic's observation.

"What were the metrics in that study?" Mrs. Kramer turned to her husband.

"Ah, the one about the correlation between

college majors and income at age forty." Jill's parents launched into a discussion about research papers they had read about lifetime earnings and college majors and career choices.

Jill relaxed back in her seat. Maybe this was the normal she was hoping for.

When the Kramers finally came up for air, I asked, "What do the studies say about amputees and lifetime earnings? Since I'll be one soon."

Jill gasped and nearly cracked her water glass.

Mr. Kramer raised his eyebrows. But Mrs. Kramer had pulled out her phone and was searching an online database.

"Here's one study about people with physical disabilities. Doesn't deal with amputees specifically…" She continued her search as the waiter took our order.

Jill glared at me. But I could barely contain my laughter. What kind of parents could show so little interest in their daughter's boyfriend? Either they truly didn't care who Jill dated, or they didn't expect me to be around long enough to matter. Were they in for a shock.

"Oh, honey, we meant to tell you," Mrs. Kramer said. "We're remodeling the upstairs this summer. You'll have to sleep in the family room."

"I won't be home this summer, Mom. Remember the internship I told you about?"

"Oh, yes, I remember now."

"I told you she was busy with something," Mr. Kramer added.

"*Busy with something*?" My temper rose. It was one thing to ignore me and show so little interest in my relationship with Jill. It was another to care so little about their daughter they couldn't remember her biggest accomplishments. "Jill has the most competitive internship on campus. She's getting paid, a lot of money, to do her own research and help out an internationally recognized project. She's a star among the stars."

"Mike!" Jill snapped, and her eyes went wide.

Jill's parents only looked at me as if I'd spoken a foreign language. Their blank stares let me know that her accomplishments weren't new information, but it wasn't a reason to get all worked up about it.

"We've always been proud of Jill. Haven't we?" Mr. Kramer turned to Mrs. Kramer.

"Certainly. She's very bright and will be successful. And the good news is she won't have to sleep in the family room this summer."

I let out the breath I had been holding. No wonder Jill didn't feel the need to tell them about my legs. Her parents couldn't look past their spreadsheets and the business section of the newspaper to even notice their own daughter. Jill needed love more than she realized.

Would she accept it from me?

JILL

Although the internship wasn't starting until the end of the semester, the rest of the lab had decided that I'd already begun working there. The amount of work they piled on was more than ever before. Everyone else had left long ago. Well past midnight and I still sat at the computer tediously typing in data.

The dinner with Mom and Dad went as well as could be expected. They didn't embarrass me any more than usual. And Mike was my champion. I smiled at the recollection of how he tried to stand up for me, tried to impress my parents with my accomplishments. I long ago accepted they would never be impressed. But Mike's indignation touched me.

My chest ached to think of it. Mike had been acting like he'd won the lottery ever since his amputation was scheduled. Try as I might, I couldn't feel happy for him. All I felt was fear. Fear for him and fear for me. How was I supposed to support him through this? He had his family, but he would want me there, too. Hospitals made me queasy. And damn it, I was going to be swamped with work this summer and next year. Right when he needed me the most. This had been exactly what I was afraid of when he first asked me out. He needed me; he needed support and help. And with this workload, and my aversion to all that touchy-feely stuff, I wouldn't be able to give it to him.

The door to the office opened, Dr. Shaffer's shadow framed in the doorway.

"Burning the midnight oil?" he asked.

"More like the two a.m. oil. I thought you had gone home."

"I did. But like most nights, I couldn't sleep. I wake up with questions swirling in my mind. I find I have to come in and get started on them. Those ideas won't leave me alone."

I nodded. "I get the same thing. I can't let go of a theory or a problem. I think the answer is there, if I just look at it the right way. I can't think about anything else. I wonder if it means I'm crazy."

"Well, genius and mental illness go hand in hand." He laughed. "I think we're all a bit nuts to think we can understand the universe."

It was so comfortable to have someone in my life who understood. Mom and Dad certainly didn't. And Mike was respectful of my desire to work hard. But he seemed to feel in competition with my work, always waiting around until I was done and could spend time with him.

Dr. Shaffer pulled up a chair next to me and looked at the computer screen. "It's a shame you have to spend your time on these menial tasks."

"I don't mind. I'm still a lowly undergrad here, and someone has to enter the data. I can't thank you enough for this opportunity. I'm optimistic about my graduate school application."

"I am too." He reached over to rub my shoulder. "You're going to do great. I wish there was some way I could fast-track you. Maybe skip some of this boring work and get straight to your project."

His hand put pressure on my neck and shoulder, easing the tension there, but it was a little strange. I wasn't used to physical intimacy from my parents, so when people reached out to me, it made me uncomfortable. But I also knew I shouldn't feel uncomfortable.

"It's okay. Really, I understand." I shifted a nanometer away.

"You're not only brilliant, but patient as well." He stood and kissed me briefly on the top of my head.

I jerked back but forced a smile.

"I'll be in my office," Dr. Shaffer said as he walked away.

That was probably how mentors showed affection. It must be normal for people to hug and kiss each other that way. I tried not to let the seasick feeling affect the way I thought about Dr. Shaffer. He was giving me a huge leg up, and it wasn't something I should question.

Chapter 17

MIKE

"And how was that for you?" Professor Shandell strode across the front row of seats, hands clasped behind his back, head bent down, studying his loafers. How could someone in a rumpled plaid flannel shirt and unkempt hair be so intimidating?

"Um." Not the most intelligent response I ever gave. I recovered a bit. "I think I could have put more emphasis on the character's confusion."

Beth and I had run a scene from a student-written play. It was part of our collaborative work project, and I thought I did a good job, but bragging about it in front of the class didn't seem appropriate.

He nodded, not taking his gaze off the floor. "And for you, Beth?"

"I think we did a great job of building the tension for the next scene. The audience knows my character is lying and the shit's going to hit the fan soon. I think I nailed it when my character plays dumb and befuddles Mike's character."

Shandell raised his head and eyed us over his reading glasses. "Yes." His voice a stage whisper. "Next time, Mike, evaluate yourself with as much confidence as you put into your lines. For next class…"

I found myself breathing again. Shandell was right. I had felt good during the scene. Beth and I made a great team; the natural chemistry between us sparked our performances.

And when I was on stage stepping into someone else's skin, saying someone else's words and experiencing someone else's emotions, I never felt more myself.

It wasn't escaping who I was. It was exploring all the ways I could be.

Class was dismissed. I zipped up my bag and flung it over my shoulders.

"Shandell's right." Beth took the seat next to me.

"I know. I don't want to seem like a blowhard. A cocksure frat guy." Having Beth near me always brought both a sense of comfort and unease. She understood all of what this art was about, but she understood a little too well.

"You memorized your final monologue yet?"

"Yep, good to go. Richard III. I'm a natural." I patted my legs.

Beth winced. "Don't you think it's a little too easy? A bit of a cheap trick?"

"If I've got it, flaunt it." I smirked.

Beth watched the last of the students file out and placed a hand on my knee when I moved to leave.

"Michael, there's no reason you need to portray a disabled character. You proved that in our last scene. You can play anyone."

"Not yet. Once I'm off these babies." I rattled my crutches. "Then I can strut, waddle, stomp, and even sashay." I winked.

"It's a done deal, huh?"

"Scheduled for right after Memorial Day." I beamed. "I've waited so long. I'm anxious to have it over with."

"You know I support you and all. I worry."

"I've got my mom for that."

"And Jill?"

"Jill's not the worrying type. I mean, she worries about her work, but she doesn't smother me." I didn't want to be talking about Jill with Beth. There were unspoken rules between Beth and myself. Beth never talked about her boyfriends with me, and I never mentioned any of my relationships with her. Everything else was on the table.

"I think you're going to need some smothering." Beth leaned her head on my shoulder. Her yellow hair cascaded over my shirt and brushed my chin.

An ache twisted inside me. It would be too easy to allow Beth to take on the role she was auditioning for. Part of me yearned for a caretaker, someone who was going to hold my hand, empty the bedpans, and help clean the wounds where my stumps would be. Jill wasn't strong enough for that. Mom would awkwardly deal with my naked body. But Beth would be a champion. The price was a romance with her, second fiddle to her spotlight performance — the disabled guy's steadfast girlfriend.

"I'm going to be fine. I don't want anyone to take care of me. After the initial period, I'll be taking care of myself. Independent in ways I haven't been in years." I stroked her hair and almost gave in to the urge to tilt her head back and plant a kiss on her. Instead, I shifted and she sat up.

"What kind of friend would I be if I didn't worry? In a little over a year, you and I will be kicking around the streets of New York, getting rejected from every audition we go to." She smiled.

"I doubt you'll be getting rejections," I said as we stood to leave. "But we'll be doing it together." I held out my hand.

She pumped it in a firm businessman's handshake. "Together."

JILL

The theater chair squeaked as I pulled it down, but I was far enough back in the studio theater that no one turned around. Besides, the audience of students and a smattering of others were so riveted on Beth.

"I wouldn't be barren if we slept together, and you wouldn't be an alcoholic if you woke up and realized that the past is the past." She slunk across the stage, her blonde hair falling about her face. She had a wildness barely contained in her body.

I had almost not recognized her when I came in, so transformed she was in posture and voice.

"I was raised on nearly nothin', but we could have so much now, Brick. So many things. So much love." She was alone on stage, but her lines seemed to be delivered to someone in the front row.

Mike had asked me to come see his final exam. He had picked some Shakespeare monologue and really wanted me to watch. I couldn't imagine anyone wanting an audience while you took a final exam, but I guessed this was a different kind of final, one in which an audience was necessary.

Beth finished and bowed to the applause. A professor made some remarks to the class gathered in the front of the theater. "And thanks to Mike Lewis for being Brick in that scene. *Cat on a Hot Tin Roof* requires a partner. And now, Mike, you're up next."

Mike stood, and I realized Beth had been delivering those lines to him. I tamped down a surge of anger. Mike and Beth were friends, he had made that clear, and I trusted him. But I didn't trust her.

"Now is the winter of our discontent. Made glorious summer by this sun of York." Mike was bent over his crutches more than usual, and he held his arm out at an awkward angle.

I had seen a few Shakespeare plays, and had been forced to read one for a class in high school. I didn't get it. It wasn't just the old style, but everything was supposed to have a double meaning, or be a play on words. Why couldn't someone rewrite it so the rest of us could understand it? But Mike was masterful. He really did ooze emotion up there. I couldn't help but get carried away in not his words, but his voice.

"Deformed, unfinish'd, sent before my time. Into this breathing world, scarce half made up. And that so lamely and unfashionable, that dogs bark at me as I halt by them."

I yelped and clamped a hand over my mouth. No one turned to look at me. I didn't need a course in Elizabethan English to understand. Tears trickled down my face and my nose started to run.

Was he the bravest person I knew, or the most provocative?

Either way, I hated to admit it, but it worked. He made me understand Shakespeare. Hobbling around the stage, he made me feel what it was like to be despised because of your shape, the humiliation that turns to resentment.

He ended, executed a crooked bow, and hopped

off the stage. While he received feedback from the professor, the next student took the stage.

I didn't pay attention to the remaining monologues. I considered how Mike had always covered his anger with charm, but once in a while I would glimpse the seething frustration.

That was when he challenged people.

That was when he decided the world had dealt him a pile of crap and he was going to chuck it right back.

That was when I admired him.

"Did you enjoy the performances?" Beth had broken away from the departing crowd and found me in the back.

"You were all amazing." I didn't lie. "I can't imagine how you do it." I scanned the students for Mike. He was in a discussion with the professor.

Beth's serene smile and lowered eyelids conveyed exactly the right amount of compassion and disdain. "Michael's brave. Don't you think? He could have chosen something safer, but he probed the sentiments of the character, exposing his own sensibilities."

"Yep." I was pretty sure I agreed with her, but couldn't be sure.

"He and I are going to take New York by storm. He's going to need me there. We're going to need each other." Beth sighed and looked over her shoulder at the thinning crowd and Mike working his way toward us.

"Yep." If I dared to say anything more, all the nasty thoughts I had about this beautiful, talented woman would gush out. And she was Mike's friend. I had to be civil.

"I should be going." Beth took a step toward the door. "Nice talking to you."

I was about to add one more "Yep," when Mike arrived.

"That was awesome." I hugged him and pecked him on the cheek.

"You liked it?" He cocked his head.

"Of course. You, uh, really explored the sentiments of the character and exposed yourself."

He chuckled. "Don't let Beth get to you."

"She doesn't. Well, she does. It's only…" I looked away from his dangerously green eyes and chiseled jaw. The room was empty save for us. The acoustics picked up my shuffling feet.

"Let's sit." Mike nodded toward the seats.

I fell into the chair. "I hate the thought of you and Beth living together in New York." I blurted the words before I could censor myself. I didn't want to be the jealous girlfriend.

Mike rubbed his face. "You'll be here."

"I know, I know. I have no reason for feeling this way and I'm sorry I said anything." I snaked my arm around him and kissed his cheek. He had let the stubble grow, I guess for the performance, and the scratch against my lips left me wanting more friction elsewhere. "Forget I said anything."

"Not sure I can." He tilted my chin back and gave me a real kiss. A spine-melting kiss.

"I didn't mean to stir things up. Not right before the end of school, and the big weekend with your family, and…"

"And the amputation," he finished. "Jill, you've got me confused about the future. I was sure what my path was before you."

"And I was sure about my path. We've both worked hard for what's coming up. Neither of us can change course. Let's focus on today."

"How about focusing on tonight?" He leaned in for another kiss. Damned if I didn't want to straddle him right there.

This man, who could strut around a stage, take a gamble with his life, and give off a gigawatt smile, was mine. At least for now.

Chapter 18

MIKE

Jill handled the winding road with ease. There's nothing sexier than watching a girl drive a stick shift. Her beat-up Ford Escort rumbled along, and she seemed to hit every dip and pothole.

"Sorry," she said as I nearly smacked my head on the roof after another jarring bump.

"No problem." I gripped the bar above the window. "There's no rush. The lake isn't going to disappear."

"We got a late start. I don't want your parents to think I'm irresponsible." She kept her eyes trained on the road.

"Jill, they're going to love you." I rubbed her knee. Her skirt slid up, and I allowed my hand to slide over the silky skin of her inner thigh.

"Ack." She jumped, and we nearly swerved into the drainage ditch.

"Sorry." I grinned, hoping to avoid her wrath.

But she took her eyes off the road to glower at me. "Behave."

"Okay, fine. But once everyone's asleep, I'm sneaking you out to the boathouse. No one will hear you scream." I waggled my eyebrows.

"No way. I'm not going to sleep with you. I'm in a guestroom, you're sharing a room with your brother, and we are not even going to shake hands the entire weekend." She set her jaw.

"What? What's the point of a romantic trip to the lake if we don't—"

"It's not a romantic trip. Your family will be there, and it's mere days before your surgery."

I stuck my tongue out at her and blew a raspberry.

"Childish antics won't work."

I wasn't really upset. I kinda guessed it would be impossible with my family hovering around. But I had to try, otherwise my manhood would be in question.

"It's right past this bend." I pointed ahead.

Dad had bought this house when I was still a toddler. I didn't ever remember not coming here in the summers. When James and I were kids, we could spend endless hours exploring the woods and building anything we imagined with whatever we found in the forest, some scraps, and nails from the garage.

It was here where my parents were their most

relaxed. I never saw them kiss and hug as much as I did when we spent time out here. Dad smiled more in one month at the lake than the entire rest of the year, and he never mentioned practice, training, studying. This was where we cooked hot dogs over a fire pit.

The perfect place for Jill to get to know my family.

She pulled the car gently into the gravel driveway, and Mom came out to greet us.

We unfolded ourselves after the long drive, and Jill graciously accepted Mom's hug. The complete opposite of what Jill was used to, but if she was going to spend time with my mother, she was going to have to get used to hugs.

Dad and James were at work in the kitchen, putting the finishing touches on their signature hero sandwiches.

"It's nice to see you again, Jill." Dad extended his hand and looked at her without his critical glare.

"What's up?" James nodded coolly. But out of the corner of his eye, he gave her the once-over. He glanced at me, and I returned a hard stare. He didn't stand a chance, but a little brother likes to think he's worthy of inciting his older brother's jealousy.

"Mr. and Mrs. Lewis, thank you so much for inviting me." Jill held out a bouquet of flowers for Mom.

Mom sputtered a thanks and nodded to me.

Manners approved by Kathy Lewis. No praise came higher.

We sat down to eat and have all the usual polite exchanges. No, we didn't hit much traffic. Yes, the last few days of school had been fine. No, I didn't need help with my stuff. It was all packed up, and we could leave it until next year. Yes, swimming after lunch sounded like fun.

"So what's on your class list for next year?" Dad sat back and took a last swig from his beer bottle.

"I've got dramaturgy and set designing—"

"Mike, we've been over this. I can't see why you're wasting your time on a minor in theater. There's no law school that's going to be impressed with those classes. I can't see how it helps. Maybe a minor in a language for international—"

"Michael," Mom interrupted. "We're at the lake."

It was enough to stop him. The rules at the lake were different. This was why Jill had to meet them here.

"And you, Jill?" Dad asked.

"I've got my hands full with an independent study and a paid internship. I'm in the physics department and will be busy applying to grad school. Hopefully staying here."

Dad nodded. "Good plan. Well, let's toast to you, Jill. You got Mikey to pass calculus and obviously are a good, stable influence." He raised his bottle and the rest of us clinked our glasses.

"To Jill," I said, and I didn't care if everyone saw my goo-goo eyes and goofy smile. I was head over heels and didn't care if James ribbed me for it later.

JILL

One night down, one to go.

How could these people stand all this togetherness? We talked at lunch, at dinner, and after dinner there were card games. Then more talking at breakfast. Even when we went swimming, there was chatting.

Did no one ever take a book and go off in a quiet corner by themselves?

But they were happy. Seriously happy. And it was hard not to have that joy rub off on me.

Mike was amazing in the water. There he could allow his strong arms and thigh muscles to do the work. Plus he looked nice in his board shorts.

I came out of the bathroom toweling my hair.

"Let's take the rowboat out." Mike stood waiting for me.

"Your parents are getting dinner ready." I peered down the steps at the noises coming from the kitchen.

"Perfect. They'll be occupied."

He led the way down the steps. I pulled my wet hair into a clip and followed slowly as we descended.

"We're going out for a row before dinner," Mike called as he headed for the back door and the path to the lake.

"Cool. I'll come." James bounded off the stool at the counter where he had been slicing vegetables.

Mrs. Lewis put a hand on his arm. "I need your help, Jimmy." Her tone was firm and held a note of warning.

I felt my face flame with a blush. Mike snickered and continued toward the dock.

Once he shimmied into position and pushed us off with an oar, he effortlessly rowed us out around an outcropping of rocks.

"There. No one can see us from here." Mike wedged the boat against a tree root and patted his lap.

"I'll upset the boat." I refused to move, but his lap did look inviting.

"I stayed in my tiny twin bed listening to my brother talk in his sleep. I kept my hands to myself when you sauntered out in that bathing suit. And now I'm looking forward to another lonely night with nothing but my brother's hidden porn magazines. Come over here." He said it with authority, but with yearning in his eyes.

I scooted low over to his bench and nestled between his legs. He wrapped his arms around me from behind.

"Mmmmm." He buried his nose in the space between my ear and my neck. "Why do you smell so good?"

I melted into his embrace and rested my cheek against his chest.

"We can't be long." I squirmed as his hand traveled under my shirt.

"I'm dying." But he moved his hand back. "Are you having fun this weekend?"

"I really am."

"Surprised?"

"Yeah. I kinda thought it would be both dull and nerve-racking hanging out with your family. But they are so sweet, and interested in talking to me. They ask me about myself, but aren't too probing."

"They have manners, but are still curious about you. Mom's a little overprotective of me."

"I've never spent a more involved weekend. It's certainly more active and busy than my family."

"This is nothing. You should see when Mom hosts all the aunts and uncles and cousins for Fourth of July."

"How come you haven't told them yet about your plans?" I felt his torso stiffen, and he pulled back farther.

"I can't. Not until the surgery and after I recover. I can't risk Dad losing his mind and kicking me out." He stared past the trees to where the dock jutted out.

"He would never do that. You describe him as some kind of tyrant. But he's cooked every meal and made sure your mom never washed a dish. He was so funny teaching me poker last night."

Mike mumbled something in my ear. Damn, those vibrations almost made me not care if we were late for dinner.

"What did you say?"

"Lake rules." He sat up. "Dad relaxes here. Lets his guard down."

"We should get back. Your parents aren't that relaxed."

"Okay, but once we're back in Chicago, I'm ravishing you."

I giggled and scooted back to my side. Mike slid the oars into place and steered us back.

"Will we have time?" I asked.

"It only takes about five minutes to row back from here."

"No, for the ravishing. Aren't you going back in your parents' car tomorrow?"

"I hadn't thought about it." Mike put his back into the strokes.

"It makes the most sense. The surgery is in two days. Did you want to stay at my apartment?" I held my breath. I would drive Mike to the hospital if he really wanted me to. But I would have to do some serious deep-breathing exercises to get through it.

He shrugged. "Doesn't matter where I sleep the

night before. I just can't eat anything."

"Will you want all your stuff at your parents'? I'd have you at my place, but the stairs."

"No, I can't stay at your place afterward." Mike's silly grin faded.

"You're brave, you know that?" I reached out to touch his arm flexed with the effort of rowing.

"I don't have a choice. I can't endure the pain any longer. And I won't get cast in any role as long as I'm on crutches. Except maybe Richard III." His cocky smile appeared. Time for his big cover-up routine. *Let's make jokes about my disability.*

"Except for Richard III," I agreed.

We bumped against the dock. I got out first and held the boat while Mike hoisted himself out. He lay flat to retrieve his crutches.

The smell of grilled steaks and buttery corn hit us as we approached the deck. The outdoor table was piled with food and the meat was just coming off the grill. We seated ourselves around, and even though I had gorged myself at lunch on pasta, I found my mouth watering.

"Jill thinks I should go home with you guys tomorrow." Mike shoveled a forkful of coleslaw into his mouth.

"I didn't say that." I squeezed down my bite of food, now a lump in my gut. "I only asked where would you be more comfortable sleeping the night before the surgery."

"Don't think it much matters." Mike didn't take his eyes off his steak as he shredded it into pieces. "I expect I'll be even more uncomfortable after the amputation."

A clatter of silverware drew my attention to Mrs. Lewis, who recovered by patting her mouth with her napkin.

"Mike, you're sleeping at home where your mother can look after you. And we'll drive you to the hospital." Mr. Lewis's voice took on the tone I'd heard the night of the show. Lake rules seemed to disappear when Mike's surgery was the subject.

"Okay." Mike chewed his meat.

The amputation always seemed so far away—an abstract idea. But now it was really going to happen. I was made a part of the family by joining them at the lake. No getting out of this. Not that I wanted to, but still, I was in deep.

My love for Mike, his parents' acceptance of me, and Mike's need for support all conspired to rope me into a full-fledged relationship, with emotion and all.

"Excuse me." James pushed back from the table and fled inside.

"He's having the most trouble." Mrs. Lewis stared after her younger son's retreating back.

"We're all having trouble." Mr. Lewis downed his beer and got up for another.

I nudged Mike's leg under the table.

He looked up and smirked his charming "See

what I can do" smirk. I guess he was entitled to one last tantrum. After all, he was about to get his legs chopped off.

Chapter 19

JILL

I wore the only pretty sundress I owned, yellow with white flowers. It was a hot Chicago summer day. The dress was likely to get all sweaty and wrinkled before I made it from the air-conditioned car through the parking lot and up to the hospital room.

I had agonized over what to bring. Surely he wouldn't want flowers. Not because they weren't manly, but because it was so impersonal. I needed to bring something that showed I was truly thinking of him. Something that would bring him comfort, but not be too sentimental.

I settled on a falafel pita. It wouldn't stay warm in the time it took to get to the hospital, but it wouldn't be ice cold, not in the middle of June. I picked up a few news magazines from the lobby, too. I was chicken shit and stalling.

I had called Mike the previous night — we exchanged whispered, loving words, and his old bravado was there, barely covering his fear.

I had been too freaked out to sleep. And at six a.m. I sat straight up in bed, knowing the procedure had begun.

As steadily as my legs would take me, I approached the automatic doors, and they whooshed open.

The woman at the information desk gave me directions, and I waited at the elevator bank. The hallways were busy, doctors and nurses briskly walking past. Patients in wheelchairs being transported around. I wrinkled my nose at the smell. It wasn't a dirty smell, but the antiseptic did little to rid the air of the stale, sick scent.

I stepped out of the elevator and went up to the nurses' station.

"I'm here to see Mike Lewis."

"Room two-forty-five," a nurse said, without looking up from the chart she studied.

I nodded and walked in the direction the nurse had indicated with her pen. The door was ajar, and I pushed it open the rest of the way. Mike lay back on the bed. An IV tube went from a bag of fluid into his arm. His eyes were closed and his mouth hung open. He snored quietly.

My eyes traveled down his broad chest barely covered by the light blue hospital gown.

"Oh!" I said it a bit too loudly, but when my eyes came to rest on the place his legs would have been, there was nothing. The sheet that covered him outlined his body, and the silhouette simply ended at his knees. Of course, I knew he was having his legs amputated. But my gaze was transfixed, to see his body end abruptly where once it tapered down to calves and feet.

"It does take a few minutes to get used to," a whispered voice said.

I hadn't noticed Mike's mother huddled under a blanket, uncomfortably curled up in a chair at the other end of the room.

"Sorry."

"It's okay. You didn't wake him." She looked lovingly at her son as he lay in the hospital bed. "I haven't wanted to leave him alone. He's on a lot of painkillers, so he wakes up on and off. I like someone to be here when he does wake up."

"Of course." I still hovered in the doorway.

Kathy Lewis got up and stretched her arms and back. "*I'm* going to need surgery if I sleep in this chair too long. Would you mind staying for a while? I could use a walk and to get some food from the cafeteria."

"No problem. I have all day." I took a few steps nearer to the bed. Up close I could see Mike's usually bright face was pale. His skin was pasty white and his lips were dry and cracked.

"Really? Maybe I'll run home for a shower," Mrs. Lewis said. "Are you sure it's no problem?"

"Of course. I'm happy to do it." I must have managed to sound convincing, because Mrs. Lewis gathered her purse and quietly left the room.

How hard could this be? Mike might not even wake up while I was here. Hopefully, his mom wouldn't be gone long.

I took Kathy's place in the chair. I set the bag of food and the magazines on the table and looked out the window. My mind wandered to our first meeting in the library. Was that really only eight months ago? His confident smirk, the bet he forced me into — that was how I fell for him.

"That's a nice smile to wake up to." Mike's voice was soft and rough.

I leapt up.

"Your mom went home to wash up. She'll be back soon."

"Hmmm," he said, and rolled his head to the side.

I thought he was going back to sleep, but in a moment he opened his eyes. He looked into my face. I hoped I hid the worry, but it was difficult to smile.

"So?" he said, his eyes holding that challenge he made to anyone remotely uncomfortable with his disability.

"Are you in pain? Should I get a nurse?"

"I'm fine. I can't feel much, and my head is clogged with these meds." He lifted his arm that had the IV running in it.

I tried not to look, but again my eyes traveled halfway down the bed, to the end of his new body.

When I returned my gaze to his face, his jaw was set tight. His teeth clenched. His eyes shot daggers. *He's daring me to say something. I won't feel sorry for him. I won't worry for him. But I can't ignore it.*

"Well, you're half the man you used to be." I waited and watched him anxiously.

He gave a hoarse, bitter laugh, but it was a laugh.

"There's my Jill," he said. He too glanced at the place his legs should be. "I keep forgetting." He shut his eyes. "I can still feel them."

I winced. Glad that his eyes were closed, I tried to steady myself.

"Must be scary," I said.

"Yeah, freaks me out. I wiggle my toes. I swear I'm wiggling my toes." His breathing was shallow and his voice was raspy.

"I brought you some magazines, and a falafel." I pointed to the table.

"Thanks, I'll have them later. I think…" His eyes fluttered closed.

I almost ran out to get a nurse, but a moment later his breaths were deep, and the rhythmic rise of his chest told me he had fallen asleep.

The relief his unconsciousness brought me should have made me feel guilty, but relief won out. I could avoid talking about his legs that weren't there, his pain, his frail state. I rarely prayed, but I looked up to heaven hoping someone would make Mike strong again, because, sure as hell, I couldn't be strong enough for him.

MIKE

As much as I was glad to be home, it was not so easy to let Mom see me naked. At the hospital a stream of nameless professional nurses had cared for me — washing, changing bandages, emptying bedpans.

And even though a visiting nurse would stop by once a day, Mom was the go-to person for my care. So, not only did I have to let her see my stumps up close and personal, she also discovered I had grown pubic hair. I was sure she'd realized that at some level, and it wasn't like she hadn't bathed me before, just not since I had become a man.

But after a full day at home, we both got over the awkwardness. Dad returned to work, James was picked up every morning for football camp, and Mom and I struggled through the physical challenges of post-op.

Kathy Lewis had always been a model of efficiency, and she had planned well ahead for this. All the shopping and cooking had been complete. Meals sealed up in Tupperware awaited warming.

All the furniture had been repositioned to allow for a wheelchair. Dad's office had been repurposed for my bedroom until I could tackle the stairs.

And now I prepared for Jill's visit. She'd come to the hospital twice. Once I barely recall, except to see her beautiful face serenely smiling and gazing out the window. That image made it all worthwhile. The second time I had been completely awake and able to talk. She held up her end of the conversation but was clearly still a little freaked out.

That was okay. I was going to slap the brave Mike Lewis face on and charm her out of her discomfort.

"Mikey. You ready?" Mom called from the closed study door.

"Yeah, come in." I wiggled myself to the edge of the bed. "Did Dad leave already?"

"Yes, I think he'll be late for dinner." Mom placed the bandage box on the bed and wheeled the office chair to sit in front of me.

"He didn't say good morning." I winced slightly as the tape pulled off my thigh tugged the hairs.

"He thought you were resting, didn't want to bother you."

"Uh-huh. He hasn't said two words to me since I got home. Hasn't even had the stomach to look at me."

"Don't give me that, Mikey. Did you expect your father to change into a different person overnight?"

"You're right, sorry." I peered over and studied the stitches. Everything looked less swollen and decidedly less gross. "Thanks, Mom. This isn't exactly what you want to be doing either."

She sat back with the tube of antibacterial ointment poised in her hand. "Do you mean when I gave birth to you did I ever expect to be caring for your wounds after a double amputation? No, I don't think any parent expects this. But life handed us this situation and there's no point in dwelling on it." She wrapped clean gauze around the sites. "There, that should hold for a while. There's hardly any goo coming out now."

I laughed. "You're the best."

"Do you want to wear shorts?" Mom stood and rummaged through the pile of clothes she had brought down.

It was a hot Chicago day and shorts would have been welcome, but I wasn't quite ready for Jill to see the bandages.

"The air-conditioning is cool in the house. I think those sweats are fine."

Mom helped me wriggled into them. She held me under the arms as I scooted to the edge and slipped onto the wheelchair.

"Let's get ready for Jill." She pushed me to the living room and parked me by the TV while she went to the kitchen.

The recap of the Cubs game didn't hold my

attention. If Jill could handle this initial visit, then she could probably handle the whole thing. If we got the chance, I'd hike up my pant legs. What was the right balance of throwing her in the deep end to test her resolve and giving her a chance to adjust?

I wasn't getting any adjustment time. The physical therapy was starting tomorrow and the wounds were supposed to heal soon, and then the initial fitting.

The doorbell chimed and Mom scurried to open it.

"Hello, Mrs. Lewis." Jill's cheery voice jolted me. I nearly bounced in my wheelchair, a kid excited for a cupcake.

"Mike's right here." Mom waved Jill in, and to her credit, Jill didn't bat an eye.

"Hey there." She leaned over and pecked me on the cheek. If Mom weren't around I might have received a little more, but I'd take it as her loose hair feathered along my ear and tickled my nose.

"Hey, sexy." I grazed her arm with my hand.

"Shhh. Your mom's here." Jill glanced behind her.

"Nope, she's in the kitchen giving us some space." I nodded to the couch, and Jill sat down as I switched off the game.

"How are you feeling?" She patted my arm and folded her hand in her lap.

"A million times better, now that you're here.

Come on, you can do better than a peck on the cheek. What's a guy got to do to get a little tongue?"

"Nehhhh." She stuck her tongue out at me and gave me a childish grimace.

"Not what I had in mind." I waggled my eyebrows.

"Don't you have restricted physical activity?" Jill crossed her arms and tried to banter back, but the tone of her voice let me know her heart wasn't in it.

"Tell me about the new job." *Subject change to safer ground.*

Jill's face lit up. She relaxed back into the couch. "It's great so far. I've made huge progress on my senior thesis. Dr. Shaffer is spending a lot of time helping me get started. And even the grad students have eased off from dumping on me."

"But not completely."

She huffed. "You don't understand. I'll never get out from under that burden. It's the way it is."

"But once you're a grad student, they can't still dump on you."

"Well…" She looked away. This had always been a touchy subject. Maybe I didn't understand the pecking order of a science group. But at some point Jill should be able to say no to those guys, especially that Robert jerk.

"Do you want to come to my brother's game next week?" Another subject change. "He's starting quarterback. We're having a cookout at the fields."

"I'm super swamped right now. It's the first week and I'm just setting up my project and timeline. But I'll come visit whenever I can." Jill searched my face. Would I be cool with her backing off for now? Maybe she couldn't handle this change.

"Whenever you want. I'm not going anywhere." I tapped the wheel.

"Mike, I love you," Jill whispered. "I know you need a lot of help. You're probably stir-crazy here with only your mom, and I'll come by when I can. But even today, I have to run back to the office after—"

I held up my hand. "Jill, I love you too. I understand how it is. You're busy. I'm stuck in a wheelchair. Let's see how the summer goes. In a few months I'll be bounding around better than before, and things can go back to normal."

"You two want lunch?" Mom called very loudly from the kitchen, announcing her entrance to the living room, giving us plenty of time to stop what we weren't doing anyway.

Jill blushed. Damn, I loved that color in her face. Her normally pale skin turned all peachy, evidence of the blood coursing through her, that throbbed and engorged the parts I so wanted to be buried in.

"Thanks, Mrs. Lewis." Jill stood and straightened the hem of her shorts.

Mom came in and wheeled me to the dining room. "I made Mike's favorite meatloaf." She parked me at the table, which wasn't quite the right height for me to eat comfortably.

"It smells great," Jill said, and took the seat next me. She eyed my position critically.

"When Mom comes out, she'll help me into a regular chair."

"Do you want me to help?" The trepidation in Jill's voice was enough to kill my appetite.

"No." I didn't mean to sound gruff, but it was getting hard to control my temper. If she couldn't handle it, she shouldn't have come. I'd rather not see her at all than endure this skittishness. Her brazen attitude at the hospital led me to believe she'd be okay with this.

"Here, let me." Mom set the platter of food on the table and came behind me to hoist me under my arms.

All I needed to do was sidle to the dining chair and scooch on. I dropped the side armrest of the wheelchair and allowed Mom to grab me.

I was pushing myself off when the wheelchair slipped out and crashed into the wall. Mom, not strong enough to hold my entire weight, went down to the floor and took me along with her.

I didn't feel any pain at first, just the shock and the thump to my ass when I landed. But then the searing tear of flesh shot through me. The warm blood seeping through my sweatpants was the second sign that something was wrong.

Jill's screech was the third.

"Call 9-1-1," Mom barked at Jill as she ran for the bandage box.

Jill fumbled for her phone, and I held my left stump, putting as much pressure on it as possible, considering how squishy my sweatpants were with blood.

Mom knelt to the floor and wrapped a towel tightly around my stump; with all her might she pressed down, and I could feel the constriction. Jill's voice wavered as she gave the address to the emergency operator.

"He's bleeding. A lot." Her normal singsong voice was strangled with panic.

"I think we got it to stop," Mom said, more to herself than to anyone else.

"I'm okay. I'm fine. It doesn't hurt." And it didn't, not much, not any more than anything had hurt over the past few days.

"What, what, what should I do?" Jill fluttered around the room.

"Move the wheelchair out of the way. Then get me some more towels from the hall closet." Mom kept her voice even and didn't flinch. For a woman who spent most of her time anxious about every little thing I did, when the chips were down she had no trace of alarm.

Jill reappeared with an armload of towels.

"Drop them here, then go to the street corner to

wave the ambulance down," said Mom, cool as a cucumber.

Jill nodded and tripped over her feet on the way out.

"Sorry, Mikey." Mom grabbed another towel and placed it on top.

"Not your fault. I forgot to set the brakes on the chair. This probably happens all the time."

"It's almost stopped, but we're still going to the hospital to have those stitches fixed up." Mom shook her head. "Remember when you busted open those stitches you got above your eye?"

"Sorry I'm so much trouble." The words gagged in my throat.

"Shut up. You're never trouble. Except when you let your laundry pile up. They're here."

Sirens wailed outside, and Jill threw open the door. The paramedics were some quick workers. In no time, I was strapped to the gurney and being bumped outside to the ambulance.

Mom ran along beside me, and as I was being loaded in the back, I caught sight of Jill standing in the doorway to my house, worry creasing every line of her face. I guessed she would clean up my blood and lock the door behind her.

She'd told me from the start she had no time for a relationship. And despite that, I'd pestered and goaded and flirted and got her to fall for me. Were we really in love? Did love make it possible to overlook a spurting wound from an amputation site? If she had no time for me before, she certainly didn't have time for all this.

Mom hopped in the ambulance beside me. "Jill will meet us there," she said.

"No, she won't."

Chapter 20

JILL

Running back home for comfort was a ridiculous idea. There'd never been much comfort at home in the first place, and who the heck runs away *to* home?

But after a call to the hospital, Mike assured me he was fine. He would only need to spend the night there for observation and making sure the new stitches held. I made a quick stop at the office, grabbed some drives with data to work on, hopped back in my car, and drove to Madison.

The two and a half hours flew by. Probably because it only took me an hour and fifty minutes. When I slammed to a stop at my parents' front door, I flexed my right foot, stiff from smashing the gas pedal to the floor.

I hadn't brought any clothes, but I wouldn't be staying long. Just long enough to get my bearings. That scene in the Lewises' dining room had seared itself in my brain. The pool of blood, not to mention the splatter. I shivered.

My old room, my old stuff. Even my old relatives would at least be familiar, if not reassuring.

I unfolded myself from the car and stood. A contractor's truck was parked in the drive and the front door was propped open. A pair of workmen carried boxes of tiling in, and another pair threw debris from my bedroom window into a dumpster positioned below.

"Jill, what are you doing here?" Mom had followed the workmen outside to their truck and inspected the material they were hauling in. She wore a ripped pair of jeans and a stained t-shirt.

I blinked to clear my vision. I knew Mom owned clothing other than gray and navy suits. But Linda Kramer at home in the middle of a workday, wearing grubby clothes, added to my muddled thoughts.

"Hi, Mom." I met her in the middle of the brick walkway. "Sorry I didn't call."

"Is everything okay?" She hugged me.

"Yes—no. I needed to get away for a few days."

"Oh." She turned to look over her shoulder. "Um, come in. We'll find a spot for you."

I followed her through the door and into the back room. It had once been a playroom, the one place in the house where I could keep my toys and make a mess. The rest of the house was off limits to Lego, trains, markers, and dolls with tiny shoes. After I had outgrown a playroom, it was converted into a guestroom and family room. Not an apt name, considering the family never spent time here. But it had a foldout couch and an old television.

She perched on the edge of the loveseat, and I slouched into the easy chair across from her.

"It's nice to see you. I only wish you would have let me know so I could…" She waved her arm toward the hammering of the work crew.

"It's my fault. I should have called. And I forgot you were redoing my room. Or the extra room. I don't know what to call it." I had my own place, my own life. This shouldn't upset me.

"All your stuff is saved. I boxed it up. You said it was all right."

"I know. I remember you asking. I didn't bring anything."

"No clothing?"

"Where're the boxes?" Maybe settling in with a change of clothes for tomorrow would be enough to calm me down.

"In the study." She got up, and I trailed behind her to the room off the kitchen where my parents each had a desk. "We decided it was best in here for the summer. Until you could take what you wanted and we could store the rest."

She wove around towers of boxes, and I squeezed in next to her.

"Here," she said. "These should be clothing."

I pulled open the flaps. Old crap I hadn't worn

since high school billowed out. That was when the tears started. If I had to wear my high school neon leggings, I would collapse for sure.

"Jill?" Mom's alarmed tone hit my ear, and I fell over the edge.

Heaving sobs shook my body, snot trickled out of my nose, and I buried my face in the pile of musty t-shirts from the science club.

Mom put her arm across my back and pulled me away. She led me to the desk and we sat side by side on the few inches of cleared space, our feet dangling over.

"Can I help?" Her question wasn't so much asking if I needed something. It was more was she capable of giving what I needed?

"Mike fell out of his wheelchair. There was blood from the stitches. I had to mop it all up when his mom took him to the hospital. I threw about four blood-soaked towels into a garbage bag and cleaned the floor, and the wall. Mom, he had his legs amputated."

"I know, you told us." She sighed and wiggled closer to me. Her fingers tapped against her thigh. She was gathering courage. "Jill, I love you more than anything. We don't talk like that much, but I think you know it's true."

I nodded as she shifted her weight on the desk and cleared her throat.

"Dad and I are proud of you. You've

accomplished your goals thus far and worked hard toward your career. If we did nothing else, we instilled in you a good work ethic and an appreciation of learning." She patted my knee. "Taking on Mike." She shook her head.

"You think it's a bad idea. Do you think I can handle it?"

"I couldn't. But you." She laughed. "When you were little, you were full of emotions, up, down, sideways. It was elated one minute, devastated the next. Dad used to call you a Klingon born into a family of Vulcans."

"I remember." It had stung. I used to imagine I was adopted. But over time I tried to fit in. I tried to tamp down my emotions, focus only on facts.

"You *feel* everything." She shrugged. "Just because you're not like us doesn't mean we don't admire you for who you are. And loving Mike is admirable."

"I didn't do such a good job today."

"So apologize." She hopped off the desk.

"It's not that easy. Some things hurt so much you can't be forgiven."

"Really?" Her confusion was sincere. She was as befuddled by emotions and relationships as Mike was by math.

"I didn't go to the hospital. I spoke with him. He said he'd be fine and didn't want me to come see him. I think he was ashamed. He has a long recovery ahead of him, and I have so much work." The laptop I'd left in the guestroom could keep me busy for days.

"Your work is important. I can't tell you what to do. You probably wouldn't benefit from my advice anyway." She patted my knee. "Let's find you something to wear. You're always welcome here."

Maybe she was right. Maybe I did have the emotional range to help care for Mike. I didn't belong in this house. I had my own apartment, my own job, and a boyfriend whom I supposedly loved and who certainly needed me.

"I'm only staying the night. I'll go visit Mike again tomorrow and get back to work." If only to prove I was more than what my parents raised me to be. I could be the woman with a full range of emotions and a career. I could be Mike's girlfriend, no matter what happened. I loved him, and that would make everything else easier.

MIKE

"Come on, Mike. Give me one more."

Grunting with exertion, I raised what remained of my right leg again. My upper body shook with the strain. After counting to ten, I released the hold and let it fall against the floor with a thump.

It had only been a few weeks since the amputation. In some ways, the time had flown by and I was making huge progress. But the individual days dragged on with nothing to do but knock around the house and wait for Mom to fetch things for me.

I also used Mom as a shield. She had kept everyone away. I wanted no visitors. Even Jill. Even Beth. I'd convinced them both that I needed time alone, to heal. I needed time alone to get used to my new body. Jill accepted it a bit too easily, but I was relieved when she consented to talking on the phone for a few weeks. Beth took some cajoling, but she also agreed to give me some space.

"Great job!" the physical therapist said. "I can recommend you're strong enough to get those prostheses. Did the doctor say you're healed?"

"Yeah," I said, still panting. "I went in yesterday. He said the skin is pretty much healed and scarred over." I reached down and felt the smooth lumps below my knee.

"Can I help you up?"

"Please," I whispered.

I hated all the extra help I needed. But I had finally agreed to allow Jill to come over, and I didn't want her to see me sprawled on the floor, flopping around like a fish. She hadn't been to visit since the gruesome scene a few weeks ago. Her new job kept her busy, which was a good coincidence for me. With time, the shame of that bloody scene had faded. With time I had accepted my new self and could present a brave face for Jill. Now I had to see if she would accept it.

I couldn't withstand the anxious, pitying looks she would wear as I rebuilt my strength. It was better that she'd been away. But man, was I ready for her to return.

The physical therapist expertly lifted me off the floor and into the wheelchair. He wasn't particularly strong. It was more that I now weighed a whole lot less. Who knew legs weighed so much?

The cumbersome wheelchair didn't negotiate inside the house well. Mom and Dad had done their best to move all the furniture out of the way. A ramp had been built outside the front door. Dad still insisted it was no problem for me to live in his study. But Michael Lewis Sr. glanced in every once in a while to take stock of the room's contents.

Outside the house was a different story. That was when I loved the wheelchair. My strong arms pushed the chair at speeds I hadn't felt since I could run. As long as the sidewalk was even and the curbs had ramps at the crosswalks, I could outpace anyone I was with. Wind through my hair, fluid motion, I was alive.

Today, the weather was great, and I'd mapped out a path to the park. Mom had helped me pack a picnic lunch before she took James to football camp.

Poor kid looked like he was being sent off to a labor camp. Jill and I would go to the park. I'd scoped out a shady spot by the pond. I went yesterday with James, to make sure I could get my chair there and back.

The therapist left and I was alone, waiting for my Jill.

I was finally feeling physically better. I no longer needed pain meds, and my strength was back. I was doing the exercises three times a day, not the recommended two. I would get the prostheses soon. I couldn't wait to tell her, to show her, that I was going to be even better than before.

When the doorbell rang, I called for her to come in.

The air was sucked out of me. Framed in the doorway, the sunlight lit her from behind, creating a glow around her. My own angel.

"Hey," I said, still trying to catch my breath.

"Hey, yourself. You look great." She came forward and bent down to kiss me. Her sweet mouth opened, and her tongue made quick work of exploring mine. "Sorry, is your mom here?" Jill straightened up and took a few steps back.

"No, she took James to camp," I said with a leer.

"Really?" Her eyebrows arched. "We have the place to ourselves?" She sashayed toward me.

"No one's around for hours." I hadn't expected this, but I was ready. More than ready.

"I've missed you."

"Me too."

"You made me stay away too long." She ran her finger along my arm. "How does this thing work?" She pointed, and it took a moment for me to realize she was pointing at the chair.

Deftly, I flipped the arms up and out of the way. "Everything works as it should, sweetheart." I patted my lap.

Jill sat down and wiggled her bottom against my crotch, and I immediately got hard.

"It was so hard being away from you," she whispered in my ear.

"You're here now." I nuzzled her neck, then she brought her face to mine.

Kissing her was a release in itself. Her soft, moist lips set my senses on high alert. Wrapping her in my arms and drawing her close, I let go of the fear that I might never hold her like this again.

I slid one hand under the hem of her dress and to her panties, already damp. I lifted the edge of the fabric and explored her delicate folds with my finger. She gasped when I found the right spot. She ground her hips and pressed her chest into mine. It didn't matter that the pressure was too much and it dug into my sore muscles. I had my Jill back, and everything would be as it was before. I worked her clit until she shuddered in my arms and clenched around my finger.

I withdrew my hand and slid it up higher, using my expert moves to unfasten her bra. I filled my hand with her breast, quenching my need for contact. With the other hand I brought her head down for another kiss. A moan escaped Jill and vibrated off my mouth.

Her hands raked my hair, and she pressed her mouth into mine. Finally ending the kiss, she pulled away.

She didn't say a word, but her smile and slanted eyes showed her mischievous thoughts. Jill scooted down so she knelt in front of me.

"You're in the perfect position for this," she said as she unzipped my pants and yanked them open, bunching around my hips. My cock sprang forth through the gap in my boxers. She held me as she licked her lips, and I anticipated her next move. But when she did cover me with her mouth, I wasn't prepared. Dizzy impressions swam before my eyes, and I let go of the breath I'd been holding. I'd barely noticed she had stopped, when I looked down and watched as Jill took a condom out of her purse and in an instant rolled it over me.

She straddled my lap and slowly lowered herself. Each inch driving me maddeningly closer to release. At first, I let Jill do the work. She ground against me; the friction and her hot tightness took my breath away. But then I bucked up and held her bottom in my hands. Not for nothing did I do all those physical therapy exercises. My strong thigh muscles lifted me up to meet each of her thrusts.

I couldn't hold on long, and when I came, I gripped her, keeping her close to smell her scent and feel the heat from her skin.

"Phew!" Jill said, rolling off and falling onto the couch next to me. "Isn't the air-conditioning on?"

"Babe, it's turned up high." I took a moment to come back to Earth before ditching the condom and wriggling my hips to close my pants and zipper them.

"Need help?"

"I got it. I'll only need help taking them off." I winked.

"I gotta say I'm relieved," Jill said.

"Relieved? I was hoping for senseless, or at least sated—something a little more than relieved."

She laughed. "You know what I mean. I'm glad you were *up to it*." She winked back and grabbed her panties from the floor and pulled them up under her dress. "Let me use the bathroom."

"Sure, and then we're going on a picnic. It's all packed and ready."

"Great."

JILL

In the bathroom, I re-clipped my bra and tried to fix my hair. My face showed more than relief—sated, and senseless, and thrilled. Mike was back. The light inside him had returned. True, he would still need time to adjust, and he'd have some rough days. But it was good to see his true personality, his humor, his confidence. It was all coming back.

That wasn't so hard. I giggled. If there was something about this I could share with my mom, I would. I'd done it. I was the girlfriend Mike wanted and needed me to be. Sure, there would be some bumps in the road. But probably no more bloody incidents like before. I had missed him more than I had expected. Even the distraction of the internship wasn't enough. But I had to respect his wishes. If he wanted some time to heal, I'd give it to him.

We had this last year of college. If all went well, I would be staying to do my PhD. If everything worked out for Mike, he'd be in New York studying theater. Projecting into the future did spoil the moment, but I couldn't help it. I wasn't one of those people who enjoys the present, appreciates the now, blah blah, the future would take care of itself. *Yeah, right.*

I could apply to PhD programs in New York. Columbia had a great program. I shook my head. *This is what you get when you allow someone in your life.* I was losing focus. Next thing would be dashing off for a weekend and forgetting to complete my applications. And I knew where that would lead me.

Dr. Shaffer had the best lab around, and I stood a good chance of being a part of it. I tried once more to pretend that next year was a long way off.

"Are we ready?" I asked when I found Mike in the kitchen.

He was hanging the handles of a large straw bag on the back of his chair.

"All set. Everything's in here." He looked up and there were his gorgeous green eyes, his hair brushing his forehead, and that jaw line I loved to run my mouth over.

"Then let's go." I let him lead the way. He was pretty good with the chair, maneuvering around the furniture and out the door. He easily controlled his descent down the ramp.

The entire way to the park, I marveled at his strong arms pushing the wheels along. It seemed effortless, and a tension I had held all morning finally eased.

"I'm glad it's working out for you."

"Thanks." He smiled. "I'm finally out of the woods. The hard part's over. I'm getting fitted for my legs next week."

"So soon? That's great."

"I might have to use a walker for a while at school, but in a few months, I'll be mobile."

The park was beautiful. Mature trees lined the paved path. A pond was ahead, and seemed to be where we were headed. In the middle of the day, the park was empty of people except a few mothers and toddlers at the playground. It had rained the previous night, so the air was cooler than usual for August and the scent of moist grass was in the air.

Mike directed me to a bench off the path under a huge sugar maple. He guided his chair to rest on the ground directly beside the bench.

I helped him unpack the food his mom had made. Delicious fresh mozzarella and tomato sandwiches on baguettes, grapes, and his mother's famous chocolate cake. We didn't talk much while we ate, but enjoyed the quiet sounds of the ducks quacking and the breeze through the tree.

"I never knew you were such a romantic." I broke the silence and leaned over to rest my head on his shoulder. We were perfectly matched for height now.

"You never gave me a chance. Jumping on my bones every time I came to your apartment."

I sat up and playfully punched him in the arm. "You're so annoying."

"You love it."

"I do," I admitted with a sigh, and leaned against him again.

"I was thinking about next year," Mike said after clearing his throat.

"I was too, but let's not."

"Really, we should at least talk."

"Okay. You first." I didn't look up, refusing to meet his eyes.

"I really want to go to the theater program at NYU, but there's a good program at Northwestern too."

"Uh-huh."

"I thought we could each apply to schools that, you know, were nearby, and we could, we could see…"

"Settle for our second choices?" I straightened and tugged at the fold of my dress.

"Would being with me be a second choice?"

"No, of course not, I didn't mean it like that."

"It was just a thought…" He looked out across the park, turning his face away.

"It's a good thought. I'll have to apply to more than one program anyway. There's no guarantee Dr. Shaffer will accept me." The sandwich sat like a rock in my stomach.

"Yeah, but would you go somewhere else to be with me? Even if you were accepted at Dr. Shaffer's lab?" His voice held no plea, just a straightforward question.

I paused. I didn't want to pause. The answer should be immediate, one way or the other. This was not a topic for hesitation, but I couldn't answer either way. "You should know what it's like to work so hard for something. I'm not sure I could give that up."

"Of course I know what it's like to struggle toward a goal." He waved his hand at his wheelchair. "I don't see how going to a different school would be giving up."

"It's confusing. Can we put off this discussion? I'll apply to other schools, you will too, and we'll see what works out. Okay?"

"Yeah, okay." He started wrapping up the food, still refusing to meet my gaze.

"You mad?" I reached out and touched his shoulder. His muscle tightened.

"No, I'm fine. You're right. We shouldn't make any decisions now." He snapped his mouth shut and ground his teeth together.

We packed up the containers and wrappers in silence, but not the easy silence as before.

"We should get back," Mike spat out.

"Yeah." I hooked the bag back onto his chair and turned to get back on the path.

Mike grabbed the wheels and pushed. But it didn't budge. He checked to make sure the brakes were off and tried again.

"Need help?" I called.

"No, no, the ground's a little soft. I tried it out yesterday, before the rain. Before the grass got all soggy."

The more he forced it, the more he seemed to push the wheels deeper into the mud.

I walked back to where he was. "Come on, I'll

get you started." I grabbed hold of the handles in the back and gave a shove. I grunted against it, and the chair moved a fraction of an inch. "I think I almost got it."

"Just leave it. Don't try any more. You're going to make it worse!" Mike yelled.

I stopped. Mike had never lost his temper. He'd never raised his voice for anything except a cheer for a home run.

"What's your plan then? You're just going to sit there?" I yelled back.

"Go! Go away, leave me." Mike wouldn't look at me.

I walked around to the front of the chair. The pants he wore had ridden up and his stumps poked through. Forcefully, he pulled the ends of his pants down, ripping the seam up top.

He lifted his face. *Shit.* His eyes glistened with tears.

Mike wasn't supposed to cry. Mike wasn't supposed to feel low. He was always on top of his disability. His humor and his cocksure attitude kept him from feeling sorry for himself. *Fuck him.* He wasn't vulnerable or needy.

"You don't want help?" I said, not sure if I wanted to help or not.

His voice grew steely cold. "I don't need you."

I shook my head and turned. I walked away.

MIKE

"Are you sure you're okay?" Mom hovered in the doorway of Dad's study.

"Fine. Tired from all the exercise." Since Jill walked away from me yesterday, I'd been in almost constant motion with my physical therapy exercises.

There was little else I could do. Any time I stopped for too long, my mind went to work. I needed to be too tired to think.

At first when Jill left, I had felt triumphant. Good riddance. I told myself I didn't need her help and didn't want her to think I even needed help. But after her first twenty paces away, my heart twisted inside.

I doubted it would ever get untwisted.

Mom shifted from foot to foot. "Is Beth still coming over today?"

"Crap! I'd forgotten." The last thing I wanted to face was Beth and her poignant monologues. "I guess I'd better change out of these stinky sweats."

Mom didn't say anything, but came straight into the room and went to work. If she had a purpose and could be useful, she'd feel better, even if I didn't.

A moment after Mom arranged my pant legs and unlocked the brakes, the doorbell rang. She fluttered out to answer it, and I wheeled myself into position to greet Beth.

"Hello, Mrs. Lewis." Beth breezed in. She carried a bag full of what looked like paperback books and a grocery bag overflowing with chip bags.

"Michael." Her volume was set to projection from an un-miked stage.

"Hey, Beth." I leaned forward to peck her cheek when she rushed toward me.

"You look great. Doesn't he look great, Mrs. Lewis? I thought you'd be pale and wan. But your muscles are so bulked up."

I had discouraged Beth from visiting until I thought I'd be healed enough to not bleed on her.

I motioned for her to sit on the couch, and Mom disappeared to the kitchen.

"Michael, I am so happy to see you." She set her bags down. "I brought your favorite snacks and a whole pile of plays to read."

"Thanks. How're rehearsals going?"

"Community theater has its highs and lows." She tossed her hair. "It's always good to have any role. And I'm grateful for the opportunity. But I don't feel the director is wholeheartedly in the spirit."

"It's *Annie*, right?"

She waved her hand. "Enough about me. Tell me how you're doing. And before you say anything, I don't want the answer you've rehearsed and repeated to all your buddies and relatives."

I opened my mouth, but nothing came out. This

was what I had been afraid of. Beth knew I had some snarky remarks at the ready. Deflection of any question too personal or likely to touch a nerve.

"Michael." Her tone was practiced, but it didn't alter its effectiveness.

I hiccoughed and found my cheek damp from tears. "It sucks." I gasped. "I wanted this and I don't regret it, but it sucks." I grabbed my stump. "There's still phantom pain, but that's not the worst. What if…what if it doesn't work?"

Beth moved closer and wrapped her arm around my heaving shoulders.

"What if I can't walk?"

"You will. If there is anyone on this planet who can do this, it's you. You're the bravest, most hardworking person I know." She leaned her head against mine.

"I think Jill and I broke up." The words came out so softly I thought I might not have uttered them.

Beth stiffened but continued to maintain contact. "What happened?"

I shrugged. "We got into an argument about the future. I guess I pushed too hard. We've only been going out six months. It's probably too much for her to take on — a disabled boyfriend asking for a long-term relationship." I shifted away.

Beth removed her arm and unloaded the chips. "The woman who wins your heart will be worthy of it and won't think you're a burden. Seeing you in a wheelchair must have shown her the reality of life with you." She neatly arranged everything well within my reach, then took a small throw pillow from the couch and shoved it behind my back.

"It's probably the last thing I need right now. I'm going to be busy with getting fitted for the legs and learning how to use them. I've got no time for dating."

"Isn't that what she said to you when you first met?" Beth slipped a potato chip between her teeth and held the bag out to me.

I croaked out a laugh and grabbed a handful of chips.

"It's not that you don't have time to date." Beth daintily wiped her fingers on a tissue. She handed me one and indicated that I had crumbs on my shirt. "It's that you don't have time to deal with a girl who can't cope with life's realities."

"My reality is a little more extreme than most people's."

But Beth was right. It was going to take a special person to want to be with me. I thought I had found that in Jill. But her freezing up when I needed to go to the hospital and her inability to plan for anything other than working for Dr. Shaffer showed me. She wasn't the one.

Would there be a woman willing to take a guy who needed frequent doctor's appointments? Refittings? Not for the first time, I wondered if my gait would be steady enough to tote a baby around. How could I ask Jill, or anyone, to take all this on when I wasn't sure myself what "all this" even would be?

Chapter 21

JILL

This wasn't how it was supposed to be.

I meandered through the campus, sunlit and warm in the early autumn. Everywhere students excitedly greeted each other after a summer apart. Freshmen still consulted their campus maps to find their next classes. The line outside the bookstore was filled with anticipation. But my sour mood prevented any enjoyment.

Even my first fat stipend check from the internship couldn't lift my spirits. I approached the physics hall and shoved the door open. The whoosh of air-conditioning stung my face after the flush from the heat outside.

I hadn't heard from Mike since the incident at the park. I had tried calling and texting, but he'd ignored me. How could he expect me to give up on my dreams? Why had I spent the last three years working my butt off if I was going to throw it all away for a guy? Of all people, he should understand the most. Mike had kept his nose to the grindstone to make excellent grades in pre-law to distract his father from finding out about his theater plans. What would Mike say if I asked him to toss aside his theater dreams to stay close to me?

And on top of that, he was undertaking this huge, life-altering, body-altering change. He was going to have to spend the next few months learning to walk on prostheses. It wasn't like he'd be so happy if I asked him to stay in a wheelchair. It was the same thing. Right?

I shook my head and dropped into my seat at my desk. *My* desk, *my* computer, to use whenever I had free time. It didn't bring an immediate smile to my face, but it did help to alleviate the gloom.

Searching through my email, I sorted the ones from Dr. Shaffer and prioritized the tasks he wanted taken care of. Maybe I could talk to him about my problems. He seemed to struggle with balancing his home and work life, too. Yet he'd managed to stay married all these years. Pictures of sons at various ages crowded a corner of his desk. He must have fit fatherhood in there as well.

Certainly, my own parents were ill-equipped to help.

"It's not the same as in high school." Nikki had come in and stood behind me.

"What?" I didn't turn away from the computer

screen.

"Seniors. In high school it's the best—you rule the school. Everyone has to get out of your way. Everyone looks up to you. You're leaving home and off on adventures. Now it sucks." Nikki sat at the edge of the desk.

"Tell me about it." I rested my chin in my hand.

"No adventure. No one is envious. You know why? Because we have to somehow support ourselves and *get jobs*." Nikki gasped dramatically.

"Heaven forbid," I replied with equal drama.

"At least we're legal to drink. Although there's no joy left in it anymore."

"No, the fun is gone. Remember when we were young and carefree?"

"Those were the days…a few months ago. Hey, did Mike ever call you back?"

"No. I'm moving on. I've got things to do. Jobs to find. Grad programs to apply to." The twist in my gut caused the words to catch, but if I repeated it enough, I'd believe it.

"Uh-huh. And I'm going to win Miss Congeniality. What have you said on your messages?"

"That I want to talk to him, see him. The usual."

"The guy has to learn to walk again and you've said the usual? Don't you think he deserves a little extra something?"

"This is for the best. He made it clear—he wants

more than I can give. I can't give up on my first choice of programs to hang out near him." I waved my arms to keep them from shaking with frustration.

"Of course you can't, that would be some kind of compromise. Like you were in some sort of relationship."

I rolled my eyes. "You're a relationship expert?"

"Kenneth and I have been together for months now. We're developing quite a domestic pattern." Nikki smiled. "Go over there and visit. Think of something nice to say. You know you're not over him, so at least give it one more shot."

"You're right." I sighed. "I'm not over him. It's killing me. I miss him more than I thought I could. Plus, I have to figure out how to apologize for being such a jerk the last time I saw him."

"So keep trying."

"I'll reach out to him again." My chest burned with shame over how I had fallen short for Mike over the summer. But shame was a good motivator to do better.

"And not by text."

"Okay, okay. I'll grovel for forgiveness. If you really want me to visit the Theta Chi house, I will."

"Oooh, and tell me what it's like in there."

MIKE

Another twenty crunches and my abs would combust. A benefit of living in the jock house was a fully equipped weight room. I toweled off the sweat from my face and took some deep breaths. Physical exertion was nothing new. I'd trained in sports since I could run. Despite all the pressure from coaches and Dad, I was unprepared for this.

A sense of urgency infused this training. It wasn't about being bigger or faster than the next guy. It wasn't about winning the game or making it to the playoffs. Even the pressure of having the team's expectations resting on my shoulders as quarterback was nothing compared to this.

This was about if I would walk again. How much muscle could I build and maintain? Would I support myself in the prostheses? I needed not just the muscles in my legs to get bigger. I needed support in my stomach and back. I needed my arms to lift myself upright. I had to be able to maneuver around without the use of my legs at all. I had grown tired of the walker and was anxious to get rid of it, but what if I always needed it?

If I did, it would have all been for nothing.

"Hey, Mike. Someone's at the door for you," Steve called into the workout room.

"I'll be right there," I answered. *Right there*. I shook my head. It was going to take about five minutes to get strapped into my new legs, and another three to get upright on them. And then I was going to have to walk all fifty feet into the living room. I glared at the walker and decided this was the day I left it behind.

As I struggled to get vertical, voices drifted in from the living room. A female voice, light and airy, answered Steve's request to sit and wait. I hadn't responded to Jill's calls or texts. She had made it clear her work was going to come first, and she'd never consider any compromise. I was going to be busy trying to get on my fake feet but still, I held hope that we could make it work.

My halting gait got me out of the room and into the far end of the living room. Working double time to feed my desire to see Jill.

Beth stood up from the couch, her mouth hanging open.

"Look at you! You're amazing. You're walking." Her eyes lit up and she beamed.

I couldn't help but smile. I was never going to get tired of the surprise on people's faces. I continued toward her, jerking as I went and wobbling to maintain balance. Beth took a few steps toward me to shorten the distance, and she held out an arm. I fell into a hug and felt her shake with laughter.

"This is too much. I had no idea it would happen so fast."

"Well, it hasn't all happened yet." I allowed her to lead me the rest of the way to the couch. "These are temporary legs. They don't articulate the way my permanent ones will. But they're sturdier and get me used to the sensations."

I pulled up the leg of my sweats to reveal the solid prosthetic made of plastic and metal.

Beth's eyes widened, but she didn't pull back. "I'm impressed. I was scared for you. But you did it, and it seems like it was the right decision."

"I'm relieved. It's going to be a lot of work, but it'll be worth it."

"Too much work to be assistant director of *Midsummer Night's Dream*?"

"What?"

"We need someone to assistant-direct. Professor Shandell put out a notice that he wants people to apply for it. I think you'd be perfect. But it means a million hours at the theater."

"And you're playing Hermia."

"Well, there are auditions, but I think I've got a shot at the lead. But really, won't I look awesome as the fairy queen, Titania? I mean, all that glitter. And I'll be doing costumes. Come on, it will be fun. Our senior year, Shakespeare, great credits to use in grad school applications…" She leaned forward to emphasize her point. Her face was so close to mine that I could smell her perfume, and her full red lips were dangerously close.

"Okay, I'll send in my application to Professor Shandell."

"Yes! We'll have so much fun." Beth threw her arms around my neck. Her hair tickled my nose, and her warmth eased some of the aches in my muscles. The embrace lasted long enough for me to feel Beth shift next me, move closer, and rub her breasts against my chest. With one hand I reached up and held the nape of her neck.

"I guess he's a popular guy today." Steve's voice came from the front door.

I hadn't heard a knock, but in the doorway stood Jill. She wore a blue dress that ended mid-thigh and showed off her shapely legs and smooth skin. The top was tight around her chest, and my mind recalled how she reacted when I would caress her breasts. Her long neck was accented by the necklace with the galaxy pendant I had bought for her last year at the planetarium. Her black hair fell loose around her face, on which was the sourest expression I'd ever seen her wear.

"Jill," I said, blowing the few strands of Beth's blonde hair still scattered across my mouth. I was half in her arms, and I moved to the edge of the couch to be able to propel myself up.

"Don't bother," she said, holding out a hand.

"Jill," I said again, hoping to stall her long enough to collect my thoughts. Beth didn't move.

"I came by to see how you were doing." Jill didn't come any farther into the room.

"I'm-I'm good."

"Michael was telling me about his new legs. And showing off how he can walk now," Beth said.

"Oh, you got them so soon." Jill's face dropped. She'd worn a look of anger when she had come in, but now her eyelids fell and her lip quavered. She might cry for the first time since I'd known her.

"Well, these are temporary." I lifted my pants again to display the prosthetic.

Jill moved forward with an outstretched hand as if to touch it, but stopped herself.

"I'm happy for you," Jill said, looking between us. "I'll catch up another time." She turned and walked toward the door.

"Jill, wait, I—" But it was too late. She'd quickly left without turning around.

"Sorry, did I make that awkward?" Beth asked. She had a pained expression on her face, but she never left my side, and I felt her leg press against my thigh.

"No, it's not your fault. I haven't returned her calls lately."

"I thought you two broke up?" Beth wore a sorrowful expression, but I knew she hoped I would say we had.

"It was never officially off. She's busy with her work and trying to get a good spot in the grad program here. And I, well, I've been wrapped up in trying to walk."

"It seems like she doesn't have her priorities

straight."

"It's not her fault. I wouldn't want her to give up on her dreams. Just as she wouldn't want me to stop trying to get upright. We've drifted apart, maybe." My throat tightened around the words.

"Well, there's always a place for you in the theater with us. I hope you know we'd do anything to help you. You only have to ask."

"I know. Thanks, Beth."

Chapter 22

JILL

My pace caused my dress to billow out behind me. Nearly knocking over the people on the slate pathway, I strode up to the physics building.

I shouldn't have expected anything less. I did walk away from him that day. And even though he insisted I leave, I should have stayed. Or at least waited for him.

Abandoning a disabled boyfriend in the park wasn't going to win me the humanitarian of the year award.

I'd called. And called. And texted. And sent a card.

School had started. I had braved the Theta Chi house. My apology all rehearsed, groveling included.

I missed Mike and was prepared to promise to do better.

And Beth had swooped in.

Mike had repeated to me that they were just

friends, and I had no reason to doubt him. It was Beth I doubted. She'd wasted no time.

I trooped into the office and plunked down at my desk. Focus on the work. Stay close to my goals. Don't get distracted by a man.

When the first tear splattered the keyboard, I knew focusing was impossible.

I laid my head on my arm and hoped people chalked it up to exhaustion. I kept my breathing even and let the tears soak my sleeve.

"Worn out from partying already? School's only been in session one week." Robert's voice grated my brain.

I sat up. "Just heartsick. Not that you would understand."

"Whoa. I seem to recall you broke it off with me. No matter." He dismissed the jab and raised an eyebrow when he observed my tear-splotched face. "Now that you're here on a more regular basis, Dr. Shaffer and I have worked out a priority list for you." He handed me a piece of paper. "I emailed you a copy as well. You can see my work on background radiation is first. Of course, you'll be busy with your senior project, but Dr. Shaffer feels that your brilliance with data sets would be an asset to me."

"I'm working for you?" Yep, this day could get worse.

"We all work for Dr. Shaffer. He makes the assignments." Robert crossed his arms over his chest.

"I thought we were past the awkwardness."

"So long—" I stopped myself from yelling and lowered my voice to a whisper. "So long as you continue to hold over me the fact that I...I *cheated*, it will always be *awkward*."

"I never held anything over you, Jill," Robert whispered back. "If I helped you in a major way once, I only ever expected you'd return the favor."

"I'm going to talk to Shaffer."

Robert shrugged and walked away.

Dr. Shaffer was in heated conversation with another professor. They stood at a smart board, each with a marker in his hand. Each erasing the other's equations.

I stood in the doorway. I'd been so sure I could barge in and demand someone else work with Robert. Now faced with the prospect of confronting Dr. Shaffer and interrupting an argument, I started to turn on my heel.

"Jill, do you need me?"

"I, uh, only wanted a quick word. But I can come back."

"No, Dr. Colby and I were finished."

"We'll just have to see whose paper gets published first." Dr. Colby marched from the room.

Dr. Shaffer smiled. "Jill, come sit down. You saved me from a prolonged conversation with a dimwit."

I took the seat adjacent to his desk.

"It's hard work, academia," Dr. Shaffer continued musing. "The competition never ends. Grant applications, publications, prime computers and office space. I hope you know what you're signing on for."

"It's the science I care about."

He nodded. "That's what we tell ourselves. And yet the politics… But what did you need to see me about?"

Politics. Now it seemed petty. How could I explain I couldn't work with Robert because we had dated, when clearly Dr. Shaffer had to endure more than an awkward relationship?

"It's, um, you want me to work with Robert…"

Dr. Shaffer broke into a huge smile. "Love affairs when you're young seem so important. I know you two dated briefly. I thought it would be okay now. You have a new boyfriend. A better-looking one, if you ask me. And judging by the ordeal he's going through, I would guess he has a better character than Robert. But if —"

The sobbing I had just got under control hadn't been enough to empty my eyes.

"Oh." Dr. Shaffer reached an arm out, and I fell into his embrace.

He stroked my hair, like Mom used to when I was sick. Why did it take illness or crises for people to offer me affection? Or for me to accept it?

"We broke up," I said.

"I guessed as much." He pulled away and handed me a box of tissues.

I cleaned my face. "It's my fault, really. He wanted to plan for the future and I freaked out. And I wasn't as supportive as I should have been during his recovery."

"I'm sure you did what you could. You're not a nurse or a therapist. Plus, you're a little young to be planning much of a future." His kind eyes weren't enough forgiveness. I knew I needed Mike to absolve me. But it was a start to know someone understood how ill-equipped I'd felt to help Mike.

"I'm so sorry. This is awful of me. The first week back, and I'm melting down in your office."

"It's true, this is a job for you. But I know college is learning more than just the subjects. And I'm glad you trust me enough to let me comfort you."

I tried to smile, but my face wouldn't move that way.

"You're an intelligent, beautiful woman. You have plenty of time to find love. And the man who deserves you will recognize your genius and give you the space you need."

Dr. Shaffer was right. There was no rush to find love. But I was no longer sure I wanted the space.

MIKE

The scent of apple pie wafted up into my room. I sat at the edge of my bed glaring at the carbon-fiber-and-silicon contraptions dangling off the ends of my legs. Already, I could hear Aunt Judy's voice raised in greeting. It was Christmas and I was hiding, looking for a quiet spot. Last time I hid from my family, I was trying to find some quiet place to call Jill. Today, it wouldn't be the football game or bad caroling that created a commotion — it would be me. The family was getting together, like they always did. But I sensed a different anticipation than the food and gifts. They wanted to see me walk.

I'd been working out for hours each day. The prosthetist had tweaked and re-tweaked the fitting. Each pressure point carefully sculpted. The socket firmly secure, and still I stumbled. After years of learning to place my center of gravity low, between the crutches, I felt almost dizzy holding myself up so high.

Once upon a time, balance and coordination came naturally. Closing my eyes, I recalled the sensation of throwing a football, in a perfect spiral, right on trajectory, even as I was hit by a left tackle. Hanging in midair, I could still make a pass. But now I looked like a newborn foal wobbling to stay upright.

The voices grew louder downstairs, and soon I heard footsteps approaching my room. There was knocking.

"Mike? Are you okay?" Mom called from the hall.

"Fine, Mom. Come in."

Mom entered, still in her flour-dusted apron. "Do you feel up to coming down? Everyone is asking about you."

"Of course they're asking. They all want to see some inspiration porn."

Mom's normally sweet, gentle face morphed into a drawn-brow, narrow-eyed warning. "Listen here. That's your family down there. They love you no matter what. So all this feeling sorry for yourself has got to stop."

"Huh?"

"You heard me. I've had about enough from you. Since school started up you've been moping around. You're the one who wanted this surgery. You can't get them sewn back on."

I laughed despite her tone. "I know, Mom. It's been harder than I thought."

"And since when did hard work get you down? Aren't you the kid who built and rebuilt a model of the White House out of toothpicks, even after the first three attempts fell apart? Even though it was for extra credit in a sixth-grade history class where you already had an A?"

"Yeah, that was me."

"And I had to clean up all that glue." Mom

sighed and sat next to me on the bed. "Mikey, does this have anything to do with Jill? She hasn't called since you've been home."

I shrugged. "I guess we broke up."

She nodded. "I thought so. It's too bad. I thought she was the type of girl who could handle this."

My eyes stung. "It doesn't matter. She's got plans to stay here after graduation."

"And you? What are your plans?"

"Mom. You know the plan."

"I know what your father wants. I know you too well to know when you're shining him on."

I didn't say anything and stared at my hands in my lap. I never came out and lied about not putting in any applications for law school. But I never said I had either. I certainly hadn't told them about the application to NYU theater school.

Lies of omission were just as painful when it came to looking your mother in the eye.

"I think anyone who has the courage to go through what you did has the guts to go downstairs and greet his relatives for Christmas, even if he has trouble standing." She stood and brushed her hands over her apron. "As for standing up to your father..." She eyed me doubtfully. "That takes even more courage. We'll see if you've got it."

She left and shut the door behind her.

I coughed to loosen pressure in my chest and closed my burning eyes. Mom had managed to comfort me, encourage me, and challenge me all at the same time. How did she do that? She was right. I wasn't the kind of person to stay up in my room, hiding. What was the worst that could happen?

I pushed off the bed and held on to the headboard until I felt steady enough to lurch for the door. Turning the knob, I leaned against the doorframe. Stepping backward while pulling the door was an especially tricky move, but I accomplished it. I walked to the top of the stairs, and held my arms out to the sides for balance.

The staircase never seemed so steep. Was it really only fourteen steps? Past the last step, I spotted my cousin Dave taking off his coat.

"Hey, it's Mike, and he's gonna walk down the steps."

Immediately, the talking stopped and everyone crowded around the foot of the stairs. Why did I have to have such a big family? I hadn't planned on walking down the steps. I had thought I would do what I'd been doing these past few weeks. Bump down the steps on my ass, then use the last few steps as a chair to push myself up.

But with this big audience, the performer in me won out.

"Ladies and gentlemen, and children of all ages, including you, Uncle Carl," I called out in a deep baritone. "I draw your attention to the center ring, where the Magnificent Mike will perform a death-defying act of" — I slapped my hands rapidly on the railing to simulate a drum roll — "Walking Down the *Stairs*."

By now everyone else had gotten into the spirit and cheered along. I picked out Mom; she had her nervous smile firmly in place. She knew I'd never come down the steps before. Dad was in the back, frowning. No doubt wondering why everyone was standing around the entryway, when there was a good game on.

My first careful step, I planted my "foot" down and quickly moved the other to meet it on the same step. So much of my weight was on the railing and my grip was so tight, I thought I might pull the whole thing apart. It took about ten seconds to find my balance.

"One step," I called down.

Applause went up, and my face flushed from embarrassment and exertion.

The next step I twisted sideways as I lowered my leg. I slipped and was sure I'd go ass over end crashing down. Gasps and "Oh nos" reached my ears as I firmly planted my foot sideways on the second step. The other foot met that one.

"Two steps, ladies and gentlemen!"

The cheering was louder this time. And I found I could balance better with the toe part hanging off the front.

I continued this way, taking each step as a baby

would, one at a time, with my feet carefully placed for balance. The family got into the act and began calling out the numbers of the step, their calls growing louder with each one. Damp patches formed under my arms. I panted, my thigh muscles burned, and my sweaty hands threatened to slip off the rail.

When they shouted, "Fourteen," I was mobbed with hugs and slaps on the back. A few wet kisses found their way to my cheek. I didn't need to worry about keeping my balance—I was held in place by all the bodies and practically carried to the couch to rest.

Christmas dinner was served and gifts were exchanged. The younger cousins convinced me to play every new game. I didn't even mind Aunt Judy's singing. At one point, I thought about Jill's funny stories of her family holidays. I felt a twinge in my chest.

Part of me wanted to call her and tell her I'd walked down the stairs. I wanted to look forward to meeting at the same restaurant we had our first date, after I won the bet, and have a falafel when the next semester started.

Dad was having a pointed discussion with my uncle. Most likely about the flaws in the current penal code. Judge Lewis put his ambitions first, and look where that got him. Sure, he has a financially successful life, but his sons resented him, and his blowhard manner kept people at a distance. I wanted more from life. Even if I never made it as an actor, I wanted a wife who wasn't scared of me and kids who could talk to me about anything.

"Miiike," whined Danny, the four-year-old. "You said it was my turn next." He held out a brand-new Candy Land game.

"You got it, little guy. I'm green." I gladly allowed myself to be distracted by the fuss.

Chapter 23

JILL

I studied the earrings in the box.

"They're twenty-two karat," Great-Aunt Molly said. "See, they're little teddy bears, because you used to love that bear you carried around with you. It was filthy and still you wouldn't let your mother wash it. I remember it so clearly."

"They're lovely, thank you." I fought back the urge to correct her that it had been a monkey I carried around.

"I wonder if you still have that teddy bear," Molly went on.

"I think Mom threw it away."

"Well, what does she want an old toy for anyway?" Mom had come in with a tray of bland cheese and saltines.

I took out the gold hoops I wore and replaced them with the bears. It was ridiculous; a grown woman didn't wear teddy bear earrings. It would be the only time I ever wore them.

"Oh, they look adorable." Molly clapped her hands in delight, which startled Uncle William out of the nap he was taking in the recliner. With a snort, he woke up and announced he needed to "tinkle."

"I'll go put these away." I held up the hoops and made a dash for the stairs.

"Come right back down," Mom said. "Betty found the old photo albums from Great-Great-Grandmother's house. We're going to look through them."

"Okay," I called, already halfway up to the second floor. I shut the door to my old room, now a library for my parents' books. I sank onto the pullout couch. I wasn't going to last the day, let alone the entire break at home. Thank goodness I had the lab to go back to. It was not only a good excuse to get away from home, but Dr. Shaffer had promised a post-holiday party that was sure to be more stimulating than this.

I'd worked in the lab for six months, as a real member of the team. I could appreciate what I had been missing my whole life—belonging. My parents had done nothing as I was growing up to create a sense of unity. We never joined a church. They never brought me to Girl Scouts, never had parties with lots of friends. Work and quiet family events punctuated with the occasional trip—usually to visit some other elderly relative in another state.

But at the lab, I belonged. Sure, Robert took advantage of my position and dumped work on me. Sure, I worked my ass off and got little to no credit, but I was accepted. Everyone had lunch together, and when we all stayed late, we ate dinners together. More than ever, I was looking forward to next year, when I'd be one of the graduate students, a full member of the team.

I opened my jewelry box to put the gold hoops away. The necklace Mike had bought for me at the planetarium was there on top. Gently, I touched the galaxy pendant. It was a cheap souvenir, but it moved me. That day when he had playfully ignored all my explanations. The time we met on the quad for lunch and the sky opened up, soaking our subs.

All the days I spent with Mike, I'd felt belonging then, too. But that belonging came with a price. I'd have to sacrifice who I wanted to be in order to stay with Mike. Belonging wasn't worth giving up your dreams.

Five more months, only five more months to graduation and then Mike would be gone to New York with Beth, and I'd be a graduate student. I could put him out of my mind. As it was, I was constantly reminded of him, the hero of campus, the guy with the bionic legs. After graduation, he'd be gone, and I could forget him.

Maybe one day I could find a man who'd support me in my goals, who wouldn't mind if I worked long hours.

Dinner was its usual affair. Soft vegetables and dry turkey.

In the kitchen, Linda and Jack Kramer had their choreographed dance to washing dishes. I didn't disrupt their rhythm, but busied myself with wrapping up leftovers.

"It was a successful meal," Dad said as he dried another platter and placed it on the high shelf.

"Everyone did seem to have a nice time. The highlight, as always, was Jill's pies."

"Thanks." I played a game of Candy Crush with the contents of the fridge to make everything fit.

"How is your senior project coming along?" Dad seamlessly took Mom's place at the sink as she moved to sort silverware.

"Great. I'm ahead of schedule, and I think Dr. Shaffer is pleased."

"Sounds like you'll get accepted for grad school," Mom said.

"Yeah. I'm applying to some other places. Columbia…"

"New York would be fun. How did things work out with Mike?" Mom asked.

"They didn't." I plopped into a kitchen chair and made designs with my finger in a pile of crumbs.

"Well, you'll find someone else." Dad hefted the trash bag. "I'll go take this out."

"Mom, why did you marry Dad?" I asked when

he had left.

She straightened at the sink and stared ahead. "I guess we had a lot in common."

"I have a lot in common with my friend Nikki, but I have no desire to marry her." I joined her at the sink and took a dishcloth.

"No, don't wipe those down. They go in the dish drain. I love your father. We fit well together."

I placed the dishtowel on the counter and realized they did fit well together. Their version of love might not be the one I wanted, but it worked for them. They could do the dishes together without communicating.

Given the vast number of humans on the planet, it should be possible to find that kind of connection with more than one person. I shouldn't worry that I lost my only chance when I lost Mike. And yet, given the vast number of planets capable of sustaining life, we still hadn't found another one like ours.

MIKE

Eventually, Aunt Judy, always the last to leave, said good-bye and the house was quiet. On the couch, I heard the clinking of Mom working at the sink and watched my younger brother, James, shuttle dishes back and forth between the rest of the house and the kitchen.

It would be pointless to offer to help. Mom wasn't going to trust me to carry anything. And besides, I was beat. The few times I did get up to move around took huge efforts of strength. I'd do my exercises tonight, but maybe not as many reps.

I hoisted myself up and wobbled to the back of the living room. My dad sat in his study, reading the *Bar Association Journal*. His reading glasses perched at the end of his nose, and the desk lamp illuminated a circle around him. He looked up.

"You okay, son?"

"Yeah, Dad. I'm fine. Just tired."

He nodded. "I probably forgot to tell you how proud I am. Took guts doing what you did. I was skeptical, but you were right. Walking—huh! You looked good out there today. You didn't even seem bothered by the way the family fussed after you."

"It's all right. I don't mind." I walked all the way into the room and settled on the leather chair across from the desk.

"True, you've never minded being the center of attention." Dad smiled. "It'll be good when you're up in front of a courtroom facing down opposing counsel."

I could see the wheels turning in his head. He was picturing me striding up to the bench and pacing back to the jury box, commanding attention.

"Dad, about law school." I took a deep breath. "I

didn't apply. I never sent the applications."

Dad furrowed his brow. "What do you mean? Didn't you have enough time? Maybe the surgery was a mistake. You've been too busy with rehab. I bet we could get you an extension, based on medical need."

"No, Dad. I don't want an extension. I'm not going to law school."

The confusion began to disappear, and Judge Lewis's face became red as Santa's hat.

"You're going, and that's that. Don't even mention the acting thing. I didn't pay a fortune in tuition for you to piss away an education."

"The 'acting thing' has been the only thing I've wanted to do since the accident. I was only eighteen, but when I woke up in the hospital and learned I might never walk again, I grew up in an instant."

"Grew up!" He snorted. "What do you know about growing up? Being an adult means having a serious job, supporting yourself and your family. Not playing pretend. It's a little too late now. You've been pre-law all four years, and will end up with a Phi Beta Kappa key." He looked thoughtful for a moment. "I suppose you could take a few economics classes this last semester and go to business school. Not as stable as law, but at least you'll make a living."

"I'm not going to business school either. Please listen, Dad." I stood up and I towered over him seated behind the desk. Even if we were both standing, I would be taller. My prostheses brought me up to the height I would have been. "I'm going to go to New York. I've only put in one application, to New York University Tisch School. If I don't get in, I'm still going to New York. I'm going to share an apartment with my friend Beth, and I'll get any job to support myself and work on my acting. I'm going to do it. I could be in another accident and lose even more. I won't waste the life I was given a second chance at by doing something I hate. You can't stop me." My pulse throbbed in my neck.

Moments ticked by on the old clock in the corner. "No, son, I can't stop you. But I don't have to sit by and watch you throw away this second chance on life. You're right, you were lucky to come out of the accident as you did. And I still say I'm proud of what you've done. But I won't support you in this. You're on your own."

"I already said I'll get a job to support myself." My throat burned as the words came out.

"And if you can't, I can't help you." He turned away from me and looked out the dark window that only reflected the light from within the room. "I've given you a chance, and you're turning it down. There won't be another offer. I can't help people who won't help themselves."

"Sure, Dad. I get it." I rasped. I tried to meet his eyes in the reflection, but all I saw was his face turned in profile.

I left the room as unsteadily as I entered. At least I could blame it on my mechanical legs.

JILL

"Welcome back, Jill. Did you have a good spring break?" Robert held a plastic cup of punch, and although he spoke to me, his eyes scanned the room for someone more important to talk with.

"Yes, it was fine. How about you?" I didn't mind much. I'd rather have his attention directed elsewhere in the crowd Dr. Shaffer had invited to his house.

"I was home for a few days but had to come right back. You know we're tilting away from Andromeda. Early spring is the best time for me."

"I came back early too, not for the party. I was thinking about that data Dr. Shaffer gathered last month—"

"Listen, I'll be headed to California for my post-doc. It's been fun knowing you and all."

"You're leaving?" Somehow I could never imagine being free of Robert.

"It's good to move around and make myself known in the wider world. I've got a sweet deal with Berkeley, major position. Should really make a name for myself. But I won't ever forget you." His gaze still didn't come anywhere near me, which was just as well. I felt a huge grin of relief spread across my face.

"I hope you get everything you deserve." A cheery note lifted my voice, because I wasn't lying.

"Yeah, thanks. Hey, Tom. How was your break?" Robert walked away without a glance.

I sipped the overly sweet fruit punch and nibbled on a cookie. Dr. Shaffer had invited most of the physics department to his house. The room was packed with people talking about work. And although I stood by myself, I felt less alone than I would have at my parents' home. Here people understood me. I fit in, had a place.

Nikki stepped through the door and waved. Kenneth was in tow, and he stopped at the refreshment table as Nikki approached.

"Holding up the wall?" she asked.

"I was talking to Robert before."

"Why?"

"Because he's leaving," I singsonged. "He's doing his post-doc in California. I won't ever have to see him again. Well, maybe at some conference. But I won't ever be under his control. Next year, I start fresh as a PhD student."

"Under the control of some other post-doc."

"No. I'm not letting anyone get the upper hand again."

"Good. At some point, you have to stand up for

yourself and demand respect."

Kenneth had come over with a plateful of cookies.

"I don't understand it, you're so thin, but the way you eat you should be five times your size," I said.

"I keep him active," Nikki answered as Kenneth's mouth was still full.

A few people from other groups came over to greet us. I didn't pay much attention to the conversation about the latest grant allocation scandal. My mind was working on what Nikki said.

I wouldn't be a pushover for the next post-doc. Whoever supervised me would have to respect my time and contribution. I was sure Dr. Shaffer would, once I was a serious grad student, doing independent work.

"I saw him walking the other day. He was moving almost naturally."

"I think they have probes on the ends that attach to his thigh."

My attention snapped back to the group. They had to be talking about Mike. Nikki was squinting at me.

"It's amazing what those applied science guys can do. I wonder what material they use. It's got to be light enough to swing naturally like a leg, but it has to be strong enough to hold up a full-grown man," someone from Nikki's group said. "How does he control the spring back?"

"Jill dated him last year." Kenneth had finally finished his cookies, so his mouth was empty enough to speak.

Nikki jabbed him in the ribs.

"You did? How does he gauge how to walk or run on those things?"

"I-I don't know. We broke up before he got them."

"Oh. Well. It's really cool. Everyone is talking about it. My roommate who edits the school paper is doing a feature on him. Some kind of incredible guy to keep going and finish school after what he's been through."

"I hear he's a genius too. Phi Beta Kappa and pre-law."

"He'll be able to get into any law school he wants."

"He doesn't want to go to law school," I said absently.

"Then why pre-law?"

I looked around the circle of faces and shrugged. I drank the last of my punch, the sweetness cloyingly sticking in my throat as it went down. The topic of conversations shifted to the school basketball team and their unlikely chance at a winning season.

Nikki's eyes softened, and it made me blush. I didn't want Nikki's pity. It was over with Mike, and that was that. Time to move on. He certainly had. He was walking smoothly and made some incredible recovery over the past few months. I was happy for him and wanted him to succeed. But my life contained no room for him.

The buffet of cookies and sandwiches gave me an excuse to move away from the group. If I focused on picking out carrots from the tray, I could ignore the tear in my chest.

"Not much left, I'm afraid." Dr. Shaffer cleared a plate with half a cookie and a pile of crumbs.

"Students and free food, not a pretty combination," I said. What a relief to see a comforting face.

"I'm happy to do it. Looks like it's breaking up anyway. I guess that's what happens when the cookies run out."

"Here, let me help." I stacked some used cups and followed him into the kitchen.

"Don't you want to join the rest? I heard they're planning to go to Epilogue, that bar outside campus. It's where all the newly twenty-one go."

I shrugged. I'd been there a few times, and it was fun, but fun didn't seem like so much fun tonight.

Students thanked Dr. Shaffer, and they shook hands. Coats were gathered and scarves wrapped to try to keep out the Chicago March temperatures.

Nikki was halfway out the door when she came back to where I was dumping paper plates into a trash bag.

"You okay here?" She raised an eyebrow.

"Yeah, I'll help Dr. Shaffer clean up and then head home. I need a night in front of the television."

Nikki peered into the kitchen to where the professor was washing dishes. "Call me if you need me."

After she left, I examined the table, trying to find something to salvage and wrap up. But the locusts had done a good job of clearing the place out.

"Thanks for staying to help." Dr. Shaffer had returned with another trash bag.

"No problem. I didn't get to see Mrs. Shaffer."

"Visiting her sister in Florida. Chicago doesn't warm up fast enough for her."

"You don't go with her?"

"I can't leave the office for long. Besides, even happily married people need a break from each other for a few weeks."

I trailed after him to the kitchen with our full bags.

"The trash cans are outside." He moved to open the door.

"Oh, I'll take them." I grabbed the bag and stepped outside. The frigid wind pricked at my face. My eyes watered from the cold. I found the bins and hefted the bags into them. The frost went right through my sweater and stung my arms. I stood for a moment taking the frozen air into my lungs. I had everything I had hoped for — a bright academic and professional future. I would find someone else when I was ready. When my career got off the ground, then I could focus on men.

I reentered the house shivering.

"Your lips are blue." Dr. Shaffer moved away from the sink and rubbed his hands vigorously up and down my arms.

"Thanks. I needed a bit of fresh air." I gulped the last words and shook my head.

Dr. Shaffer brought me in for an embrace. "I heard them talking about your ex-boyfriend. It must be hard."

I steadied my breathing and pulled back. I wiped my eyes with my sleeve. "It'll be okay. I have so much to work toward now."

"You and I are a lot alike." Dr. Shaffer kept his arm around my shoulders, and I leaned into his side.

If I'd had a father who held me, or a mother who tucked me in at night and got under the covers with me to stare at the glow-in-the-dark galaxies on my ceiling, then I wouldn't need to rely on professors for affection.

"Thanks," I said.

"My role doesn't just have to be your teacher." He stroked my hair. The warmth of his hand dashed away the chill.

His hand rested on the nape of my neck. Shocked, I looked up at him and was about to ask what he was doing when his mouth covered mine.

Because I was about to speak, my lips were apart and he didn't waste a second shoving his tongue inside. I choked on saliva and gargled a protest.

I twisted free. The ham and cheese sub sandwich threatened to reappear.

Dr. Shaffer's smile didn't waver. "We're adults. These things happen. There's no need to call this anything more than it was."

"What…what…" I couldn't form a question.

"It's okay. I understand you were upset about breaking up with your boyfriend. I offered a shoulder to cry on. Frequently, students misunderstand my intentions to give support and guidance." He held up his palms and shrugged.

"But I didn't…"

"Who's to say?" His smile widened. The soft, fatherly eyes I had so often looked to for advice were now out of place above the artificial grin.

"I could tell the dean about this." I wasn't going to let anyone take advantage of me anymore. Nikki was right. Robert was gone, and there was nothing to manipulate me with. I squared my shoulders.

"I'd hate for you to do that. As I'm sure you'd hate for me to delve into your final project from the cosmology class."

"Wh-what?" Ringing in my ears made me unsteady.

"Jill, proofs are like fingerprints. I've known

Robert his entire college life. If you don't think I can't recognize the work of someone I've taught…" He waved his hand. "No matter. You gave me some mixed signals. Stayed behind when the others left. Rested your head on my shoulder. Let's call it even."

"Even?" My blood boiled hotter than a fusion reaction. "You took me in your arms, offered me comfort." I shook, my arms straining not to slap him.

"You don't want to ruin our working relationship, do you? We'll be working a lot closer now that you'll be my grad student. I think this is your coat."

I grabbed my coat, for lack of anything else to do, and wobbled out the front door.

I didn't zip up my coat, and the arctic air that had refreshed me before now hurt. Everything hurt.

Chapter 24

MIKE

The controlled chaos backstage let me know that everything was as it should be.

Beth as Titania looked stunning. She was already in character, her face crafted in a perfect combination of haughty and mischievous. Her gown was trimmed with iridescent ribbon, and her breasts, almost spilling out, had enough body glitter to shame a stripper.

Professor Shandell sat in the back row, and I gripped my clipboard as a drowning man might hold a buoy.

"Mike, we're ready to dim the house lights." Shandell's voice came through my headset.

I nodded, and the stage manager cued the music.

Assistant-directing this play had been the highlight of college. Even better than the kegger at Theta Chi sophomore year when I hooked up with Lauren. I shook my head. It wasn't, however, better than an ordinary day with Jill.

But that was over.

Jill was always going to put her ambitions first, and I didn't want to come in second.

Beth brushed past me, head held high, and entered on her cue.

She and I had grown even closer over the past few months. Our upcoming trip to New York would cement our plans. Auditions at NYU scheduled, hotel and plane tickets booked. I wasn't nearly as nervous about the prospect as I thought I would be.

Having a buddy in Beth would be enough.

At the scene change, I hobbled over to the chair I had placed toward the back of the alcove. It took every bit of strength to soundlessly lower myself into it. The intense friction from the sockets on my stumps urged me to drop hard to relieve the pressure. But any noise could be detected in the audience.

I didn't dare remove my legs. They might clank to the ground. Instead, I closed my eyes for a moment and breathed the pain away.

Gaining my balance and finding my gait hadn't been as hard as I thought. My new legs fit better and were lighter. But still, as the swelling went down, the fit got looser. I tried adding the socks, but I'd need new sockets again. If dear old Dad was good for something, it was for footing the hefty bill for blade legs. Soon, I'd be running.

I opened my eyes and listened to the actors perform their lines. The timing couldn't have been better, and with intermission coming up, I could almost relax.

When the curtain did come down. I went to the dressing rooms to give one more needless pep talk. Then I went into the house to check in with Professor Shandell.

I scanned the crowd and spotted Jill. She stood with her friend Nikki and tore into a package of Twizzlers. Why my body should choose that moment to panic and break into a sweat, I could probably guess. Sweating was not good for a stump-to-socket connection.

I hadn't mastered the art of finding the right number of socks to keep it all tightly together without the leg jangling loose once in a while.

I felt the leg go unstable and sank onto a nearby bench.

Peeling the silicone sleeve off while in the lobby was not on my list of things I would enjoy, since I'd probably have to take my pants down.

I cursed Cameron, who seemed to allow intermission to last an hour before he flicked the lights, indicating people should return to their seats.

Please let her be sitting on the left side of the theater.

Nope. Jill and Nikki made a beeline for the door to the right aisle and would pass directly in front of my safety bench. My heart slammed against my ribs.

And I desperately tried to conjure the cocky, overly confident Mike.

"Enjoying the show?" I flashed a smile, but it didn't seem to feel right.

"Mike, it's great. Nice job." Jill stepped out of line and stood so close that her warmth nearly enveloped me.

"Did you sew the costumes too?" Nikki flipped through the program. "Says here you sewed."

"Yeah, Mike of all trades."

"You okay?" Jill narrowed her eyes. She scrutinized my legs and noticed I gripped one.

"Yeah, taking a break. Go ahead in. Cameron's having a fit with the lights trying to get everyone seated."

"Sure, see ya." She looked at me over her shoulder as she passed into the theater.

Once the house doors were shut, I reattached my leg and headed out the front door to the alley and the stage door.

See, that wasn't too hard. Jill and I could pass each other and it would be no big deal. It wouldn't impact me at all if I ran across her in the library or the dining hall.

But the knot in my gut told me that wound would take a lot longer to heal.

JILL

"What do you think he meant by 'enjoying the show'?" I tried to keep pace as Nikki's effortless long strides took her to my top jogging speed as we exited the theater.

"I think he was asking if we were enjoying the show. You're not going to get all seventh grade on me, are you?" Nikki took pity on me and slowed down.

"Did he look okay to you? I thought he looked anxious."

"He was directing a play. I'm guessing he was getting graded on it, too."

"But why was he gripping his leg?"

Nikki stopped short, and I stutter-stepped to a halt.

"You're not his girlfriend. You don't get to worry about him anymore." She started walking again.

"I can still worry," I muttered behind her back as I followed.

"Why don't you try getting back together?"

"Because he made it clear he wanted more than I could give. Plus, I screwed up so bad over the summer. There's no apologizing for some actions."

We walked in silence through the dark quads. Lamps lit the pathways, and a few students trekked from dorms to libraries and back. The chill air gripped and wouldn't let up for a few months. At least the snow had been minimal. How many more Chicago winters would I endure? Kennedy Space Station in Florida held more appeal than simply for my career.

Nikki stopped again, outside the physics building. I stood searching the windows for signs of life.

"Well? Didn't you want to go back to get some work done?" Nikki pointed to the door.

I counted the floors. "Looks like Shaffer's in his office."

"When is he not?" Nikki took out her phone. "I'm texting Kenneth to see if his roommate is out."

"I think I'll go home."

Nikki's finger paused in mid-typing. "You're skipping out on work and an opportunity to show your boss how dedicated you are?"

"Let's go." I turned and stomped toward the edge of campus and the street where my apartment was.

"Whoa, slow down there." Nikki caught up and grabbed my arm. "Spill."

An icy wind blew past and rubbed my cheeks raw. "You have to promise not to do anything, or say anything, or, or any anything."

Nikki glowered. "What's going on?"

"Dr. Shaffer kissed me. The night of the party. When I stayed to help." I didn't look at her. Nikki would only say "I told you so" or drag me to the rape crisis center or the dean's office.

"Oh, Jill." She pulled me to her, and I was crushed against her leather jacket. "You rely on him for so much. And now all that support seems so fake. You'll have to turn him in and switch groups now."

I heaved a sigh but allowed her to continue to smush me in her version of a hug. "It's worse than that."

She pulled away to look me in the face. "Worse than wrecking your years of slaving away for him and pinning your hopes on his recommendation?"

"I can't switch groups. He knows about how Robert helped me. How I cheated."

"So you're not turning him in?"

I shook my head.

"And you can't change groups?"

"Not now, not a few months from graduation. Maybe for the grad program. If someone else will have me. If he'll even let me work somewhere else." I glanced up at his office window.

"No Mike, no mentor. You're stuck with me as your only supportive person. Man, that's a bad place."

I giggled. "Thanks. Now go meet Kenneth. I'm headed home."

"Sure you don't want to hang out? I think girls are supposed to eat ice cream and complain about boys at moments like this."

The image of Nikki curled up on my sofa trying to gab all night was frightening. "No, please see Kenneth. I'll catch up with you later."

The wind had died down, but I still hurried back to the relative warmth of my drafty apartment.

Once inside, I checked my messages. I rarely used my Facebook page, but I was still friends with Mike on there.

He'd updated his status with pictures from the show. It really had been a good show, and I would have stuck around to talk to him afterward if he hadn't given me the brush-off at intermission. I didn't know what I had expected. Part of me hoped we could pick up again.

A moment later, his status changed.

Packing for NYU audition with Beth Matthews.

My mouth went dry and my near-empty stomach threatened to heave.

No wonder he gave me the brush-off. I could hold on for a few months until graduation. Then I'd never see him again, and I could move on. But I had no opportunity for change, and not much likelihood for any kind of movement.

Chapter 25

MIKE

I paced the hall outside the studio theater. My audition had gone about as well as it could have gone. My monologue from *Richard III* still rocked, and the pages they gave me to read were right up my alley — a sarcastic but charming character.

Beth was still inside. We'd arrived so late the previous night that we hadn't had time to do any exploring of New York. But today she had an itinerary that took us to some of the touristy spots and some off-the-beaten-path landmarks, including where the Lion's Head Tavern used to be.

The doors flew open and Beth emerged, a huge smile stretching her face.

"Do I even need to ask?" I said.

"Ask me anyway."

"How did it go?"

"They all but came out and said I'd get in." She jumped, lifting both feet behind her.

"Me too." I waited for her to return to earth before sharing a hug.

"We need to celebrate." She hooked her arm through mine and steered me out the building.

New York in March was only marginally better than Chicago. A freezing rain pelted down on us. The ground was slick in spots, and although I was now quite adept at walking, I would lose my balance at the most unexpected times and crash to the ground. This made me edgy all the time.

Beth kept her pace even with mine, but it didn't take more than two blocks before she was ready to give up on major sightseeing. "We could go back to the hotel. Maybe the weather will improve in a few hours."

I nodded, and we walked the additional two blocks to the almost no-star hotel. I hadn't bothered to ask my parents for money for the trip. The contribution from Beth's parents was what kept us from unrolling a sleeping bag in Grand Central Terminal.

"Phew," Beth said when she used the key card to open the door to our room. The two double beds were separated by a nightstand, and the one window overlooked the alley and straight into the bedroom of a young couple in the next building. We'd seen them fighting the night before.

"Ugh. I'm soaked." Beth pulled at her blouse, which had gotten wet even under her thick coat.

"I think I'll change." I opened my duffel bag and rummaged around to find dry pants and sweater.

"I can use the bathroom." Beth carried her clothes into the bathroom and shut the door.

The gel packs I'd been using to cushion the connection had shifted, another sign the swelling was still decreasing. I tore them out and decided I'd rather feel the bumping against the socket than deal with the lumpy packs. I peeled off my dripping pants and hung them over the arm of a chair. I had only packed one other pair and needed these to dry by the morning.

I slipped on a new pair of pants and had removed my shirt when Beth came out of the bathroom.

"Oh, sorry, I should have knocked." She eyed my chest and her lips parted. She wore leggings under a long sweater that drooped off her shoulder, exposing her creamy skin and a red bra strap.

"No problem. I'm almost changed." I twisted to grab my dry shirt from the bed. Her delicate, warm palm pressed against my shoulder.

She retracted her hand. "Sorry."

"It's okay." I looked down into her amber eyes. She had the fullest pink lips.

"Michael?"

She didn't need to finish the sentence. I tossed my shirt on the floor and pulled her to me. The kiss was wild, a tangle of teeth and tongues. She smelled of flowers, a heady rose scent.

The angel on my shoulder told me this was wrong, that Beth was a friend, that this would ruin our relationship. I didn't feel this way about her. The devil didn't state his case too enthusiastically. It must have been my cock leading the decision.

I bunched up her sweater so I could ease my hands underneath. Her body reacted immediately to my touch — she arched into me and I cupped her tits, small but perfectly round.

She didn't seem to notice my expert move of unhooking her bra, as she worked on the fly of my pants.

"Beth." I paused in my explorations. "I need to take them off." I searched her face to see if she'd accept this. My legs could easily hurt someone if I wielded them around in the throes of passion.

"I'll take care of you, Michael." She gently pushed on my chest, and I fell to the bed.

She did a brief striptease that got me hard, merely because she was naked. I'd rather have her rip her clothes off or let me do it. But Beth did things Beth's way.

I shimmied out of my pants, peeled off the silicone sleeves, and took off my legs. She didn't blink, didn't even look down. Her eyes stayed locked with mine as she licked her lips.

"I didn't bring a condom." I reached for my pants, coming to my senses before things went past the point of no return.

"I always have some. Every girl should." She sauntered to her overnight bag and bent over it.

It was a very nice view, her tight ass displayed. Too bad she was too far away for me to grab it.

She placed the condom on the bedside table and pushed me back again. My body must have been that desperate, because the reel in my mind keep playing "don't do this."

"Let me," she said.

"I can do anything you want." At least I hoped I could. I had made a few attempts at humping my pillow, like a twelve-year-old, to see if I could do it. It was a balance thing, but I felt confident.

"No. *I* can do anything *I* want to," she purred.

I was half propped up on the pillow and watched as she licked my abs and worked her way up. I wish I could have felt turned on, but I only felt clammy where her tongue had left a wet trail.

"Beth. I can be on top." I nudged her shoulder.

She peeked through her blonde tendrils. "But I want to take care of you. I want to make you feel good."

Somehow her wanting to please me wasn't for my own sake. Not the selfless way Jill had about her. I wasn't the type of guy who always needed to be in control. But my manhood was at stake. I may have lost my legs, but I could still take care of a woman in bed.

At least I hoped I could.

Beth reached down and covered my cock with her hand. I wouldn't deny that the stroking felt good. But as she flashed her wicked grin and moved to take me in her mouth, I went a little limp.

"I-I think I'm not ready." I pulled the floral bedspread over my stumps and sat all the way up.

"Mike, you don't have to be self-conscious with me." She released me and splayed her long fingers against my chest. "It's me. I want to help you get over any discomfort you have."

"I appreciate that. Really, I do." *I don't.* I wanted to be with a woman because it was part of our relationship, not just to get over my uncertainty. "You're beautiful. But I don't want to wreck our friendship. And to tell you the truth, I'm just not ready. I don't think I feel comfortable, yet." I gestured to my legs.

"I understand, Michael. I don't want to pressure you or rush you." She turned to sit next to me propped in bed, like it was the most natural thing. "If you do need my help, you'll let me know."

"Of course. I know we're there for each other."

"No matter what. We're in this together. We're taking on the Big Apple."

"Together." I leaned to the side and pecked her cheek.

She gathered her clothes and sauntered into the bathroom to dress. I went to work putting myself together.

It was good to know I had someone to lean on. But Beth would never be a true partner. A good friend, yes. But I could never be with someone who saw me as something delicate to be taken care of. I wanted an equal. I wanted someone who expected me to fuck her just as hard with or without my legs. Someone like Jill.

JILL

My fingers tapped furiously at the keys, trying to make the deadline Dr. Shaffer had set.

"And Jill, don't forget to send those results to Robert. He'll need them." He strode back into the inner sanctum of his office, leaving me at my cubicle with a burning face.

"Sure thing, Dr. Shaffer." I nearly ground my molars to nubs.

Ever since he'd shoved his tongue in my mouth, he'd begun a torture campaign to load me with more work and pair me and Robert as often as possible. Either it was a test to see if I could handle the stress or he was a sadist.

Didn't matter—the result was the same. I was miserable. The thawing of the weather and shedding my winter coat didn't ease my mind.

I opened the documents he wanted me to update before passing them on to Robert, but I had to read them three times before they made sense to me. The spring sunshine poured through the window across from where I sat. Students dotted the quads, still wearing sweaters but hanging outside.

From instinct, I searched for Mike. He was easy to spot, and I spotted him everywhere. Marching across campus, carrying a backpack over one arm—his hand free to hold the strap. Even up the steps to the lecture hall. Something inflated in me when I saw him. I guessed it was pride. I'd done nothing to be proud of, but Mike had accomplished so much.

And there he was again. This time jogging on his blade legs. Funny how they didn't look like legs at all, but functioned better than mine when it came to running.

It only took a minute for him to pass out of my range of vision, but I stared at the spot he had just left. He must be happy.

"Shaffer said you'd send me those results." Robert's cloying aftershave wafted into my space.

"Working on it now," I grumbled.

"Don't bite my head off. It's him who's pushing us at double speed."

"What's up? All of a sudden there's a rush?"

"It's the grant application cycle. He always gets like this when trying to beat out his colleagues for money." He rested his hand on the back of my chair, and I flinched.

"I'll get it to you by tonight. I don't have classes for the rest of the day. So I'll sit here until it's done."

"Thanks." He tapped my shoulder. "You're a team player. Always knew that about you. When I'm in Berkeley, I'm sure I'll never find someone as easygoing."

Or as stupid.

But after a few minutes I did delve into the work. And that was when I liked it—the figuring, the calculating, decoding. If I forgot whom I was working for, I could enjoy myself.

"Ready to go?" Nikki pushed her way into the cubicle so as to almost block my view of the screen.

"Why does everyone interrupt me?"

"Kenneth is waiting downstairs. He said he'd drive if we split gas money."

"Crap, I forgot." Kenneth had invited Nikki and me to some literary event on the North Side. He was all excited about some well-known authors being there. Nikki was all excited because she thought I needed a new boyfriend, and not some science guy.

"Forgot? Not likely. Probably you blocked it out. I think you have some underlying fear of social success. You're never going to get over him unless you start with someone else."

"Thanks for the vote of confidence. I really do have a lot of work. And I don't want to be a third wheel."

"That's the point of this outing, to get a fourth wheel." She pulled my chair away from the computer and spun me around. "Now save your work and let's go."

"Can't. I promised Robert and Shaffer I'd have this done tonight. Go without me."

"Ugh. Don't make me sit through some spoken-word poetry nonsense without you."

"I think they'll be reading from their books."

"Whatever. You hit the right formula for you with Mike. He was an artsy guy. You need an artsy guy. Like me and Kenneth. Too many analytical brains in a relationship is no good. Let's find you some hot dude who talks about imagery or symbolism or form versus structure. Some shit like that."

I pulled myself back into the safety of the cubicle. "I don't think the reason Mike and I got along was because of how different we were. It was because we were similar in the important ways."

"Sexual ways?"

"Nikki, you're my closest, and probably only, friend. Get lost so I can work."

She huffed. "Fine. But no more moping around. I gave you a perfect opportunity to find a nice piece of ass, and you're blowing it."

"Love you too," I called as she stomped away.

The truth was I didn't want to be distracted from Mike. A sick part of me enjoyed the morose, lovesick angst that came over me when I saw him jog by.

That pain let me know I had loved. That I was capable of strong emotion, not like my parents. As long as the pain was there, there was hope that I might love someone again.

Chapter 26

MIKE

I flipped open my laptop, nearly knocking over Jeff's bowl of sugary flakes.

"Hey, watch it. What's the rush?" Jeff slurped up a spoonful of milk.

"NYU sends out the acceptances today." I logged into my email.

"Well, is it there?" Jeff swigged the last gulps of juice from the carton.

I searched my inbox and clicked on the message. I didn't get past *We are pleased to offer* before I slapped my palm on the table and whooped.

Jeff sprang out of his seat. I stood too quickly, but Jeff was there to steady me. We exchanged a man-hug-chest-bump and sent out a cheer that brought the other Theta Chis into the kitchen.

I had no problem receiving more man hugs and back slaps. My legs supported me perfectly. And I'd never stood taller. My face grew warm with the attention and excitement.

"I'm going to call—" I stopped myself from saying "Jill." "My parents," I continued.

"Sure," said Jeff.

The crowd allowed me to go into my room.

I pulled out my phone and scrolled through the contacts. Jill's number was still there. I passed it and went to "Mom."

"Guess what?" I said when she answered. I had hoped I could have hidden the quiver in my voice.

"Everything okay?" When would I be able to hear Mom's voice without the anxiety?

"I got accepted to Tisch. Mom, I'm going to New York." It came out as more of a question than it should have.

"Mikey." The pause seemed to last minutes. She took a deep breath. "I am proud of you. I don't know how many amputees have been accepted to theater schools, but you are the bravest person I know."

"Thanks," I choked out, not wanting any tears to come. "I love you, Mom."

"I love you too. And I am the luckiest mother." The uncertainty that had veiled everything she'd said dissipated.

"You're okay with this?" I held my breath.

"I can't say I'm thrilled with you being so far from home. But with the way you bound up and down steps now, I guess you can handle the New York City subway. But don't stand too close to the tracks. I read an article where people are getting pushed in front of the trains."

My smile hurt my cheeks. I rubbed my face to make sure there was no crying in the Theta Chi house.

"What about Dad? When are you going to tell him?" I exhaled.

"If you're going to bring two sets of prostheses to New York City and enroll in a theater program, then you have the courage to tell your father. No way am I getting in the middle of this. You two haven't spoken since Christmas, and I am not going to play peacemaker."

She was right. I was going to face plenty more difficult conflicts than telling my dad I was going to theater school.

"He doesn't listen. He keeps coming up with plans for a 'gap year.' As if this isn't the real plan."

"Your father is a stubborn man and may never accept your choices. But if you're making this choice, you'd better be sure and stand by it."

"You're right. Next time I come home, I'll talk with him." Better face to face. Then he would see how mobile I'd become, and he'd have more faith in me.

After I ended the call, the reality of going to New York set in. Leaving Chicago for college was impractical after the accident. There would be no problem finding doctors and amputee services in

New York. But I'd have to learn to negotiate a whole new set of streets and stairs and jogging paths. I'd have to find a whole new set of friends. People who could look past my disability.

Not a whole new set. If I got a message today, then so did Beth.

I grabbed a hoodie and waved to the brothers in the weight room on my way out into the early spring day.

The walk to Beth's apartment wasn't long, and I needed the exercise to burn off some of the adrenaline from the news. All the decisions I'd made until this point had been clear. The amputation, the theater classes, the master's in fine arts program. Even with some minor ambivalence, I had been sure of all these plans.

Once I'd accepted the loss of my former body, I'd never looked back, never let fear encroach on my dreams. But now they were no longer dreams. I was going to have to go through with it. Tell Dad, move to a new city. At least I had Beth. Our one almost night together hadn't interfered. If anything, it made our friendship stronger.

I came to the front door of her building and pressed the security buzzer.

"Yes?" Beth's voice sang through the intercom.

"It's me, Mike."

"Thought I'd hear from you." The buzzer sounded and the lock clicked back.

I pushed through and bounced up the flight of stairs.

Beth stood in the doorway. An oversized t-shirt slipped off one shoulder. She wasn't wearing a bra, and her nipples were visible through the thin fabric. Her yoga pants clung to her legs.

Nothing stirred in my pants. We'd been down that road, and it wasn't us. We were buddies again.

"So?" I asked.

She nodded and smiled a half-smile. I came forward and picked her up in a hug.

"Whoa. You've gotten strong," she said, standing back to look me up and down. "Come in. No one's here. We have a lot to talk about."

She led me to the musty couch in the apartment she shared with two other theater majors.

I accepted a cookie from a plate as she came to curl into the couch next to me.

"Did you call your parents?" she asked.

"Just my mom. I'm going to tell my dad in person. If he wants to kill me, it will be easier for him that way. I bet your family wasn't surprised."

"No. But…well." Her gaze darted around the room. I recalled the same action from when she played Nora in *A Doll's House*.

"Beth…"

"I didn't want to tell you. I didn't tell anyone, so as not to jinx it. Not even my parents." She took an exaggerated breath. "I went out to LA. I auditioned for an agent there and he…he…wants me to move there. He's got a lot of auditions lined up for me. There's a commercial that's almost a sure thing. And he's talking about feature films from the big studios."

"You're going to LA?" A breeze came through the gated window off the fire escape and prickled my skin, damp with sweat.

"I don't know. I haven't made up my mind completely. The thought of you all alone in New York…" She shook her head. "I can't endure it."

"You need to do what's best for your career." I coughed around the words. "Do you trust this guy?"

"Michael, would I go with a small-time agent? He's represented Christy Roberts and Brian Patton since before they were big." She jiggled against the cushions and her breasts made themselves known. "He's famous for spotting new talent. But theater is my first love." Her voice wound around the last word, thick with a plea.

I held her hand. Her delicate fingers rested in my calloused palm.

I cleared my throat. "Your decision should be made without me in the equation. You have a chance, and if you want to take it, you should. I'll be fine in New York." I released her hand. She drew it back to rest in her lap.

"You don't want me there?" Her head downcast, a single tear hit her shirt and absorbed into the fabric.

"Beth, I want you there. But not at the expense of

giving up your dream. I know what it's like to have a passion and not let anything stand in my way. I'm even going up against Hanging Judge Lewis."

"Are you sure? I couldn't live with myself if you were abandoned to gritty New York all by yourself."

"Really, I'll be fine. NYU has dorm rooms for disabled students. And you're not abandoning me. You're grabbing a rare opportunity." My chest ached.

We talked some more. I reassured her. She reassured me. We parted.

As I walked back to the house, my body shook, not from the breeze, not from the physical exertion. Alone. I was doing this all on my own. Without my parents, without my football teammates, without the Theta Chis, without Beth. And without Jill.

I would have never gotten this far without the support of others. At home, at school, there was always someone to help, even if I complained and insisted I didn't need it. And now, no one. But I guessed that was to be expected at some point.

Besides, Beth wasn't the first person to choose dreams over me.

JILL

I spread the two letters out on the table in the library

study room and reread each one, going over each word. Searching for hidden meaning, an omen.

When the letter from Columbia came, I wasn't surprised. I'd given a great interview there. They were looking for someone who was interested in studying exoplanets. Rarely did I feel as confident as I had after meeting with the committee at Columbia.

What shocked me was the acceptance into Dr. Shaffer's group. After all that, he still wanted me there. Was it to keep me close so I didn't spread rumors? I couldn't damage the reputation of the principal investigator of my own group. Was it because he was going to try again to get me into his bed?

"Thought I'd find you here." Nikki waved a piece of paper in the air, crackling over her whispered voice.

"Shut the door," I whispered back.

Nikki released the doorstop to the small room.

"So?" I asked.

"Stanford, baby!" Nikki cheered loud enough for heads to turn from the carrels outside the little room.

"Congrats." I got up to hug Nikki. An awkward embrace immediately turned into a true hug when I didn't give up after Nikki's initial squirm.

"And you?" Nikki plunked into the other chair and arranged her bag at her feet.

"Columbia."

"You knew that, but still good to get

confirmation."

"And Dr. Shaffer wants to keep me on. I was accepted to the grad school here."

Nikki's eyes widened. "No shit."

"Yeah, I can't figure that one out." I flipped the corner of the letter with my thumb.

"Well, you can't stay here." Nikki flailed her arms.

"Why not? Dr. Shaffer hasn't come on to me again. It's like he's forgotten the entire thing. His lab is the best in the country outside NASA for my area of interest. I can put the whole thing behind me." I searched Nikki's face for assurance. I needed my friend to agree, to tell me that I could forge ahead with my plans.

After a prolonged moment, Nikki relaxed into the tattered chair. "You have a choice to make. Your integrity or your plans. Those plans have run your life and dictated all your decisions."

"Exactly why I shouldn't abandon them now. Columbia doesn't have the base I want. The professors there aren't focused on my areas of interest."

"They're focused enough to offer you a spot." Nikki waved her hand as I was about to defend myself. "Never mind. I'll only be able to Skype with you no matter where you go. It's no sweat off my ass. Let's get out of here and celebrate."

"Okay." I gathered my things and folded both

letters into my bag. It wasn't only my career plans dictating my decisions. New York City might be the largest city in the country, but knowing Mike was at the other end of the island of Manhattan might be harder to bear than Dr. Shaffer's threats.

Chapter 27

MIKE

The hall was decked out in maroon bunting. Professors and national Phi Beta Kappa representatives sat on the dais and murmured together before the ceremony was to begin.

I twisted around, scanning the crowd for my parents. Despite the fact that I'd done all this to appease my dad, I couldn't help feeling pumped up. Who doesn't like to get rewarded for hard work? As an actor, all experiences are worthwhile. And all the classes I took for pre-law were enriching. I admitted to some things I needed to thank my dad for. For pushing me academically, for believing I could meet any challenge. For never giving up on a goal. Even if it wasn't the goal he set out for me.

Mom and Dad came in and were looking for seats. I wound my way through the crowd and accepted a hug from Mom and a handshake from Dad.

"Proud of you," Judge Lewis said. "With this on your résumé, I'll have no problem getting you an internship with the DA's office this year. Then next year—"

"Let's sit down, Michael." Mom took Dad's hand and tried to steer him into a seat.

"No, don't bother staying." Now was the day.

Manhood can sneak up on you. There's a moment when you realize that it doesn't matter if it's a good time or an appropriate place—adulthood demands you be ready.

"Dad, if you can't stay here and support me in my plans, then you need to leave. I've made my decision, and you need to accept it and accept me."

His icy stare told me all I needed to know. "Kathy, we needed to leave early anyhow. There's no point in only staying for a few minutes." He nodded at me, turned, and walked out.

Once in high school, I'd been slammed by a linebacker, and not just the wind had been knocked out of me. I really and truly couldn't breathe for what felt like minutes, but was only a few seconds. That same inability to get oxygen to my lungs rooted me to my spot.

Worse was the sorrow on Mom's face. "I'll stay," she said. "He's not really expecting me to leave."

"No," I croaked. "It's best if you go. Having you here makes it worse for me." The pained look she wore reminded me too much of how she'd looked when I woke up in the hospital after the accident. A mixture of sadness, worry, and an overlay of false bravery.

I hugged and kissed her, then walked to the humanities table and greeted some classmates.

Focus on the moment. The way an athlete stays in the game, ignores distractions.

I took a seat and opened the program.

Jill Kramer's name was among the physical science students.

Great, that won't be distracting.

I wasn't surprised. She'd worked her butt off and deserved it. Plus, her past tutoring work and volunteering in the department had to have factored into her invitation to join.

The remaining students filed in. A familiar shape came into my periphery. She might be short, but I would never miss that figure in a crowd. Her full breasts and ample bottom were lusciously encased in a dress that made me think of sunflowers and apple orchards.

Crap! Why did she still affect me this way?

Plenty of girls would get with me. It would be easier to move on from Jill, after graduation, when I'd be a thousand miles away and not likely to spot her at the coffee shop, or the library, or walking across campus with her dark hair reflecting the sun, the wind spraying her hair across her eyes, her gentle hands brushing the hair away to reveal her sweet face. Her rose-red lips forming words as she talked to a friend while she sat on a bench on the quad.

I cleared my throat and placed the program strategically in my lap. The speaker had come to the podium and the audience fell silent.

The back of her head was visible between the other students. The pinkness of her ear showed she was emotional about something. Whether it was the excitement of the event, or—please, I silently prayed—that she'd seen me, too.

Yes, it would be better for both of us as soon as I put some distance between us.

JILL

I settled in to listen to the speeches. But frankly, they were dull. I hadn't even planned to come to the induction. It wasn't my parents' fault that they weren't there. I never bothered to let them know.

The air-conditioning inside the nineteenth-century hall barely made a difference. Despite the droning noise, the space was nearly as humid as the late spring day outside. Chicago could go from frigid, wintry gusts to thick, pollen-heavy heat.

The sundress clung to the backs of my legs. It wasn't the weather.

Yes, I'd spotted Mike when I entered. And yes,

he looked gorgeous. His shoulders seemed to have gotten even broader, no doubt from all the physical exercise. I'd watched him run around the track on his cheetah legs, his quad muscles so huge and defined.

Goosebumps rose on my arms and I shook myself. *Focus on the speech.*

It was no use. I missed him something terrible. And I was lonely. It didn't matter that I was friendlier with the people in Dr. Shaffer's office, and that the grad students almost counted me as one of their own. It was knowing that this was where I would stay for the next few years. The same faces, the same issues of secrecy and the same expectations of me—Jill the wonder student who helped everyone at her own expense.

Mercifully, the speeches ended, and one by one the inductees were called to accept the pin and certificate.

Effortlessly, Mike walked up the three steps to the stage. An extra burst of applause sounded when his name was called, and he shook the president's hand. Long pants covered the prosthetics he wore, but I could hardly notice a difference in his gait from the other students. My seat gave me a good view of his strong arms and corded neck, and when he turned for a picture, his green eyes made my stomach flip.

He bent his head to sign his name into the leather-bound book that held all the names of inductees into this chapter dating back to 1891. His dirty-blond hair fell across his face. But he looked up and directly at me. His eyes heavy-lidded, a sad smile crossed his face, and a buzzing started in my ears.

He kept his eyes on me as he stepped to the side of the stage. And when he broke his gaze, I exhaled.

I couldn't recall walking up and receiving my certificate, but I must have, because I sat again with it in my hands.

The obligatory punch and cookies followed in a crammed side room. The crush of bodies at the table forced me to grab a root beer, which I hated. Hopefully, I could get away with a quick word to the head of the physics department and scram.

"Hey."

I felt his presence before I heard his voice. Turning, I faced him and discovered he was mere inches from me.

"Mike." My voice came out raspy and exposed my longing for him.

"Congratulations." He nodded at the leather folder in my hand that held the certificate.

"Thanks. You too."

Someone jostled him, and he shuffled even closer. He smelled of soap, and he'd nicked himself shaving just in front of his ear.

"Are your parents here?" I avoided looking into those eyes or I'd be lost.

"No. Yours?"

"Really? You need to ask?"

He smiled. "Sorry. I guess I'm getting a taste of your world. Dad's...not really speaking to me because of my going to NYU." His brow furrowed and he seemed to lose his strong posture for a moment.

"So it's settled, then. You decided for sure?"

"Yes, I'll be in New York studying what I really want. It feels great to be open about it now. Even if my dad disowns me, and I have to make do in a new city, it's a fresh start."

"What about Beth?" I did meet his eyes.

"She's not coming." Mike's lids lowered and he peered into me. "She's going to Hollywood."

I shouldn't have been pleased to hear that, but I was. It shouldn't have mattered, but it did.

"You were always a brave person. And going to New York on your own shows there's no end to your courage." My throat tightened.

"Thanks." He placed a hand on my shoulder. "Your opinion means a lot to me."

The skin of his palm resting on my bare shoulder sent a pulse of photons through my body.

"Looks like we both ended up with what we wanted. I've got a place here."

"You hate root beer." He ran his hand down to my wrist, took the can out of my hand, and wrapped my fingers in his. "I've missed you."

"Me too." I let my fingers play against his hand and watched the reaction on his face.

"Let's get out of here." He cocked his head toward the door.

I nodded and let him lead me through the crowd and out into the sunlight. Without speaking, we set off for the three-block walk to my apartment.

"Is there a reason we're not together?" he asked. He had placed my arm through his. Keeping pace with Mike's slightly bouncy gait was awkward at first, but I soon found the rhythm.

"You wanted me to go to New York with you."

He nodded. "I did. But I understand now. If someone asked me to give up my dreams… Beth has to follow hers in LA. I guess we all have to go our own direction."

We arrived outside my apartment. It wouldn't hurt to talk to him, to catch up for old times' sake.

"Do you want to come in for a while?"

"Yeah, let me show you how I do steps." He waited while I unlocked the security door and held it open for him.

Going in ahead, he bounded up the steps. His hip kicked back with each step, but except for that hitch, it was like anyone else running up steps.

I came puffing up behind. I went up and down this same flight every day, and I was the one winded.

"Impressive," I said, and unlocked the door. "Can I get you iced tea?" I waved to the couch.

Mike sat in the corner he'd always sat in, and my chest tightened to see him in the familiar spot.

"Sure, thanks."

Pouring the drinks gave me a moment to collect myself. There was no reason we couldn't be friends. Or even more. It was clear we weren't going to see each other after next month. Graduation would come and then it would be good-bye forever.

I handed him a tall glass and his fingers brushed mine. His Adam's apple jumped in his throat as he took a long swallow.

Taking a spot on the other end of the couch, I folded my legs under me.

"I've seen your blade legs. You look good on them."

He blushed. "Thanks. I love running again. It wasn't easy. It hurt a lot getting used to these things." He slapped his leg.

"I'm sorry I wasn't there." I looked into my lap and felt tears sting my eyes.

"Crap. I didn't mean that. It was too much to ask anyone to have to go through that with me. Besides, I think part of me wanted to do it on my own. I would have hated for you to see me helpless."

"I wouldn't have minded. I…" The words choked inside. I should have been the one to comfort him, but instead it was *his* hand that rested on my arm and slid down to my hip.

When I looked up, the familiar smug but sexy

expression crossed his face.

If I couldn't get him out of my head, I might as well have him in my body.

"Would it be weird?" I scooted toward him on the couch and kissed him lightly on the lips.

Too cool to look shocked, he merely grinned. "It would be the most natural thing."

I stood and reached for his hand. He allowed me to lead him to the bedroom.

He unbuttoned my dress and it slipped to the floor. I held my breath as he hooked his arm behind my back and deftly undid my bra.

A rush of air left my lungs.

"Mmmm." He hummed as he cupped my breasts. I became incapable of thought, and with frantic fingers I undid his shirt and unzipped his pants. He stepped back to pull his undershirt over his head. His chest was even more defined than it had been before. Blond hair dusted the hard planes. I splayed my hands against it and he rolled his head back.

"I've missed your touch," he murmured.

He sat, and I knelt before him. I grabbed the waistband of his pants to pull them off. He clutched my wrist and delivered a warning stare.

"I want to see," I whispered.

The mechanical legs and springboard feet didn't bother me. There was no use in touching them, but I did, to see what it felt like. I knew some students in the engineering department who would probably be interested in how they worked. But his erection pushing against his boxers was the most fascinating thing I could see.

I sat on his lap. He took the back of my head in his hand and tilted my face. The kiss propelled my body into his. I ground my bottom against his lap and he groaned.

He let go of me to take off his legs, and I heard them fall to the ground.

I went to straddle his lap.

"No way. I do my best work when you're underneath me."

"I seem to recall that." A huge smile spread across my face. Mike could work magic with his tongue and a finger.

I allowed the magic to happen, writhing into the sheets. And then he stopped. I groped for the bedside table, and the new box of condoms purchased in a moment of optimism.

I sat up. "Do you want me on top? Can it work?"

"Jill, I'm highly motivated to make it work."

I lay back down, and he did make it work. It wasn't long before his thrusts had me hurtling toward my release.

I think I screamed. It might have been my head exploding with passion I hadn't even realized I'd missed so much.

A moment later, Mike flung his head back, his

neck strained, his chest gleaming with sweat.

Panting, he rolled to the side and pulled me into him.

"You're right. It is magic," I said into his chest. His heartbeat echoing in my ear.

"Because it's with you."

Chapter 28

MIKE

Her hair tickled my nose, but I didn't dare move. She was exactly where she belonged, curled into my side.

Jill had explored every inch of my new body with abandon. She wanted me on top, and it worked. I had known it would—well, I had hoped it would. But I'd pulled it off, and the next chance I had with a woman I could face it with confidence.

That next opportunity wouldn't be Jill. Yeah, we might hang out until graduation, but she wasn't interested in developing something long-term, especially long distance. All her dreams were here in Chicago.

She did shift her position so she could look at me. Her wide, natural smile I had only seen in these intimate moments returned. She saved this smile for me. The one where her face relaxed and her lips parted. She probably didn't even know she had it.

"That was fun." She kissed my cheek and

propped herself up, pulling the sheet over her chest.

"More than fun." I threw my arm around her and drew her to my side. "Thanks." The word croaked out.

Jill shook her head. "Shut up. I should be thanking you." She leaned in for another kiss, this one lingering on my lips.

I let out a breath. "I knew getting Phi Beta Kappa would be a good day."

She giggled. "You have a place to live in New York?"

"Yeah, there's accessible grad student housing. I'll get my own room, no roommates, no sharing a bathroom, no worries about furniture getting in the way..."

"Most people would be thrilled. You sound bummed."

"I've always lived with someone, usually lots of someones." Crap. I didn't want her to hear that catch in my voice.

"You'll miss Beth." She fiddled with the hem of the sheet.

"I'll miss you." I took her hand and caressed her fingers. "We'll have these next few weeks, and then I'll know you're following your dreams. I'll know you're with supportive people who care about you. Dr. Shaffer has been your mentor, and he's lucky to have you and you, him."

She took her hand back and shoved it under the

sheet. Color rushed to her face, and she turned to look out the window.

"He kissed me." Her voice was so raspy, the words barely audible.

"What?"

"Dr. Shaffer kissed me. At the department party. I stayed to help clean up. His wife was away. I…"

My stomach constricted and a knot formed in my chest. "Son of a bitch."

"I didn't do anything about it. Nikki said I should report it to the department. But then what? Jeopardize my whole future because he had a little too much wine and made a slight pass at me?"

"A slight pass? He's your boss, the principal investigator of your project. You have to work closely with him for the next four years." Every inch of my skin crawled with the urge to hunt that man down, take off my leg, and beat him with the carbon frame of my foot.

"That's just it. I have to work with him. Because…because he knows I cheated on a project once." Jill sat up and twisted away.

"So?"

"So? He could get me brought up to the ethics council. I could lose everything. Everything I've slaved away for."

"You're going to ensure you're slaving away forever if you stay."

"You want me to come to New York with you.

Don't you? That's what this is about." She swung her legs off the side of the bed, grabbed her robe, and shoved her arms through.

"I don't care if you go to the moon, as long as you don't continue to kowtow to that manipulative, power-hungry professor." I eyed my prostheses on the floor. It was going to take a few minutes to make an exit. And not the dramatic exit this situation called for.

"What choice do I have? Columbia doesn't focus on the kind of work I want to do."

Her stare hit me like a punch to the throat. I couldn't speak. I inched farther down the mattress so I could grasp my legs from the floor. When I jerked on the sock, my finger went through the fabric. I took extra time with the second sock. Carefully monitoring my breaths, squelching the curses I so wanted to let loose. Instead, I deliberately fitted the first leg on. Jill paced the room eyeing me and chewing her fingernail.

"You got into Columbia? A place where no one has sexually assaulted you? A place a short subway ride from where I'll be?" I had intended to sound accusatory, but the words came out too soft, and instead I heard myself pleading. Self-hatred wrenched my gut.

"Mike." Jill stopped pacing. Her deep blue eyes misted over. But crocodile tears wouldn't work on me.

"It's one thing to choose your dreams over our relationship. It's another to twist your values around to stay in this city with that letch hanging over you day after day."

"You knew from the beginning what the deal was. I never lied to you." Tears did roll down her cheeks, but I turned away.

I yanked the second leg on, and although anger blurred my vision, I felt the socket fit into place.

"What are you so afraid of, Jill?" I pulled the loose-fitting pants easily over my legs, sprang up from the bed, and faced her, head-on.

"I'm not afraid of Dr. Shaffer. That's why I'm staying." She crossed her arms.

I grabbed the rest of my clothes from the floor and stalked past her through the living room to the front door.

"You should be scared of Dr. Shaffer. Instead, it's me that frightens you." I threw open the door and let it slam behind me. At the bottom of the steps I got dressed, glaring at the neighbor who gave me a questioning glance.

Outside, the heavy floral scent of spring choked me. My lungs refused to open to allow in air. I pounded the sidewalk with my feet. When I walked quickly, my bouncing gait was emphasized. It didn't matter. Jill hadn't ever lied to me, that part was true.

But how could I ever let my heart go to someone who had no idea how to hold it?

"Man, your room is huge." Carlos, another Tisch student, entered my dorm room.

"The benefits of being an amputee." I watched Carlos wince, and regretted my words. "Don't worry about it."

"Didn't mean to put my foot in my mouth," Carlos said.

"You've got two." I smiled, slapped my new friend on the back, and indicated Carlos should sit in the desk chair while I perched at the edge of the bed.

Besides the twin bed, the desk, and the wardrobe, there wasn't any furniture. But there was plenty of room to hold my wheelchair and for it to maneuver around in the middle of the night so I didn't have to put my legs on to go to the toilet. I had my own bathroom equipped with rails, a sink at wheelchair height, and a roll-in tub. In many ways, it was easier to live in the specially designed dorm room than at home.

"Is it hard for you? Getting around?" Carlos shifted in his seat, and his sincere concern was reflected in his face.

"It's a lot more walking than I'm used to, but I'm managing. What do you think of Professor Shane?" I didn't want to start a new friendship in the way my old ones had. The smart remarks, the challenging stares—those were all masks to keep people away. To truly be an actor, I had to stay in touch with my feelings and allow others to be authentic with me.

"Bit of a hard-ass, but should be an interesting class. You wanna go out with us tonight? We're going to check out a band at Irving Plaza." Carlos relaxed into regular conversation mode.

I calculated the trip to Fifteenth Street on the East Side.

"Maybe. I might want to do the reading for set design."

"Sure. Give me a call. And if you ever need any help…just ask. It's not a burden on us, you know. We're in this program together."

"Thanks." I stood on my new vacuum-sealed prosthetics to see Carlos out.

Once alone, I tore off the prosthetics and rubbed at my skin.

I might be able to live with the tingles at the end of my stumps, but the irritated skin was something I needed to fix. I reached into the drawer of my desk and pulled out one of the many tubes of ointments. The appointment with the prosthetist three days away couldn't come soon enough. Not that there was much they could do. I had every type of lotion, sock, and gel packet made. Their advice would be to go in a wheelchair for a few days, give my skin a chance to heal.

Not likely.

Carlos, the other students, and the professors had all been more than welcoming. My disability wasn't an issue to be worked around. It was an aspect of me they embraced. In fact, in playwriting class we discussed incorporating my cheetah legs into a character I could play versus casting me as a non-disabled person and still having the prosthetics.

I smiled at the memory. But it faded as I lay back and stared at the freshly painted ceiling. Everything about the new dorm room was fresh. I should feel lucky, as Carlos said. The other grad students were crammed together in dorm rooms or dilapidated Chinatown apartments. I had this whole place to myself. And I was miserable.

The frat house might have been difficult to navigate, but there was always someone around. Not only to help me if I needed it, but to talk to or work out with, or just silently study with.

I was truly on my own. And the amount of walking on hard pavement was taking its toll on my skin.

I shut my eyes. Back home, Mom would be there to drive me to appointments. James would be there to hang out with. But what would I do? Dad might let me move back home until I got on my feet—metaphorically. But then what? Michael Lewis Sr. was not going to support his older son forever. He would force me to apply to law school, with an "I told you so" attitude. My stomach clenched at the thought.

The absence of my family and buddies created only part of my loneliness. I could admit to myself that one person would have changed my outlook completely. Sharing all my new experiences with Jill would have melted away my concerns, would have evaporated my isolated feelings.

The many friendly new faces couldn't make up for the space she still held inside of me.

The coursework at Tisch was no problem. Compared to the double major, this workload was nothing. It was the traveling around, the movement class, and doing it all on my own. What was going to happen when winter came and the New York streets got slushy? No frat brother to come help me in and out of a car. I would be reduced to wheelchair use.

I'd be that guy who held up the bus while impatient passengers watched as the driver got up from his seat and slowly lowered the rear entrance ramp. The whole point of the amputation was so that I would walk like anyone else. And I could, most days.

I rubbed more lotion onto my stump. I ran my fingers over the skin flaking in spots, the protruding blisters.

My phone beeped and I checked the text message.

It was from Beth. *Here's my apartment.* The picture showed a tiny, clean efficiency behind Beth's perfectly proportioned face. Her golden hair still radiant. The second text came in. *Look for me in the new Ford and Budweiser commercials.*

Nothing stirred in me. Sure, I was happy for her. But I didn't miss her or envy her.

The only one I envied was Jill. She was back home in Chicago following her dreams, and among familiar people. More than envy, I craved her.

With a deep sigh, I hoisted myself up to do some reading. I wouldn't be able to distract myself from wanting her. But I could at least do what I came to do. Accomplish the goals I set for myself. Put one foot in front of the other, sort to speak.

JILL

The crisp fall air bit at my ears. I hadn't expected New York to be as cold as Chicago. But I also hadn't expected Columbia to be as good a match.

I pushed open the door to the astronomy building. On the short flight up to the office, three different students greeted me. It didn't even faze me anymore, this camaraderie.

I took my place in my cubicle and dove right into the Physics 101 problem I was grading.

"Hey, Jill—nice job in that lab demo today for the undergrads."

"Thanks, Steve." I smiled because I would never get used to calling my boss by his first name. The fact that the textbook he wrote was the most used in colleges across the world didn't stop him from being a humble and cooperative man.

"Don't forget the social tomorrow," he called as he walked away.

"Sure." I would go, even though it was the second social in as many weeks. This department and these students didn't compete with each other—they supported each other, and me. I couldn't have asked for a better situation.

But when I had a few quiet moments, my mind strayed downtown, to the other end of Manhattan.

He was there. I knew it, felt it.

One night I joined some classmates at a bar, and a group of students in NYU sweatshirts sat at a different table. It was silly considering the thousands of students enrolled there, but I searched their faces and legs for any sign of Mike.

I'd calculated the probability that I would run into him. With over eight million people in New York City and about fifteen hundred days in the graduate school program…I decided not to let fate take the lead.

"Jill, when you're done, you wanna grab some coffee?" Three other grad students stood at the other side of the office.

My new friends. I liked them and saw a great

future here. This had been the right decision. But still something was missing.

"If someone were living in grad student housing, how would you find them?" I asked.

"Huh?" Confusion took over their faces.

"I need to find a friend at NYU." I closed my laptop and stood. "I'll catch you later at the social."

I walked the few blocks from the number one train and now stood outside grad student housing for NYU.

The campus map showed three buildings used for grad housing. I couldn't tell which one Mike was in. But I had to see him.

Seeing him would help put the memories in perspective. Once I had a normal conversation with him, I would remember how difficult he was to be around. How much of a smart-ass he was, how he kept people at arm's length, how good his arms had felt around me. No, not that.

He was going to be needier than ever. No family, no Beth. All on his own, the danger of falling into a caring-for-Mike trap was there.

But he'd never asked to be taken care of. All he had ever asked for was mutual support. I got that now. I saw it at the astronomy department here. Such a thing could exist.

The first building on Third Street was a bust. The stoop in front told me that it couldn't hold accessible housing. On my trudge to Mercer Street, it started to rain. I hadn't grabbed a jacket, and of all the street corners in New York, this was the one without someone selling cheap umbrellas.

The second building had a list of buzzers but no names. A security guard sat behind a desk. I tapped on the glass door and waved. He scowled but buzzed me in.

"I'm looking for a student named Mike Lewis." Water dripped off me and formed a puddle in front of his desk.

"I can't give out names."

"If Mike Lewis did live here, could you get a message to him?"

"Miss, I'm no message service."

"Please. I need to see him. I need…"

I had to get Mike off my mind so I could move on. We could be friends or never speak again. Seeing him would put an end to the torment.

The guard's face softened. "Press number three." He indicated the row of buzzers. "It's on the first floor."

My lungs constricted. But I managed a "thanks." I pressed and waited.

"Carlos?"

His voice sent a shock wave to my gut.

"It's Jill."

The only answer was the buzzer unlocking the door.

The guard pointed down the hall.

He stood in the open doorway, his face a blank page. He stepped back and ushered me in. "I thought you were a friend who had just left."

His room was small, but I guessed it was big enough for one person.

"It's good to see you." Mike's formal voice.

"How are you doing?"

He lifted his palm up. "Great. I'm loving it so far." He narrowed his eyes. "What are you doing here?"

"I'm in the grad school at Columbia."

His eyes got even narrower than before. "Why?"

That steely stare was usually reserved for people he challenged, people he didn't care about, people he wanted to feel uncomfortable around him. My heart sank knowing I had dropped to that level.

"I didn't want to take any more crap from Shaffer. Turns out here is better." I took a deep breath, preparing myself to say good-bye forever. He didn't want to give me another chance.

"You didn't tell me." He sat on the edge of his bed. He didn't invite me to sit in his desk chair, so I shuffled my feet.

"I didn't know what to say. Mike, I'm making friends in the department. The work is interesting and I'm finally comfortable. The other students respect me. There are no secrets."

"Sounds wonderful for you." He picked up a book and flipped through the pages.

I knew it was a long shot. A one-in-a-quadrillion chance that he'd be happy to see me, that we could start again. But his reaction cemented it for me. With one more statement out in the air, I could move on.

"It's not wonderful. I need you." There, I'd said it. A ton of weight lifted off my chest. Floating without gravity's pull.

Forget moving on. Forget trying to be friends. With him in front of me, I knew what I really wanted. What I really needed.

"I need you," I repeated. "I thought all I needed was my work, my goals. That love would come at some point later. But love came when I wasn't ready, and I was too stupid to recognize it. I need your smug looks, your challenges to my rigid ideals. If it's too late, I'll accept it. But I had to ask."

Mike placed the book back on the nightstand. He stood, closing the space between us. His soapy scent didn't mask the underlying trace of masculinity.

"I don't need you," he said in monotone.

My heart turned to a lead block. It might not ever soften, but at least I'd tried.

"Okay. I understand." My throat was raw, and I wanted to leave before the flood of tears came.

"But I want you. I'm desperate for my Jill. The girl who won't take any crap from me. The girl who is so brilliant she can comprehend the cosmos and make a kickass lasagna, but who is so clueless and innocent she becomes a wallflower at parties, when she should be shown off as the most beautiful woman in the universe."

Happiness overwhelmed me. His hands gripped my waist and I linked my hands around his strong shoulders. "The universe is pretty darn big. You know, there are so many planets that could sustain life. We haven't found it yet, but sometime soon I bet we discover —"

His kiss cut me off. And there was nothing I wanted more than to be interrupted by the big, hunky jock who returned my love.

THE END

Dear Reader,

Thank you for reading STANDING UP. I'm not sure what Jill and Mike are up to these days, but I like to think they are leading successful careers in New York City, with occasional trips to swim at his parents' lake house.

If you don't want to miss my next release, sign up for my very occasional, but informative newsletter. Guaranteed to not clog your inbox (http://www.kateforestbooks.com/bio).

Or follow me on Facebook https://www.facebook.com/KateForestAuthor.

And turn to the end of this book to find out what the side effects are to falling in love, from INTERIOR DESIGN and OTHER EMOTIONS.

I love hearing from readers, so feel free to reach out to me on my website (http://www.kateforestbooks.com).

Wishing you a Happy Ever After,
Kate

ACKNOWLEDGMENTS

My critique gals, Veronica Forand, Susan Scott Shelley, Lauren S. Strauss, Kate Lutter, and Maria Imbalzano, are always there for me in a pinch or a slap. I couldn't ask for a better group of women standing beside me.

A very special thanks to Jim Concannon. He allowed me into his home and into his world. His work to support amputees is amazing, and his open, honest discussions with me invaluable. And thanks to David Lawall of Harry Lawall and Son, Prosthetics & Orthotics. He let me play with all his legs and took time from his busy day to talk with me. Any inaccuracies are mine due to artistic license or error.

My family is so important in everything I do. They are the reason I am able to do it all. Thanks, Mimi, Pa, Andrea, Tom, Ben, and Leah.

ABOUT KATE FOREST

Author Kate Forest has worked in a psychiatric hospital, as a dating coach, and spent a disastrous summer selling aboveground swimming pools. Everything she does gives her fodder for stories of rocky but hilarious romance. She lives in Philadelphia with her husband, two kids, and a fierce corgi.

You can find her at:
www.KateForestBooks.com
Twitter: @KateForestBooks
Facebook:
https://www.facebook.com/KateForestAuthor

INTERIOR DESIGN and OTHER EMOTIONS

There are side effects to falling in love.

Gina Giancarlo is an interior design genius, fast as lightning with numbers…and autistic. Yearning to be just like everyone else, she joins a drug trial that promises to help her experience a full range of emotions.

With the ink still wet on his MBA, Chris Rinaldi has only two goals—make bags of cash and bag lots of women. Dancing on the edge of insider trading, he pushes his company to buy stock in a pharmaceutical firm because of its promising new autism drug.

As Gina's understanding of the world blossoms, she forms a connection with the Wall Street hustler, who appreciates her—quirks and all. And for the first time since his sister's death, Chris experiences true emotions with a woman who has recently discovered passion herself.

Gina believes that the pills are responsible for her awakening. Chris knows they're responsible for his success. When the drug is discontinued, the cost of "normal" might bankrupt their future.

1557777r

Advanced Praise for
Interior Design and Other Emotions

"This book is really much more than a conventional romance… Kate has lovingly crafted a story about the power of the human heart to affect more change on its holder than any drug could hope to affect." — **Katy Regnery, *USA Today* and *New York Times* bestselling author**

"Characters are charming and the story is so original and fresh. I fell in love with this very special woman." — **Mariah Stewart, *USA Today* and *New York Times* bestselling author**

Available on Amazon

Proof

Made in the USA
Charleston, SC
13 February 2017